EVERY NIGHT
I DREAM OF HELL

BOOKS BY MALCOLM MACKAY

The Night the Rich Men Burned

Every Night I Dream of Hell

The Glasgow Trilogy

The Necessary Death of Lewis Winter

How a Gunman Says Goodbye

The Sudden Arrival of Violence

EVERY NIGHT I DREAM OF HELL

Malcolm Mackay

MULHOLLAND BOOKS

Little, Brown and Company
New York Boston London

Mulholland Books / Little, Brown and Company
Hachette Book Group
1290 Avenue of the Americas, New York, NY 10104
mulhollandbooks.com

First United States Edition: April 2017
Originally published in the United Kingdom by Mantle, an imprint of Pan Macmillan, a division of Macmillan Publishers Limited, August 2015

Mulholland Books is an imprint of Little, Brown and Company, a division of Hachette Book Group, Inc. The Mulholland Books name and logo are trademarks of Hachette Book Group, Inc.

The publisher is not responsible for websites (or their content) that are not owned by the publisher.

The Hachette Speakers Bureau provides a wide range of authors for speaking events. To find out more, go to hachettespeakersbureau.com or call (866) 376-6591.

ISBN 978-0-316-27177-6
LCCN 2016940859

10 9 8 7 6 5 4 3 2 1

LSC-C

Printed in the United States of America

CHARACTERS

Gary Aldridge — A tough piece of work, willing to throw his considerable muscle around, providing Adrian Barrett keeps on paying him for it.

Adrian "Dyne" Barrett — The little drug ring he tried to build in Birmingham tanked, sent him into a spiral. He was pulled out of it by a beautiful woman with a lucrative plan.

Taylor "Original" Carlisle — Oh, he thinks he's right on the cutting edge of criminality, running boiler-room scams. Fake tan and fake accent, only a small percentage of him real.

Ben Carmichael — Works as Kevin Currie's second in command. The quiet and reliable type, just looking to get through the industry with money in his pocket and a functioning pulse.

Lee Christie — A mid-level drug dealer, podgy and in love with the party life. He may be married, but if pretty girls think he's a rich and well-connected man, you can bet he'll take advantage of that.

Nate Colgan — A relentlessly tough man, maybe the strongest reputation in all of Glasgow, and there's nothing that can bring him down. Everyone believes that, because nobody really knows him.

Rebecca Colgan — Perhaps the only person who knows him that doesn't have a shred of fear for Nate Colgan, her harmless, goofy father who cares about her so much.

Russell Conrad—Steadily built a reputation as a freelance gunman, and with so many organization men falling by the wayside, it was inevitable someone would make him an offer.

Zara Cope—When she and Nate were together, when they had their daughter, she thought that might be her life. The thought of domesticity appalled her, so she ran.

Stuart Crockley—Used to be that John Young would handle the process of ensuring all dirty money was cleansed of its sins, a role now filled by Stuart.

Kevin Currie—With his boss Jamieson in jail, Kevin's taken on a lot more responsibility. Smart enough to handle it, but there's a lot to get a grip on.

DC Ian Davies—Still clinging on to his career, praying for that pension to hurry up and arrive. If he could spend the rest of his working life in the office, he cheerfully would.

Jake "Lonny" Donezak—One of Lafferty's right-hand men. Young and smart, trusted despite his lack of experience because if you're good enough, you're old enough.

DI Michael Fisher—Occasional big victories and constant small defeats. He got Jamieson sent away, but his organization continues to function. And that nagging little obsession, Zara Cope.

Jess Flowers—All she had wanted was a bit of glamour, a bit of fun while she tried to find her way in the world. She never realized people could be so evil.

Neil Fraser—A big, dumb lump of muscle, slowly working his way down towards the gutter. Someone stabbed him once; many regretted that he got back up.

Mark Garvey—One of the higher-profile gun dealers in the city, of whom there are few to choose from. Garvey is well connected, always looking for a good deal.

Melanie Garvey — Marriage to the older man had seemed convenient. Money and stability in her life, but, my God, it became boring fast.

Paul Greig — He used to be a cop; now an information gatherer for anyone who can pay. Couldn't be any more bent now than he was when he wore the uniform.

Conn Griffiths — Been a long time since the ability to punch someone really hard was enough to make you good muscle. Conn epitomizes the new breed of smart hard men.

Keith Henson — A hard man, he thinks, who's come up from England with Barrett and his crew. He's there for the money, not the camaraderie.

Peter Jamieson — He ran the fastest-growing organization in the city, and one talkative gunman took it all away from him. He might be in jail, but that's temporary, and he's only ever a phone call away.

Adam Jones — Twin brother of the increasingly influential Marty and still bathed in his shadow, a fact he's increasingly coming to resent.

Marty Jones — If you knew Marty a few years ago you'd be amazed by the transformation, from a rotten little pimp to a key leader of the organization in Jamieson's enforced absence.

Angus Lafferty — Jamieson's biggest drug importer, and possibly the biggest in Scotland. Has enough legit business to live off, but can't seem to pull himself away from the criminal life.

Aaron MacLennan — Experienced, but that counts for nothing when you remain incompetent. Working with Adam Jones, which doesn't say much for Adam.

Ronnie Malone — He was working at the St. John Hotel when he met Nate Colgan. Nate spotted talent and pulled him in under his wing, a place nobody had been before.

Esther Mayberry — Lives with Ronnie, and will build a future with him, but she can't pretend she likes the way his life is going. The new work, it just seems wrong.

Jawad "Nasty" Nasif — He's been tight with Barrett for years, been through it all with him. Nasty does the dirtiest work, even if he's no fan of their new surroundings.

Kelly Newbury — She knows the business, and she's seen its bleak consequences at close range, but that doesn't stop her seeing something in Nate that she wants to have near.

Don Park — More than just a senior man in Alex MacArthur's organization, he's the ambitious shark with big teeth circling his ageing boss.

Elliott Parker — Barrett's right-hand man and the one who considers himself the brains of the operation, with a heartbeat that neither rises nor falls, no matter the circumstance.

Billy Patterson — Always ruthless. Always. Saw the need to refocus that ruthlessness when Alan was killed, the need to form the smartest alliances.

Charles Simpson — Every smart criminal has an even smarter lawyer, and Simpson is Jamieson's. Kept the sentence down, and is now helping to make sure Jamieson's messages get to the right people.

Mikey Summers — Hired by Billy Patterson to work alongside Conn Griffiths as a second pair of brutal hands. Now that Billy's joined up with Marty, Mikey's taking orders from various sources.

Brendan Thorne — Controls the Jamieson housing stock, useful properties that any criminal organization needs. An old man who's seen it all before and is impressed by none of it.

Owen Turner — Been a good mate to Ronnie since schooldays, and they still look to help each other out. Sometimes the best help a friend can give is to do nothing.

Trisha "Tish" Turner — The driving force behind the gadget shop she and her husband Owen run, trying to prop it up with the financial help that Ronnie organized for them.

Kirk Webster—He changed phone records for Jamieson at the call center he works at, and he admitted it to the police. Helped put Jamieson away. Been living in fear ever since.

Lewis Winter—Zara had almost persuaded herself she could build a life with Lewis, and then ambition pushed Lewis to make an enemy of Jamieson. He didn't live long after that.

John Young—Jamieson's right-hand man, his trusted lieutenant. Stood beside him on the rise and was beside him on the fall. Now in a different wing of the same prison.

EVERY NIGHT
I DREAM OF HELL

1

"People are terrified of you. You've given them good reason. We know how valuable that is."

I sat listening and didn't say anything. This was the preamble to the subject that mattered: business. I already knew what was coming next. We were sitting in Kevin Currie's office, and I was listening to him speaking someone else's words.

"I don't need to tell you that there's a lot of stuff going on, a lot of stuff that needs to be sorted out," Kevin went on.

I liked Kevin, but he was wasting my time. I knew there was a lot that needed sorting. He knew it. If he'd stuck his head out the window to alert a passer-by, there was a good chance they would already have known. Peter Jamieson ran the criminal organization Currie was a major part of, but Peter Jamieson was in jail. That meant people were trying to pick scraps from the organization, profit from temporary vulnerability while it still existed.

"There's a lot of little stuff," Kevin went on, "but even that's become more complicated. A man with your reputation, you can simplify all that. That'll be the first thing we want from you."

There were shelves on the wall behind Kevin, and most of them were filled with what looked like folders. Supposed to make him look like the legitimate businessman nobody was dumb enough to believe he was. Maybe once he could fool people, but not since Jamieson went away. That change had made Kevin a bigger player than ever, one of the group of men running the organization day to day. So the neat little office of a legit businessman probably wasn't cutting it anymore.

But it wasn't the folders I was watching. There was a little gold trophy at the end of one of the shelves, tucked in behind a leaning folder. Looked like the sort of thing you would give a mediocre amateur sportsman. I couldn't stop myself wondering what that was for. Kevin wasn't a sportsman; he was a guy in his late forties getting slowly fat and jowly.

"None of that sounds like a problem," I said. I wasn't looking to sound nonchalant, but he was reading from a not particularly interesting script.

It was obvious what had happened, I probably don't even have to tell you. Peter Jamieson knew that I, Nate Colgan, was already doing work for the organization, and doing it well. He knew that he needed someone with a reputation to start throwing some weight around on his behalf, scare away the vultures. The serious attacks needed more defending than I could provide alone, but getting rid of the opportunists would remove the sense of weakness. So he made a call to Kevin, told him to hire me permanently and told him what to say.

"I didn't figure it would be," Currie said, nodding his head and letting his relief show. "We need good people around us right now, Nate, we really do. Feels like we're taking shots from every side and I don't know where the next one will come from."

"Anything new?"

He looked left and right, like someone might have snuck into that cramped little office. "There is something. I mean, Jesus, you know what people are like, always complaining about something or other, but this seems different. We've had a couple of guys complaining about being pushed off their patch. Couple of other guys seem to have crossed over."

"To?"

"Don't know. That's the problem. Well, we sort of know.

Outsiders. Can you believe it? Like there aren't enough local sharks in the water. Some English guy seems to be trying to pick off business in the city."

"You have an ID?" I asked. Knowing who the threats were was a big part of my job, and this was the first I had heard of this one. For the first time since I arrived in the office, Kevin had my interest.

"Just a name, Adrian Barrett. You heard of him?"

I shook my head, which I didn't like doing.

"English guy, like I said. We're trying to work out where he was before, who he might be working for, if anyone. Seems like he's putting the word around that he's in charge, but that could be a screen. The guy in charge doesn't turn up to do the donkey work, does he?"

Asking me, because he didn't know for himself. Kevin ran a counterfeit operation, a good and profitable one. The man knew how to run a business, let's make that clear right now. But he hadn't been involved in the dirtiest corners of the business until Jamieson's arrest pushed him there. Now he was up to his armpits in the filth and didn't know where to swim for safety.

"Not usually," I said. "Depends how big he is to start with, I suppose."

"Aye, well, he's becoming an issue. Everything's becoming a fucking issue." He was shaking his head and looking tired. The small things were mounting up, because the organization wasn't a well-oiled machine anymore. It was causing the sort of frustration that coaxed a rare sweary word out of Kevin's usually pristine mouth. "We have so many things we need to clean up," he went on. "There's stuff that still hasn't been done from months ago, stuff we should have gotten out of the way but we were too busy keeping our heads down. There's new stuff coming along all the time. You'll have to get on top of a lot of that."

"Sure. What's my title?"

"You'll be security consultant, the job Frank MacLeod was do-ing before he disappeared," he said. "You remember old Frank?"

I smiled a little and nodded. If you've been in the business in Glasgow at any point in the last forty years, you know of Frank MacLeod. I'd been in it for nineteen years, since I was eighteen. Disappeared was business speak for killed off and buried without the body ever being found. We knew he had been murdered on Jamieson's orders by a hitman called Calum MacLean, who then told his interesting little story to the police. But they couldn't peg the killing on Jamieson in any way, so that was another crime for which he wasn't convicted, despite the few for which he was.

"You'll be providing security advice for the club, some pubs, some bookies, some of the legit stuff that Jamieson has. You don't have to do anything though; the security mostly takes care of itself. We have people for that. Just put in the occasional appearance; I think that was all Frank used to do. Make sure the legit employees know your official job title in case the police ask them."

That all made sense, but I'll admit I was a little uncomfortable having to step into Frank's shoes. I wasn't going to be doing his job, not his real job. He was a hitman, and that was a line I'd never crossed. But people would see me doing the "security con-sultant" job he did and they would make the comparison. They would think I was now as important as Frank had been, and that would make me a target.

"Listen," Kevin went on, "there's a job I want you to start with, and I don't want you to laugh."

I raised my eyebrows. When you're a freelancer, you can be choosy if you really want to be. Won't do much for your reputa-tion, and your reputation is what's going to get you work, but it's up to you what jobs you do. If you can afford to say no and you want to say no, then go ahead and say no. Not when you're an or-ganization man. When you're on the payroll, you have to do the jobs you're given.

"I want you to go round and kick seven bells out of Kirk Webster. I know that's a pathetic place to start, but it still hasn't been done and it needs to be."

"Is that all that needs to be done?"

"Well" — Kevin shrugged — "for now it is."

I stood up and I shook his hand, like a new employee delighted to get through the job interview. There was something about that little office that made me want to play at being legit. That feeling had passed by the time I was out on the street, getting into Ronnie's car.

He had his little Astra parked in the single line of parking spaces in front of Currie's place. The car was too clean, I thought, maybe too new as well. It was a work car that nobody should ever spot. We were in Hillington, not far south of the river in an industrial area full of engineering firms and warehouses. Currie's was a single-story white building, brick front and corrugated roof, the office at the back of a large warehouse, surrounded by respectability on a street lined with trees. Nothing to suggest that the warehouse was crammed with tremendously illegal goods.

"So?" Ronnie asked me.

"I'm on the payroll."

"And me?"

"My first job will be to hire you in a security role. Congratulations."

He started the car and we pulled away, me telling him about Kirk as we went. I'll tell you about Kirk in a minute, but first I want to tell you about Ronnie Malone. I'd met him a good time ago, when he was working in a grubby little hotel near Central Station. He was there for Currie, helping his men get rooms for whatever little business they wanted to hide from others. He was wasted there.

Ronnie was smart, and smart shouldn't be left booking rooms in a half-empty hotel for barely important counterfeiters and suppliers. I persuaded Currie to move him into my employ, let me work him into something more usable.

"You come and work with me, and we'll make good money together," I had told him. "You'll have cash, you'll have interesting work, you'll have the chance to move up fast."

He'd looked at me like he was trying to find the world's politest way to say no. I wasn't there to hear no, however polite, so I leaned a little more heavily.

"All you're getting now is beer money, but you still go down if someone points the finger at you. You've helped dangerous people do terrible things. The dough you're making isn't worth that. Let me help you make more, help make the risk worthwhile."

He still looked reluctant, but he was a good boy, smart enough to realize that yes was the correct answer. So he came to work for me, and he was doing a decent job of it. Had a few little missteps, but every kid does when they're starting out. Kid: Ronnie had just turned twenty-six a few weeks before Currie put us on the payroll.

He drove me back to my house. "You go look up Kirk Webster, find out what rock he's living under. Come pick me up when you've found him. I'll handle him. It won't be a two-man job."

We were still at the point where Ronnie was doing the set-up and I was doing the dirty work. The process of educating him on how to get bloody was a slow one. He had to learn, because that was his job, but you don't rush a kid into it if you don't have to. I was taking my time, teaching him, because I enjoyed it that way.

2

I had a small terraced house in Balornock, on a long curving road in an area that wasn't quite as rough as it looked at a glance. Used to have the Birnie Court flats looming at the end of the road, looking ready for a fight. They had picked one with a demolition team and were gone by the time this happened. My house was the sort of place you would accept a man on a low income lives in. I wasn't on a low income, but I was happy for the world to make its usual assumptions and move quietly along. I needed just enough space for me and my few possessions and I wasn't fussy about location, location, location.

Don't get me wrong, I would have liked to share my home with someone else. More than one, actually, but there was no way I was going to let that happen. I was bursting with faults, some of which I may find time to tell you about, but that kind of selfishness wasn't one of them. I would have loved to have my daughter living with me, but I knew she was better off living with her mother's parents. I wasn't the man to bring up a young girl. And I would have liked to have a woman in my life, but that wasn't happening either. I was short-tempered, generally surly and lugging around a reputation that made me good at my job and bad at everything else. People were scared of me, and that cut bad as well as good.

There was someone sniffing around, a girl I liked, a girl I admired. Her name was Kelly Newbury, and because I liked her I was making a conscious effort to stay away from her. She wanted the security a relationship with me could give her. Have me be scary on her behalf. It was an invitation to trouble and other good things that I couldn't afford to get tangled in. Not with all this going on.

I took a sly look up and down the street as I made my way up to the front door because the habit of caution is a priceless gift. There was nothing out of place that I could spot, even if my eyesight isn't as good as it once was. It'll have to stay below its best because a guy like me doesn't turn up to his work bespectacled.

I pushed open the front door and stepped inside, already seeing something I didn't like. There was a folded piece of notepaper lying on the mat just inside the door that someone had put through my letter box when I was away getting gainfully employed. In the few seconds it took me to pick up the piece of paper I wracked my brains trying to think of any good news I had received in this way. None, ever.

Just needed a glance at the handwriting to know that this was more than bad news. This was a disaster waiting to happen. This was Zara Cope's handwriting. Messy but confident, her name scrawled across the bottom of the paper, the *Z* much bigger than the rest of it, like a dyslexic Zorro.

I sighed my disapproval loudly to the empty corridor and wandered through to the living room. Putting music on always made it less likely that I would lose my temper, so I sat with a guitar being gently strummed in the background and read the note.

Nate,

> *I was at your door but I guess you're not home.*
> *I don't have your number so I'm leaving this note instead.*
> *We need to meet. There are things we have to discuss,*
> *like the delivery I made for you some time ago.*
> *Remember that? There are other things to talk about as well.*

> *Zara*

There were little digs in there that were designed to annoy me. Let's start with the "I guess you're not home" comment, as though I was hiding behind the fucking couch to avoid her. Even mentioning the delivery was uncharacteristically stupid. What if someone else had found the note before I got to it? And saying there were other things to talk about was just a cheap tease. There was a lot more to the letter than the words.

She was desperate, was the first obvious thing. Mentioning what she had delivered to me before she was arrested was her charmless little shot at reminding me I owed her money. I didn't need to be reminded; the money was sitting in an account waiting for her to adopt it. The sooner she got it out of that account and into one of her own the happier I would be. I didn't want it anywhere near me. The money had started out its life attached to Lewis Winter, a walking catastrophe who had strolled to his early death when Zara was with him.

I should maybe give you a little history lesson at this point. Zara was the mother of my nine-year-old daughter, Rebecca. Zara hung around the business, using her looks and her smarts to make herself a fine little living. Or a living, anyway. She was a cut above the usual hangers-on, sharp as anything that's ever cut me. I fell for her hard; we moved in together; she had Becky. Didn't last though, and it was mostly my fault. Zara was twenty-one, looking for a fast life, and I was an angry and dangerous twenty-eight-year-old who wouldn't accept the world not constantly bending to my will. We were too young. She ran, and I let her. Becky went to live with Zara's parents, and it's been that way since.

Zara shacked up with Lewis Winter, a mid-level dealer, and when he was knocked off she came to me with some of his dirty cash and the last of his supply. The drugs needed selling and the money needed hiding until the dear Scottish police service kindly stopped looking for it. I did what I could to help her, because that seemed like the right thing to do for the mother of my child, and because I still didn't know how to say no to Zara Cope.

She was a special woman, one who had a power over me no other person has ever had. That didn't help her a damn when she got a three-month sentence for perverting the course of justice. Slap-on-the-wrist stuff for someone inside the industry, but she was no more than a hanger-on, and the sentence would have hit her hard. She got out and went off the radar for a while, didn't even come looking for her money. I knew she'd been away from the city for a lot of that time because I kept an eye out for her. Now, evidently, she was back. And yes, I did recognize her hand-writing after all those years. There was almost nothing of her I had forgotten.

I turned the piece of paper over and saw that she'd scrawled a phone number on the back of it. A mobile number, underlined twice as though that would be the clincher if I was undecided. I was going to call her; she would gnaw at the back of my mind if I didn't. She could also cause trouble for me, and I had enough of that to keep me company already. Zara was on first-name terms with some of the skeletons in my closet, so I had to keep her smart mouth shut. And she knew that I'd organized the sale of drugs on her behalf, and the cleaning of the money it raised.

If you're interested in how, I had taken that little stash of drugs and dirty money she turned up on my doorstep with to Ross Kennedy to handle. He worked most closely with Angus Lafferty, Peter Jamieson's biggest drug importer, but his loyalties were made of smoke. He bought the drugs from me for less than their street value but as much as I could get in a hurry. He also cleaned the money for me, because making dirty things look respectable was always his greatest talent. Since then the money, about four and a half grand in all, had been gradually filtered into an account I'd opened to house it, waiting for Zara.

I was looking at that number and looking at the phone, wanting to call and wanting to crumple up the paper and pretend she had never existed. But I was going to call, both because I had to and because I wanted to hear her voice. I wanted to know that she was doing okay. Since she'd left the city she'd left my professional radar, so I had no idea what sort of state she was in.

The phone rang for a while before she answered it and I heard her voice, cold and flawless.

"This is Nate," I said to her hello.

There was silence on the other end, the kind of heavy pause that insinuated horror. She wanted me to call so I was calling; it was up to her to say something next.

"You got my note."

"It was inside my front door, so yeah." Talking to Zara always ripped me in half. Part of me wanted to be nice to her, let her know that I still cared. The other part wanted to make sure that she kept her distance, stayed away from me and stayed away from Becky. That was the part that usually won, because protecting Becky from Zara's influence was my priority.

"Yeah. Well, we need to talk. I take it you still have the money you owe me?"

Needling away, emphasizing the word *owe* as though she had done me a favor. She hadn't; she had nearly led the police to me and had indirectly tied me to Lewis Winter through his product. It was a dangerous thing to be tied to a man whose murder was part of the MacLean confessions. It was hard to think of the last time Zara had done me a favor. Becky, I guess.

"The money I raised, cleaned and hid for you is sitting in a bank account, waiting."

"Good."

"You want the bank details? We can make this nice and simple and you can take the money without any fuss."

This was me giving her the opportunity to keep her distance, something I didn't really want but that I thought we were both smart enough to understand was the best option. But she didn't keep her distance; she kept barreling right on into my life.

"I want to see you," she said, like it was a sudden revelation. "We should meet up. There's stuff we need to talk about."

I sighed, but I kept it light enough to make sure she didn't hear. I wasn't looking to provoke. Maybe ten percent of my worry was about my own feelings at seeing her again, another twenty was about whatever trouble she was going to try and drag me into, and the other seventy was the ever-present fear that she would want to talk about Becky. Whatever the split, it was still a hundred percent of worry.

"Where and when?" I asked. I knew I was walking into trouble; this isn't me looking back and thinking I could have done something different. I knew it then every bit as much as I know it now. I went along with it because that was all I could do. The alternative was no, and no meant conflict with a dangerous woman at a dangerous time.

"Um, Wednesday, how about? I can come round to yours."

"No," I said, a little too quick and a little too hard. "Wednesday, fine, but we'll meet somewhere."

"Neutral territory, huh? Fine, if that's what you want. You know the Greek place right on George Square?"

"I do."

"Midday?"

"Fine."

She made a big effort to sigh down the phone at me. "It's always a pleasure to talk to you, Nate."

She sounded like she was about to say something else but she stopped herself and I heard a door closing in the background.

"You have company," I said.

"Yeah, well, maybe now I have a chance of a grown-up conversation. I'll see you on Wednesday."

I hung up without saying goodbye because I was feeling petty.

Resentful might be a better word for it, and disturbed by the fact that I was jealous of whoever was having the conversation with her right now. Some new man in her life, hopefully giving her a good sort of life. I looked at the letter and I thought about its desperate contents, and I knew that whatever he was giving her, it wasn't a good life.

3

We were sitting in a car park outside a big plain white building. Big windows, could have been a building for just about anything, but the sign sprawled across the wall said it was for a telephone company.

"Call center," Ronnie told me, sitting in the passenger seat. "He's something technical in there. I don't know what. Supposed to be quite senior. I think that's because most of the other people working there are students. Lot of short-term people. From what I can tell, he knocks off at five every day, goes straight home on the bus, doesn't leave the flat when he gets there."

"That usual for him?"

Ronnie shrugged. "No idea, but it's what he's doing now."

I nodded. We both guessed that wasn't the life Kirk Webster had been living before he grassed up Peter Jamieson and John Young; just the life he was now stuck with. He was hoping that keeping his head down was going to help him stay out of trouble, like trouble ever walks past you because you don't look it in the eye.

Kirk had helped the organization by placing fake calls in the records to implicate some people, removing real calls from the records to protect others. A simple precaution, but it was illegal and it was all about hiding much more serious crimes. The police knew it, because Calum MacLean told them, but it's never enough to know something. They needed more proof than they had, and they managed to get Kirk's name. They questioned him; he cracked like a dry biscuit and told them everything he knew. That added to Jamieson's sentence and played a big part in John Young's sentence. Young was Jamieson's right-hand man, and the most senior organization man Kirk had met. Now Kirk had to be punished.

"That's what he looks like," Ronnie told me, holding his phone across to me. "You'll not have trouble picking him out."

Wasn't a brilliant picture, but it showed me a thirty-year-old guy in a tracksuit, dark hair with a mini Mohawk. He looked ridiculous, easy to pick out. A man not smart enough to understand that the concept of keeping your head down included keeping your head restrained.

"Right, you can leave it with me," I told Ronnie.

I got out of the car and walked halfway across the car park to where mine was parked. A couple of minutes later Ronnie pulled away and went off to do whatever things he killed time with. He had a girlfriend, Esther, who he lived with, and it seemed like he had a good little circle of friends. I wondered how long all of that would last. As secrets grow, friendships shrink.

The boring part of the job, sitting there and waiting for someone else to stick to their schedule. Which he did, emerging from the building at about ten minutes past five, walking quickly, looking around without ever knowing what he was looking for. He was scared of everything, and that was why he couldn't see the danger. You get so wrapped up in believing that every shadow is about to jump at you that you can't pick out the real threat.

I let him get well ahead, then drove to his flat. He lived in Greenfield, a line of old council flats running down a side road with a bashed and bedraggled bus shelter at the corner. There weren't many cars on the street so parking was easy. I stopped at the top of the street, with a view of the bus stop down at the bottom. I could have made more effort to hide away, but your effort matches your need. I didn't need to die of effort outwitting Kirk Webster.

Took another ten or fifteen minutes of waiting for the bus to stop and Kirk to get off. He walked quickly up to one of the four-story buildings, dipped in brown roughcast and left to degrade, and went inside. I watched and I waited and wished I was somewhere else. This was cheap, and the world would know it.

No point sitting there wishing your superiors had better judgment. You go and you do the job, so I went and I did the job. Up to the front door, in and up the stairs to the second floor. Three doors on each floor, and I found the one I was apparently looking for, number 8. I knocked and stood a step sideways so that he'd still be able to see me when he opened the door but he wouldn't be able to see much of me. I doubted he would recognize me, but I'm a big unit and wherever I am, I look like I'm there with bad intentions.

The door opened a couple of inches, me leaning sideways against the doorframe, watching for any sign of security. There was no chain on the door, no sign that the clown had gone to any real effort to protect himself. You're living in fear of the Jamieson organization and you don't even get a chain for your door?

"Yeah?" he said out into the corridor, still only holding the door an inch open.

"Delivery," I said with a bored tone.

And he paused just long enough to let me take complete control of the situation. People always pause. Even when they're not expecting a delivery they're still willing to believe it might be for them. People want to believe that there's something wonderful arriving. I spun a half-step and shouldered the door, shoving it open and Kirk backwards.

As soon as I stepped inside I closed the door behind me, keeping as much of the noise inside as possible. Kirk was back against the wall in the narrow corridor, looking at me and shaking his head.

"No, oh no, please, no," was about as much as he had time to say.

I didn't want him to start cranking up the volume, so I threw a fast punch, straight-armed, aiming for the middle of his face. It wasn't a hard shot, but it was a silencer. Caught him on the tip of the nose and knocked his head backwards, making it bounce off the wall behind him. The shock shut him up, made him drop to his knees. This wasn't a man practiced in the art of fighting. No man who voluntarily drops off his feet when he doesn't have to is a competent fighter.

While he put his hands up to his face, I reached out and grabbed him by his stupid hair, dragging him in through the door to his cramped little kitchen. He was whining and spluttering, blood coming out of his nose.

The kitchen was already a mess by the time I got there. Food packaging, crumbs and general assorted dirt were scattered over every surface. There was a stack of magazines on the small kitchen table that looked like they'd been there a good while. Some were tech mags, others weren't. There was a laptop on the table too, probably used to view the same content as the magazines. Looked reasonably new, maybe bought with the money the organization paid him. The kitchen had old cream units, a cooker that didn't look old and didn't look used; this was a young guy not living much of a life as far as I could tell.

It was my turn to make that sad little life a little sadder. I threw him at the table. He hit it side-on and smacked into the magazines, sending them skidding off the table. He reached out and held on to the table because he thought that would help him. His legs had gotten drunk without him; he was wobbling. It was exactly what I wanted him to do, hold a position while I picked up a chair and smashed it against him. It was a dramatic move, smashing a chair against a guy, watching the legs fly off, but it didn't do a whole lot of damage. An effective scare tactic. It also had the benefit of not having to throw a punch. No need to cut my own knuckles to make him hurt.

Did the trick; he let go of the table and crumpled onto the floor.

He was saying something about how sorry he was, but even he knew that wasn't going to help him any. He had grassed up Peter Jamieson, and that had to carry a severe punishment or Jamieson would look weak. He should have been punished as soon as his evidence was used against Jamieson in court, but the organization was too disorganized to do anything about it. But they were always going to remember Kirk. Those who need to be punished don't get forgotten.

Kirk crawled across the floor, trying to make himself as small as possible. I let him get close to a cupboard door and swung it open, making it clatter off the top of his head and bang shut again. No great damage done, but he needed to know that this wasn't over yet. I stood over him, placed the toes of my left foot on the edge of his tracksuit bottoms to hold his leg in place, and stamped on his ankle.

The animal scream he let out caught me by surprise. Took me all of half a second to react and kick him hard in the mouth. Harder than I'd meant to: heard the crunch of teeth and a choking sound as one or two made their way down his throat. He did his best to cough them up while I pressed my boot on his stomach to complicate matters.

We were getting towards where we needed to be for this punishment to suffice. Kirk was trying to shuffle backward on his arse, looking to get up onto his knees. I moved beside him, let him get up to his knees with his hands on the fridge-freezer, and then slammed a knee into the back of his neck. His face hit the door of the freezer hard and he slipped sideways. I caught him by the hair, pulling him up onto his feet, but he was desperate to fall over.

I opened the fridge door and failed to get a reaction; Kirk was already at the point where he would accept any punishment that took him closer to the end of the beating. I shoved his head into the fridge and slammed the door as hard as I could. There was an explosion of plastic as the little shelf on the inside of the door shattered against the side of his head. The few items that had been in it went for a fly, dropping out onto the floor when I pulled the door open again.

Kirk's head took another couple of slams before I let him drop unconscious onto the floor. Looked like there was a little flap of skin ripped open on the side of his head, just beside the hairline. One ear looked chewed. There was blood running out of him from various places. I pushed the fridge door shut and stood looking down at him.

He was a poor soul, and if there were any thoughts running through his tiny mind right now, they would be misguided. This beating was nothing. This was a punishment that needed to be given, because the city needed to see that a punishment would come for anyone who crossed Jamieson. He got this beating, and his scars would show the world that he had gotten it. Kirk would think that this was the end of the matter. The city would think this was the end of the matter. Even the police, who must have expected Kirk to be a target, would think the punishment had been served and the issue was closed. When Kirk finally got himself out of the hospital and went back to his work, he would be happy. He would think he could go back to his normal life, the old one that was free of fear. That was the happiest he would be.

It would all be a lie. This was a temporary punishment. You can't give the police information that helps put Peter Jamieson in a jail cell and think that a casual beating is as bad as it's going to get for you. Kirk was a target, and he was going to be killed. I had no doubt about it; the organization would wait for the right moment and hit him. That they hadn't spotted the right moment yet told me they weren't running their operation as well as they used to.

The problem was gunmen. Hard to pick up a good one, and God knows Jamieson had had his fingers burnt so badly they blistered. So until they had a permanent gunman, the most they could do to Kirk was have me come round and make an example of him. It was petulant, and in its own way it was a sign of weakness. Told the world that we weren't the sort of organization who could employ who we wanted anymore.

Had its plus points though. It meant that the police and Kirk would take their eye off defense. They would think the job was done so would do nothing to stop it being done again. It would, the organization hoped, make the hit that much easier whenever it did happen.

I couldn't stop myself from shaking my head as I walked out of that flat. A piss-poor little halfwit like Kirk, thinking his life had just hit rock bottom, not realizing that he still had a grave to fall into. He was an example of what was wrong with the organization. There were some inside it that were doing a good job. Kevin Currie, who I answered to, was making money, organizing, getting things done. Marty Jones, a grubby little pimp and loan shark I had always held in low esteem, had stepped up and was running his business as well as anyone. The rest of them? I don't know; seemed like they weren't living up to their potential. Some of them because they weren't capable, some of them because they were deliberately holding back. People didn't want to put their head above the parapet until they knew how things would play out.

I drove straight home. I was done for the day as far as I was concerned, and if anything else was required of me then they knew where to find me. I didn't know who "they" would be from now on. I'd been working for Currie, and I figured it would stay that way, but I was on staff now and that technically made me available to anyone in the organization who wanted me. I could get a call from anyone who wanted to use Nate Colgan's reputation on a job.

Back in the house, and I sat down and picked up her letter again. Should have thrown it in the bin by then, but I didn't. Kept thinking about the phone call, all of the things she'd said. I was thinking about that door closing behind her, wondering where she was when she called. I had a picture of her in my mind, sitting in a bedroom somewhere, a man coming in. I didn't like that picture.

My mobile started ringing. I glanced at the screen and saw Ronnie's name.

"How did it go?" he asked me.

"Fine. It's done," I told him. Beginning to think I should have taken him with me; there were things he could have learned from it. Things like throwing chairs and fridge doors around so that you don't waste energy in the fight.

"Good. Nice one," he said. "Just wanted to check that all was well."

I could hear voices behind him, sounding like they were in another room. A woman laughed and there was the mumble of another voice. His girlfriend, his friends.

"Thanks for calling, Ronnie," I said.

Didn't tell him that his phone call had left me more depressed than I already was. Seemed like everyone else had someone in the background, while I was sitting alone in the house, listening to the silence.

Killed time and went to bed, the least worst option available to me. I hardly slept, but then I hardly ever did. A couple of hours, then awake for an hour, then an hour's sleep, more time awake, then another hour and a half asleep if I was lucky. Always waking up, always seeing things I didn't want to see. The only world darker than the one I lived in was the one I slept in.

4

They told her she'd be doing glamorous work. They told her it would be exciting. A girl she knew and trusted said it would be great fun, that she'd make loads of money and meet loads of cool people. She didn't. Like many others, she was there to be exploited. A pretty young woman, a naive nineteen-year-old. Jess Flowers didn't stand a chance with men like Elliott Parker.

Parker took her to a party at the club. Not as a favor, or for a night out. This was work. They'd invited Lee Christie to that party, and he was her target. Not a target she wanted, not a job she had any wish to do. But if she didn't, they would punish her again. As soon as Parker pointed him out, she approached Christie. She was slim, blond, wide eyes and full lips. He was thirty-six, narrow-eyed and big-toothed. Had a belly he could rest a beer can on for a laugh. If his basic good sense hadn't been overwhelmed by her beauty, he might have wondered where his luck had come from.

Jess flirted with him, danced close for nearly an hour. When she suggested they go back to her place, the *yes* couldn't jump out of his mouth fast enough. Lee Christie was a man from the industry. A man who should have understood what a set-up looked like. Sometimes, though, it doesn't matter if something's too good to be true.

She started on him in the taxi, fondling and kissing. The driver glanced in his mirror and grimaced.

"You're beautiful," Christie kept telling her, like she might not already know.

They got back to the flat she'd been told to use. Had to pretend that she knew it, that it was hers. Christie wasn't paying attention, didn't notice that she seemed unsure about which bedroom to use. He was lost in the enthusiasm of the moment. A moment that came and went quickly. Jess lay underneath him, smelling the cigarettes, booze and desperation on him, until he was done.

"You are so beautiful," he told her again, rolling over and falling quickly asleep.

Jess tried to sleep, but she couldn't. She lay and listened to the rattling in Christie's throat as he snorted through the night. She lay and thought about her mistakes. Thought about how the only way out of this situation was to do as they wanted. Whatever the cost. Maybe she drifted off to sleep, briefly. She got less than an hour's rest though, by the time Christie woke not long after eight.

She pretended to be asleep, although she was more awake than ever. She heard the scratching noise first, a pen on paper. Then she heard him getting dressed and trying to be quiet about it as he snuck out. He was on his best behavior, not waking the sleeping beauty for fear of upsetting her. When he was gone, she rolled over and read the note he'd left. There was something childish about it, something almost endearing. He told her what a great time he'd had, and that he had to leave for work. He left a number, asking her to call so that they could meet up again. He signed it with his real name.

She already knew that Lee had to be involved in the criminal industry. Elliott Parker wouldn't have been interested in him if he wasn't. They were doing this because they were going to try and make money from him. But she felt pity for him. This fat little guy, thinking that she found him attractive. He was pathetic. How could he fall for this?

Jess sat up in bed and thought about running. Throw on some clothes, run out of the flat and down the stairs. Get on a train and get out of Glasgow. Go anywhere — it didn't matter. The thought of freedom was nice, but false. She had been snared by them; it was a trap she couldn't break out of that easily. There would be someone watching the flat, watching Lee Christie leave and waiting for her phone call. They were professional, and that's what people didn't realize about them when they first turned up in the city.

Jess called Elliott.

"He's gone. He left me a note with his phone number on it."

"Good," Elliott told her. "You've done really well. You've been excellent. I'll come round right away, pick you up."

His Birmingham accent was the softest of all the group. There was something suave about him, like he was educated and sophisticated. Elliott had always tried to be nice to Jess, or at least make it seem like he was being nice. That was how it worked. He did his best to seem reasonable, so that when he demanded she do repulsive things, it was harder to say no. But there was something about Elliott Parker. The others, they ignored her, or were unpleasant towards her. The nicer Elliott tried to be, the creepier he became.

Elliott arrived at the flat within a couple of minutes. He had been outside, watching and waiting. He let himself in with his key, smiling contentedly as he watched Jess emerge from the bedroom. She was wearing the short dress she'd been wearing the night before and she looked ruffled. He thought the look suited her.

"You ready to go?" he asked her. Pretending she had a choice.

"Yeah," she said, and nodded. Pretending that she wanted the same things they did, afraid of the consequences if she defied them.

He smiled at her. "Come on, Jess."

As they walked out to the car he kept a hand on her back or shoulder. It looked, to any passer-by, like a sign of affection. In truth it was a reminder not to run, that he would always be there. He always did that if they were in public, made sure she didn't get any ideas. Being nice kept her calm, being close kept her passive.

Elliott drove back to the hotel. Hotel was rather a lofty term for a big house converted into manky rooms and let out to gullible people who didn't have the time or organizational skills to find something proper. Could have been a nice guesthouse if it had been well looked after, just down the road from Queen's Park, so it took real sloth to make it as unwelcoming as it was. They wouldn't be there long, so none of them cared much.

The bedsheets weren't clean, for a start, and the bathroom had definitely not been scrubbed since Elliott's room was last used, no matter what the owner claimed. Elliott had always been picky about these things. Where Dyne and Nasty could put up with little inconveniences on a job, Elliott saw no reason for standards to be so low. He reminded himself it was short term; they'd be moving again in a couple of days for security reasons.

They parked in one of the few parking spots outside the hotel and Elliott led Jess up to her room. They didn't see anyone, didn't talk to anyone. He let her go into the room, said goodbye, and pulled the door shut behind him. He locked it, and went downstairs.

They were all in the TV room. Four of them: two muscle, a gunman and the leader of their group. The muscle were nothing, hired help they'd picked up before they came up the road for this gig. They knew them both, Henson and Aldridge, down in Brum, but they weren't part of the group. They had always used Ricky Saunders for muscle work back in the day, but he was inside. The muscle had no part to play in the conversation Elliott wanted to have. This was for authority only. He nodded for Dyne, the head man, and Nasty, the gunman, to follow him into the kitchen.

"She do her thing?" Dyne asked him.

Dyne was looking thin these days, vulnerable. He was using, and that was bad news. Made him take risks, like this whole job. He had a narrow face that was a little too long for the rest of him, brown hair messy on top and clipped at the sides and skin that looked darkly tanned, whatever the weather.

"She did. The soppy dick left her a love note with his phone number on it. He's in."

Dyne nodded, hearing what he wanted to hear. "No need to waste time then. We can do it tonight, right?" He looked at Nasty when he spoke.

"Sooner the better," Nasty said. As much as he was likely to say. He was the most openly hostile to this job.

"Yeah," Dyne said, "sooner the better. Tonight then. Get her to call him. Get him round there. See, lads, see? Couldn't be going better." He said it with the sort of ingratiating smile that looked desperate, pleading. Seemed like he was trying to convince himself.

Nasty got up without a word and went back to the TV room. Elliott patted Dyne on the shoulder as he got up and walked past him. It was all right for Dyne—he had his girl with him. It was her who set this job up, and only she was in anything close to familiar territory.

Elliott walked back up the stairs, marveling at the thinness of the carpet as he went. He unlocked her door and went inside. Jess was sitting on the edge of the bed. She was always sitting on the edge of the bed, looking sad. Never seemed to watch TV. Never did anything other than sit there.

"You need to make a phone call. Can you do that for me, Jess?"

"Sure," she said.

"Course you can." He smiled, sitting next to her and putting an arm around her shoulder. "You've been amazing so far, Jess, really amazing." He leaned in and kissed her gently on the side of the head. When he straightened, he reached into his pocket and took out his mobile and the note Lee Christie had written for her. "Call him; tell him you want to meet him tonight at the same flat."

He flattened the paper and carefully tapped in the number, handing the phone to her. Elliott leaned in a little, close enough to hear every word.

"Hello, Lee? It's Jess, from last night."

"Jess," he said, loudly and enthusiastically enough for her to move the phone briefly away from her ear. "I'm glad you called. Listen, sorry I had to shoot off this morning, but I had work that needed doing and I didn't want to wake you. You looked so peaceful, asleep there."

She grimaced. Peaceful. This guy was clueless. "That's sweet. Um, would you like to come round again tonight? I'd like that, if you could."

There was a chuckle from Christie. "I'd love that, I would love that. How about I get round there early, say six o'clock?"

"That's great," Jess said.

"Great. Well, I'm looking forward to it. I'll see you at six."

"See you."

She hung up and Elliott put his arm around her. "It won't be so bad tonight," he told her. "You won't have to sleep with that creep. All you have to do is let him into the flat."

"That sounds better," she said, nodding.

Elliott smiled as he got up from the bed. The smile of a man who knew things she didn't and reveled in the advantage. She knew then that something worse than sex with Lee Christie was going to happen that night.

Elliott and Nasty took her round to the flat. This time they went in with her and waited. She'd been told it didn't matter what she wore and that she didn't need to do her hair because Christie was going to come round anyway. All she had to do was open the door for him and that would be it. Elliott kept repeating that to her. The more he said it, the less reassuring it sounded.

Elliott looked relaxed but Nasty was clearly nervous. He kept going into the bathroom, standing in the doorway looking out into the corridor. The two of them spoke as though Jess wasn't there.

"We need to be fast, after. Good chance of getting spotted," Nasty said, shaking his head.

"We'll be out in thirty, forty seconds, tops."

"Doesn't take that long to spot us."

"Nobody will be looking. There won't be noise."

Jess was torn. She didn't want Christie to turn up because she knew what was going to happen to him now. Didn't matter how much of a creep he was, she didn't want to see that. But if he didn't turn up they might blame her. They would blame her. Nasty had a bad temper; she had seen him lose it. And Elliott, with his calm re-assurance, always touching her. His punishment would be worse than Nasty's anger.

It was before six o'clock by the clock on the living-room wall when the doorbell rang. Everyone got up quickly. Elliott went into the bedroom and Nasty walked quickly down the corridor and into the bathroom. Jess waited until Nasty was out of view and answered the door.

As soon as she opened the door Christie stepped inside and kissed her hard on the lips. Jess wasn't expecting it; his mouth hit hers hard and hurt a little. He laughed and closed the front door behind him. Jess turned and started to walk down the corridor. She was walking with her back to him, didn't hear the bathroom door opening as they moved along the corridor towards the living room. She was in the living-room doorway and looked back over her shoulder to make sure Lee was still behind her. That was when she saw Nasty coming out of the bathroom with the gun in his hand. He raised the gun quickly and shot Lee in the back of the head. The gun made a puff rather than a bang. There was a flash of blood and Lee fell forwards at Jess's feet.

She opened her mouth, wanting to scream or say something, but nothing came out. She stood in the living-room doorway, panting with shock. Someone touched her arm; she jumped. It was Elliott, already out of the bedroom and pushing her past the body and towards Nasty, who was at the front door.

"Come on — let's go."

They walked back down to the car, trying not to rush. If anyone spotted them, none of the three noticed. They drove straight back to the hotel, Nasty complaining that they were breaking too many rules of a good job. Elliott locked Jess in her room and disappeared downstairs. From her room she could hear them shouting, arguing about the gun Nasty had used. Nasty wanted to throw it away, try and get another one in the city. This one was used, compromised. Elliott was arguing loudly that getting another gun was madness when they couldn't trust anyone here. They quietened down; Jess didn't hear how it ended.

Be a party girl, that's what her friend had suggested. Knew a guy who ran a club in the city that held private parties. You dance with guys, get them their drinks, treat them like they're something special. Maybe, if you want more money, you do more than that. Made it sound like it would always be her choice. Like she would have control. A few weeks later and she was locked in a hotel room. A man had died because she had lured him to a flat. Jess had never felt more alone.

5

His name was Lee Christie. He was thirty-six and had been a useful network guy for the organization, working a couple of street dealers and pushing some of the lower-risk stuff himself. He wasn't vital, but he was useful. He made money. And then he was dead.

There were three messages on my phone when I got out of the shower in the morning: one from Kevin Currie, one from Ronnie Malone and one from Conn Griffiths. Conn was what I always considered myself to be: smart muscle. There was a time, not that long ago, when most muscle could be dismissed as some halfwit, some thug working a short-term gig, throwing his weight around for cash. Times had changed, big organizations had gotten more sophisticated and the standard of muscle had gone up. There were still some halfwits around, but usually in the smaller organizations or working security or debt collection. There was still some use for the meatheads.

Doing the sort of thing I'd done to Kirk Webster the day before, in fact. I'd done a thorough job, the sort of job that sent the right message, but the whole job was a piece of shit. If the organization even had basic muscle that it trusted, they would have done that job a long time ago. Right down to the bottom of the ladder, people were being treated differently. The old boss, and the old certainties, were gone. Now nobody knew who could be trusted, and everyone was trying to earn the leadership's respect all over again. If they were lucky they would earn it before Jamieson got out and the leadership changed again.

What I'll try to do now is explain a little something about the food chain in our business. You look at the Jamieson organization, and you know that Peter Jamieson, in prison or not, is top dog because his name's above the door. Below Jamieson are the people that run the different aspects of the organization work; and for loan sharking and prostitution, that was Marty Jones. So Marty has trusted people working below him, handling day-to-day stuff, and the man he trusts to handle much of the debt collecting is Billy Patterson. Keeping up? Billy has a long track record of hiring the smartest muscle he can get his hands on because he figures he needs to stay a step ahead of the other bitey little sharks in his area. He hired Alan Bavidge before he got knocked off. He hired Mikey Summers and he hired Conn Griffiths. There are a few levels below people like me and Conn, the front line if you like, but we'll forget about them for now. If they were important, people would realize as soon as they went missing.

"Apparently he'd been lying dead there since yesterday, maybe yesterday afternoon. Nobody found him," Conn said when I called him. Judging from the messages on my phone, Conn knew more about the dead man than Ronnie or Currie, and I was interested to know why. "It was me and Mikey went round and found the man, lying there. We left, waited a couple of hours, made an anonymous call about a smell. There was a fucking smell as well, Nate, I'll tell you."

"What were you looking for him for?"

"Ach, business, you know. Just business."

I stood in my kitchen, half dressed, wondering what to have for my breakfast, holding the phone and letting my silence speak for me.

"Don't fucking give me that," Conn said to the silence. "It was nothing major; we weren't looking to do him any mischief, if that's what you're thinking."

"I'm just thinking, why was Billy Patterson sending his two

senior men round to visit a mid-level dealer working for Angus Lafferty? Billy isn't worming into dealing, is he?"

I could hear Conn muttering under his breath. "Christ's sake, you're gonna make me say it, ain't you?"

"Up to you."

This problem was inevitable in any organization with a split leadership—the lack of trust. I hint that I think Billy is moving into dealing when he should be sticking to debt collecting and that gets Conn all hot and bothered because he knows if I said such a thing to Kevin Currie it could spark a falling-out. This is why any organization needs a strong head, a single person who has the power to make any decision he wishes. Means people further down the chain falling out don't matter so much, because people down the chain will always fall out. Plus it gives those people someone to fear if their falling-out starts costing money.

"It ain't Billy, it's Marty, and he ain't trying to get involved in the drug business. We're not daft, Nate—you know that by now. Marty doesn't trust Angus Lafferty as far as he can throw him, so he's got us hooking up with a couple of people close to Lafferty's lot to find out what they're up to. The dead guy, Christie, was trusted by Lafferty and we were talking to him, regular like, and friendly."

"And?"

"And nothing. And Lafferty is doing what he was always doing, not holding back on anything that we can see."

That was good to know, at least. "So what about Christie?"

"Dead. Long dead and looking like it. I'll tell you this and all, Nate—his way of dying is the sort that we all need to worry about."

"Oh?"

"Bullet to the back of the head, nice and clean, single shot. No fucking about with it. Couldn't see any other marks on the man. It was quite dark so we could only get a wee look at him. Had to use Mikey's phone as a fucking torch. Anyway, yeah, it was clean, professional, I'd say. Wasn't in his own flat either. A place belonging to persons as yet unidentified."

"A lure?"

"Probably, although he didn't have any product on him."

"So how did you guys find him?"

"Had a meeting set up with him, went down to his place and he wasn't there, but his wife tells us where he was going."

"His wife knew the address?"

"Wife seems to know an awful lot; I think she did a lot of the work. Lot of the thinking, anyway. So she gave us this address, says he was going there and that was yesterday. We ask her what she's been doing since yesterday; she says she's been doing the same thing she always does when he disappears for days on end— praying his dick falls off inside whatever whore he's with."

"Nice."

"Aye. So we go to the address, thinking it's probably bullshit, but it's not. It's an ordinary wee flat with the front door ajar."

"It was open?"

"Like they wanted it to be found," Conn said knowingly. "This was a professional hit, sending a message. Listen, Marty's up to high doh. He's got me and Mikey working on this and I want you and your boy to come give us a hand, maybe take the lead in some aspects. There's more to this than me and Mikey can see for ourselves."

"Where do we meet?"

"It'll be one of Marty's offices; I don't know where's available yet. I'll call you in an hour. You and the boy come right round."

Coffee and toast for breakfast, sitting at the kitchen table thinking about this dead guy I'd never met, pushing thoughts of tomorrow's meeting with Zara out of my head. I'd heard of Christie, because it's my business to know who's who. My first thought was Lafferty lashing out because the dealer was talking to Marty, but that was shit-for-brains thinking. There isn't a man in the city works harder to keep out of trouble than Angus Lafferty, and knocking someone off for something minor like that couldn't be further from his style. The corpse had been talking, but he'd been talking within the organization.

So you think about the dead guy and who might have wanted him dead, who profits from it. Another dealer maybe. Yeah, sure, that's the natural place to leap to, but what other dealer works a lure and nails the wee bastard with a professional hit? If Christie was sticking to his own patch and not playing suicide games then he was hit by someone looking to take his patch from him. Not much of a patch for a hit like that. Using a gunman, setting up a lure, those things cost time and money, and Christie wasn't worth much of either.

But my mind was clinging on to the same thing that had mattered to Conn: the open door. You lure a guy to a flat with the promise of a good score or a woman, you shoot him dead, and then you leave. So far so professional. Then you leave the front door open on your way out. Doesn't matter if it's wide open or ajar; open is open and open means a lot. Means you want someone to come along and find the body, sooner the better. You want to send a message and you want that message out on the streets within hours.

If we're accepting that Christie being killed was a message then you and me have got to sit down and work out what the message was. Not just what it was, but who it was aimed at. Let's stick to the obvious until we have something more complicated to play with. The message was "we're coming to take over your business and there's fuck-all you can do about it." The target was Angus Lafferty, or the wider Jamieson organization. If the obvious was correct then it wasn't just a message; it was a bloody declaration of war.

6

Took until half nine for Conn to send a message through with an address for me, an office in a small industrial site out near the airport. I went and picked up Ronnie and drove us out there.

"This is all a bit over the top, isn't it?" Ronnie asked me.

It was, a bit. We could have had this meeting somewhere more convenient and saved time, something we didn't have to spare. But you can't mock careful because careful is often the thing that keeps you breathing in this business. I could understand why Conn wanted this out of the way. It was his meeting, so he got to choose the venue.

"If we're going to be poking around in the business of a dead man then we need to poke carefully," I told him. "Better if people don't know we're doing it at all. Also helps if we only meet Conn and Mikey off the radar. Make it seem like we're not working together. Trick people into thinking that only those two are looking into it—leaves us free. At least make people think we're working separately from each other."

"Muddy the waters so we can move in them unseen," he said casually, like he'd heard it often enough to know. Apparently I'd tried to teach that lesson before.

"Exactly," I said. He was learning.

The place was smaller than I had expected—a little office building in a wide open space that was presumably meant for unfulfilled industrial purposes. The building wasn't a lot to look at: not twenty years old and looked forty. Two-story, bare blocks, glass door, sat at the end of a street that just stopped there with little room to turn and go back. There was an empty patch of land next to the building that used to have a shitload of vans for hire. The building was worth buttons but the land was worth a fucking fortune and Marty was sitting on it. Picked it up from some halfwit who hit the bottle as soon as his business started to look shaky, got himself into debt with Marty and gave him the place to settle it.

We parked next to Conn's car and went inside. A little reception area with glass doors on either side. There was a shout of "through here" from the right so we went into a large empty room to find Conn and Mikey. Two big men in their thirties, Mikey younger, darker and a little softer round the gut. There was a pasty halfway into his mouth, so he could only nod a hello to us both.

It had been a workroom; Conn and Mikey were sitting on units at the side of the room. It had a bare floor and tiled ceiling and not much else to look at. It was clean; place hadn't been used or broken into since the previous owner went tits up. There was a large window that looked out the front to where we'd parked.

"You must be Ronnie," Conn said, reaching out a hand.

Mikey had met Ronnie before; helped him out of a little jam when we were chasing down a dealer working on Jamieson's patch. Conn hadn't, and was polite enough to say hello first. Politeness is often the first casualty of professionalism, so Ronnie appreciated the gesture.

Conn went back and sat beside Mikey; me and Ronnie loitered around in front of them, close enough to whisper. It was cramped; we were huddled together like we were hiding the conversation from nonexistent passersby. It felt right though, the way men like us ought to talk when we're discussing the dirty end of the business.

"What's the latest?" I asked, in a tone that said I wanted to take charge of the conversation. I knew what I needed to hear, and I didn't want to hear anything else.

"Latest is what it was," Conn said. "The police are on it. I heard DI Fisher's name being mentioned. Don't know what conclusions they're jumping to, but we'll need to keep our heads down. They see us sniffing around, they're going to think we're involved."

We were involved, of course, just not the way Fisher would want us to be. "How clean did you leave it?" I asked.

"Clean enough, I think," Conn said as I watched flakes flutter from Mikey's mouth. "We weren't gloved; didn't think we'd need to be. Touched the door and nothing else though. Took our time leaving, wiping anything we might have touched on the way in. Can't guarantee we weren't seen, but we didn't see anyone. Not a great area for going unseen, mind you."

I trusted them both; they were about as good at this as anyone in the city and they made a hell of a team. I nodded, accepting that there was no need to say any more on the subject of their professionalism.

"We went and saw the wife again," Mikey said, swallowing down the last of his brunch. "That was Marty's idea; he wants this figured out as fast as possible. We went round and had a word with her when we were sure the cops had gone."

"How sure?"

"We called her first, checked; she said they were," Conn said. "We went round, checked the area first. Seemed clear. We didn't have long with her though; the cops aren't going to leave the griev-ing wee woman alone yet."

"And?"

"And she had fuck-all to add to what we already know. She was holding it together, best she could. Said nobody had been in touch with Christie that he hadn't been expecting until this new chance came along. Said he got a call asking him to come to a meeting in-side, like, an hour, or some fucking rubbish like that. Should have smelled a rat at that."

"She says this was some new person that Christie had no

connection with, but, I don't know," Mikey said. "He wasn't daft. Got led around by the cock sometimes, but that was a problem for him and the wife to sort out. I figured with his experience he wouldn't go running off to a meeting with someone he'd never even heard of."

That made sense; even someone with little experience shouldn't run into a potential danger zone like that. A man who'd been around the business a while, he would know that.

"So what are we thinking?" I asked.

"First thing, he knew the person who called up and invited him to the meeting. Maybe someone he'd done business with before, or a woman he'd been involved with," Conn said. "The lure worked, and they had a pro there to hit him. It was someone that was good enough to get in and out without being seen, far as we know, and make a clean shot on Christie. I think we can assume a pro."

"Which leaves the why part," I said.

"Aye, that bit's what's got Marty farting fury," Mikey said with a casual smile. "He's worried that we might be under attack, that this might be the start of something big instead of all the pishy wee shite we've had to put up with so far."

We'd all been waiting for something big, expecting it to come. The fact that this much time had passed without a major attack was some credit to the people running the organization, shoring up the defenses and repelling any of the small attacks that were made. Some people tried their luck, looking to pick a little bit of the business away while Jamieson sat in his cell, but none had succeeded. Maybe that had helped to put the big guys off, but it wasn't going to stop them forever. Someone was going to roll the dice and take a shot at what he considered a weak opponent.

"He have anything to back that fear up with?"

Conn shook his head. He always did the majority of the talking for the two of them. "Just more fear. Don't get me wrong, he's done a hell of a job, wouldn't have thought he was capable, but he's been sitting there waiting for something like this to come along for a while now. He's ready for the fight, just needs the fight to get ready for him."

"Not the worst way to be," I said quietly. "So what's our part in the play?"

I looked sideways at Ronnie, indicating that I meant him and me, but mostly I was just making sure he was still there. He hadn't said a word since we arrived, which was fine if he had nothing to say, but he needed to impose himself a little more around established guys. It was way too easy to disappear into the background of a conversation when men with reputations were talking, but if he ever wanted to be taken seriously then he had to learn to speak up. Guys like Conn and Mikey meet new kids in the business every damn day, and they forget about most of them pretty quick. You have to make some sort of impression, and sitting next to me is no more than a good start. It's easy to get lost in the deep shadows of other people.

"We're going to look at the more obvious stuff, the stuff that might have us bumping up against the cops," Conn said. "We'll start with everyone around Christie and see where it takes us. You start with Adrian Barrett and try and work your way back to Christie from there. We'll see if we meet in the middle."

"Adrian Barrett, huh? Anything to support that?"

"He's flavor of the month," Mikey said with a shrug. The work we did, the world we inhabited, was all just a little too easy for Mikey. He wasn't as smart as Conn but, quiet as he was, there was nobody more comfortable with brutality than him. There was a danger that that made him sloppy, complacent, but there weren't many better in a tight spot.

"The bosses think he's here with a crew," Conn said. "I'm sure someone's mentioned him to you already."

I nodded.

"He ain't here alone anyway," Conn went on, "so he might just have the means to make a hit against Christie."

"Not much of a message though, is it?" Ronnie asked. "I mean, the message is strong, but if we have to search around to work out who's sending it then it doesn't do him a lot of favors."

Conn nodded. "True, but there's another side to it. There's nothing worse than uncertainty. Uncertainty makes us all look weak, and that helps him make more attacks in the future. You get circumstances as well when you can only pull off a move at a certain time. He knows that once the first shot is fired, everyone's going to be keeping their head down. So he pulls this now and only shows off that he did it later on when he can profit most."

"What do we have on Barrett anyway?" I asked them.

"A name," Mikey said with a smile. "Not much else, uh?"

"Not much." Conn nodded. "The rumors say he's been here for a month or two, but I don't know. I think that might have been a bluff. I think he might have had people here for a month or two, spreading the word that he was with them, but I figure he only showed up more recently. We think he has a crew with him, some serious people maybe. Got a good supply behind him as well, judging from the moves he's making. Comes from the Midlands, apparently; Birmingham or something."

"I heard not Birmingham, but somewhere close by," Mikey said.

"Yeah, lot of different stuff going round; take it all with a pinch of salt."

"We're sure he's alone, not fronting for someone else?"

"You thinking of Park?" Mikey asked, smiling.

A little bit more history for you now. Don Park is a senior man in Alex MacArthur's organization, and everyone with the power of sight can see that he's trying to edge MacArthur off a cliff so he can take control. MacArthur's old and coughing up his lungs, so he might not need much of a shove. That means Park making big moves of his own, and getting an outsider to front up a network attacking Jamieson would be a good start. Park was the one we'd all been waiting for.

"Makes some sense, doesn't it?" I asked.

"It does, but nobody's seen any link," Conn said with a despairing shrug. Somehow it would be better if it was the devil we knew. "Worth looking at though, when you're trying to find Barrett. That's all we've got," he said with a sense of finality, looking at his watch, "and we ain't got any time left either. Come on."

He and Mikey got up, headed for the door. If they were in a hurry then we would give them a head start; just good form to not all rush away from the same location at the same time. Me and Ronnie edged our arses onto the units and did our best to look like we had a clue what was going on around us.

"How do we find Barrett then?" Ronnie asked me.

I started laughing, because, come on, what else could I do? "That would be the question," I said. "He needs to stay somewhere I suppose, so we start looking round for places he might be staying. If he's brought a crew with him then we should be able to track them down. Might take some time though. Needle in a haystack."

We were driving back into the city, listing hotels and other places they might be hiding out in while they tried to crack Glasgow.

"Are those two going to be able to keep themselves out of a police station if they're sniffing round the case?" Ronnie asked with a hint of genuine concern.

"They have about as much chance as we do, which is some. They'll be careful, and we do still have some people inside the police who can help us out of a little trouble, just not a lot."

"Huh. So they're good at all this then, are they?" he asked me, fishing for something more than he was going to get. Ronnie wanted info on everyone he met. That was the right attitude to take. Best way of keeping yourself alive and free was knowing who the threats were. Threats from the bad intentions of enemies, threats from the incompetence of friends.

"Very good, and you'd be wise not to say anything to the contrary."

I left it at that, because that was as much detail as a smart kid like Ronnie needed. Mikey and Conn were two of the best in the business, Conn smarter than Mikey, Mikey more brutal than Conn. They'd both been working for Billy Patterson for three or four years and had been his top men since Alan Bavidge died. That was the business side of them, and that was all anyone really needed to know.

The personal side was straightforward. Mikey was married with a couple of young kids and I think I'm right in saying Conn was godfather to the youngest. What Ronnie was plucking up the courage to hint about was Conn's private life, which was very private. In my opinion it didn't really need to be. Nobody further down the food chain was ever going to dare question him to his face about it, and nobody further up the chain gave a damn about who a profitable employee slept with. Okay, if he stopped being good at his job then it would be open season, a stick to beat him with, but as long as he was brilliant at his work then his business was his own. He didn't seem to see it that way. Spent too much effort hiding himself from the world, but that was up to him. It wasn't Ronnie's place to try and make it an issue.

We stopped at a pub in Craigton that Jamieson owned, place that had unreachable pretensions about it. I introduced myself to the manager as the new security consultant and asked if there was a room me and my assistant could use for an hour. In a quiet back room we sat and wrote out a list of places we could check. A few hotels in there, some houses we knew Park owned, a few other decent hiding places that might be good for a long-term option.

We were about to make some phone calls when my mobile rang: Kevin Currie.

"Nate, listen, there's big things going on. Lafferty's gone nuts about this hit on one of his guys and he's calling a meeting."

"Meeting of who?"

"Everyone whose name he can remember. He wants a big meeting tonight, everyone involved in running the organization these days. Marty tells me that you and Ronnie are helping his boys investigate, so the two of you might as well come along."

"Jesus," I muttered.

"I know, it's stupid, you don't need to tell me. I tried to talk him out of it but that just pissed him off even more. It was his boy that got killed and he's getting all emotional about it. He probably thinks it makes him look weak, has to be seen to do something big about it."

Yeah, they always think they have to be seen doing something big about it.

7

She was waiting for me when I got back to the house. I wasn't in the mood for her, or for anyone else. Too much to think about, and my thinking is better done alone. But Kelly smiled at me even when she saw my scowl, and that forced me to soften a little. I unlocked the door and let us both in.

Kelly was thirty-one but could have passed for a weary twenty-five if she'd made the effort. Pretty, girlish features, long dark hair and a look around her eyes that told you just a fraction of what she'd seen. I didn't ask what she'd been through, because it was rude and because I knew some of it already. I knew her father and brothers were about the worst people I'd heard stories about in my many years of hearing stomach-turning stories. I knew she'd gotten into some sort of relationship with Tom Childs, a boy who worked for Kevin Currie. Childs got her a job with Currie too, and all was going well until Childs overreached. Tried to step up and become a gunman, got himself killed.

So now Kelly was single, and probably feeling a little vulnerable. If any one of the stories about the kind of father Vincent Newbury was were true then he was a man worth running from, and I was the sort of guy who could protect her. That might be a cynical point of view. Maybe it wasn't as negative as that. Maybe she liked me. I'm not an ugly man, a little weathered and starting to grey at the side of my dark hair, but not wholly unattractive and certainly well built. I'm smarter than most in this business, but not exactly a bundle of laughs. So I don't know. A mixed bag.

The first time I'd met her had been when her man Tom Childs had died. I was the one who took the body out of the hotel Ronnie worked in. She helped. That had to color what she thought of me now. Negative association. I had been professional at the time, cold but trying to keep it polite. She had called me a few weeks later, saying she wanted to know how the disposal had gone and whether we were in the clear from any police investigation. We met up, we chatted. I didn't tell her about the disposal, just that it had gone well. She didn't need those details, not about someone she presumably loved. She was smart and she was strong and she was pretty. The sort of woman that leaves a mark on you. She had contacted me a couple of times since, one time coming round to the house and having a cup of tea. That's how she knew where I lived. It was flattering. That's why I had let her get this close.

Thing is, I was in no mood to play nice that evening. The search for Barrett had started with me and Ronnie firing off blanks all across the city. Not only could we not find out where they were, we couldn't find anyone who would now admit to knowing about them. People who had previously mentioned Barrett and his crew were now denying all knowledge. Defensive amnesia. Information lockdown, us on the outside.

I went in ahead of her to the living room. The living room was ordinary and tidy. Laminate flooring, TV in the corner, three-piece suite, a picture of Rebecca on the mantelpiece above the fire. It was all part of my drive for ordinariness. It was designed to lull you in, make you think I was a normal guy.

"You working?" she asked me, standing in the doorway to the living room, practically inviting herself in.

"Uh, sort of, yeah. Not with any success." That was my polite way of saying that I didn't want to talk about my day's work. Sure as shit didn't want to talk about the work I would be doing that night, sitting in on this meeting that Lafferty had called.

"Okay," she said, nodding and saying nothing more about it.

And that, right there, was one of the reasons I really wished I could have made a move. She was smart enough to know how the business worked, already trusted by Currie to carry out decent mid-level work for him. But I couldn't do anything, because why would I take a woman I liked into my life? A dangerous life. The burden of my work and my daughter and now my daughter's mother. The best I could do for a woman I liked was to keep her away.

"I won't keep you long if you're busy," she said. Watching her as she looked at me out of the corner of her eye. Smart, and playing up to me, trying to get me to see how lucky I was to have her in my living room. I didn't necessarily disagree.

"I do have to go out in another hour or so. More work," I said, not adding to that.

"Oh, right, well, I'll keep this brief. How worried should I be about my employment prospects?"

"Why do you ask?"

"There's talk going around that moves are being made against the whole organization. People are talking about the whole thing finally falling down. I'm thinking of getting out before I get trapped in the rubble."

I frowned a little because I didn't like the sound of those rumors. Sort of thing someone who wanted to damage us would start, then sit back and watch panicky employees spread the word for you. It was a good tactic.

"I don't think you have anything to worry about," I lied. "There are people making moves against the drug side of the business, but there always are. Nature of the business. I haven't heard anything about Kevin's business being vulnerable."

"No, but if someone takes the drug side of the business, every other side is likely to fall down, isn't it? That's where a lot of the money and a lot of the toughest people are."

I sighed loudly. "Not necessarily, not if Kevin's half as smart as

I think he is. Most parts of the business are designed to survive without the help of the rest of it. That's the point of having all the different parts. And anyway, we'll deal with this new problem, just the same as we dealt with all the other ones."

She stood in my living room, nodding. "Word is that someone got killed."

"Someone did," I agreed. "That's the nature of the business as well, unfortunately. You know that."

She winced a little when I said it, more for show than emotion, but she made me feel guilty.

"Sorry, I didn't mean anything by that," I said to her. I moved towards her, wishing I had the good sense to stay where I was. I was about to reach out and put a hand on her shoulder when the phone started ringing.

I went over and picked it up because Kelly had seen the gesture I was about to make, and seeing it was enough. I didn't recognize the number, answered it and said hello.

"Just making sure you haven't forgotten about lunch tomorrow," came the female voice. Zara sounded exasperated, like she'd rather be speaking to anyone but me.

"I haven't forgotten," I said, and left it at that. There was something in me repulsed by the idea of talking to Zara while Kelly was standing right there in the room with me. Zara was the hard lesson I'd already learned; Kelly was me trying to put that knowledge into practice.

"So, uh, yeah, it'll be nice to see you again," she said, speaking low and trying to sound personal. That wasn't the way she spoke when we were together and I didn't understand why she was trying it now.

"Will it?" was all I said. We were meeting for lunch the following day and there were only so many things I could say to Zara; this phone call was in danger of using most of them up. I can indulge in a happy conversation with someone I like but there's a lot of sense in cutting off people that are dangerous.

"It will, yeah," she said. "You're the father of my daughter, Nate; it'll be good to see you. Been a while. Not since all that stuff with Lewis."

I had no idea what the hell this was anymore. This wasn't her just checking to make sure that I would turn up for lunch; this was her trying to establish some sort of connection. Mentioning Becky and throwing in a mention of how I helped her when Winter got killed for good measure. There was something sweet and sticky in her words, a trap I didn't like the sound of.

"Yeah, well, I'm busy right now, so I'll see you tomorrow."

"Okay, sure, I'll see you then." Cheerfully accepting my words and their dead tone as though it was the friendliest way in the world of saying goodbye. That wasn't like her at all. No snarky comment to kill me off with at the end of the conversation, nothing to make sure she had the last word. I smelled a dead rat.

I hung up and looked round at Kelly, and immediately found myself comparing her to Zara. It was a stupid thought that I stamped out before it could go anywhere it shouldn't.

"I guess I should get going then," she said with a nod. "Should I, uh, spread the word that all is well in the organization, that there's nothing too much for the people I work with to be worried about?"

That made me pause, because there wasn't an obvious answer. As soon as an organization starts telling people there's nothing to worry about, people immediately assume there's something to be worried about. Nobody trusts what their employers tell them and it's often smarter to say nothing at all than to screech reassurance.

"Maybe don't say anything at all unless people ask. If anyone says something then you can shoot it down, yeah, but otherwise let's not make a fuss about it."

"Good thinking," she said, nodding. "Better not to give people an excuse to panic." She was looking at me, waiting for me to say something that would close the conversation.

"It was good to see you again, Kelly," I said, sounding more businesslike than I'd intended.

She smiled and headed for the door, and we said goodbye. Kelly was still staying in the same flat she'd shared with Tom Childs, still working the same job she'd been doing for Currie. It seemed, from the outside, like she didn't need protecting anymore, and that she could build whatever life she wanted for herself. But if she'd been running from that family of hers it would be a hard habit to break.

I grabbed something to eat before I went out to the meeting. Meeting! What a stupid bloody thing it was, another act of petulance that wouldn't have happened if Peter Jamieson was on the outside. Only he would have the power to make people gather before him, and that was a power he was too smart to use. This was going to be a parade of bad leadership. Anyway, I went, because bad leadership was still leadership.

8

The one redeeming feature of this meeting was that Lafferty had a good place where we could hold it. He had a three-story glass-and-steel building next door to a recently renovated warehouse, on a busy, business-looking kind of street. The buildings were tall, brick affairs that shut out the light on the street and made the streetlights coming on a relief as I drove along it. A lot of them now had large glass doors and big wide windows knocked into them, but most made an effort to keep the classic feel. One stood out, and the one that stood out was the one where we were having our meeting.

On the left-hand side of the road there were two properties that Lafferty owned, one traditional brick building whose ground floor was now a car park, and a pudgy, three-story glass-and-steel mediocrity next door. That was Lafferty's office, bought not long after it was built, replacing a perfectly decent old building that had been knocked down in the name of modernization.

The sliding doors to the rusty brick building were wide open, the place well lit as I pulled in and came to a halt facing the side wall. Sort of place where cars could come and go for meetings and it wouldn't raise too many eyebrows. This was all part of his cover for the money he was making, and a damn good cover it was too. Lafferty was making enough legit money to walk away from the dirty, but having a lot of money seemed to make him want to have more.

I was busy looking at the other cars, trying to work out who was politically minded enough to get here early and who wasn't. I didn't recognize any of them, a collection of entirely predictable German luxury. I wasn't first to arrive; probably not last. There must have been seven or eight cars in there ahead of me, probably another seven or eight to come, and that just made me shake my head. Gathering everyone that mattered in one place when you're worried you're under attack. Might as well have put up a fucking sign.

There was some gormless-looking soul standing at the side of the warehouse, obviously sent by Lafferty to show people the way to the office next door. I didn't need a map to go out the side door and cross the narrow gap to the next building.

"Just go in the side door and the stairs are beside you," he said as I walked past him and ignored him. "They're on the second floor."

I mumbled something that he might have mistaken for a thank you if he was in good spirits, and kept on walking. Across the narrow road between the buildings and in through the glass side door. The foyer was a needlessly long and wide waste of tiled floor space, a large curved desk on the left tucked under one of the staircases that stood on either side. There were large paintings hanging opposite each other that looked rather like a giant had coughed up paint onto a sheet of steel. This was presumably designed to give the place a sense of personality. It failed miserably. There was a sterile, functional and contrived feel to it that I guessed hadn't been the case with the old place they knocked down to build this.

I went up the stairs, found myself looking left in through an open door to a conference room with a lot of chairs laid out for people to sit on, a group of men standing around with drinks and talking in low voices.

The room was all lit up, full-length windows all the way down one wall. Now, I was all for hiding in plain sight, but this just seemed to be pushing our luck. A couple of low voices fell lower when they saw me walk in through the door, my usual scowl on my face. I'm employed to be scary so it's always worth reminding employers how scary I can look.

Three gravitated over towards me: Mikey, Ronnie and Marty Jones.

"Some party, huh," Mikey said with a smile, nodding across to the table at the side of the room, as amused as I was disgusted.

There was wine, red and white; whisky; orange juice; tea and coffee; and a bottle of rum that was presumably intended for Damon Walker, who I knew drank gallons of the stuff. There were glasses and cups, all very neatly lined up for the happy little troops to drink, in what felt like an attempt at friendly normality.

Marty Jones stuck out a hand, one I wouldn't have wanted to shake in days gone by. Marty's always been a weasel, working in the grubbiest, cheapest parts of the business, but you have to give credit where it's due, even when it's due to an arsehole. So I shook his hand, because he'd stepped up and done as much as anyone to hold the organization together in Jamieson's absence.

"I should warn you," Marty said in a whisper, "that Lafferty ain't happy with how things have played out. Doesn't like the fact that it isn't his own people who've been taking the lead on this."

That was to be expected, so I shrugged it off and looked around the room, picking out the faces I knew and making a note of the ones I didn't. Seemed like a lot of people had come along, certainly a lot more people than could be considered important. Some had brought protection, which boosted the numbers, and others had brought company to give the impression that they were too important to travel alone.

Never a good thing to see faces you don't recognize and realize that they're important, but that was happening. I leaned across to Mikey and asked him who the cluster in the far corner were.

"Guy with the grey hair and the earring is Davey the Robot. You heard of him, yeah?"

"Fuck's sake, what happened to him?"

"Got old fast is what happened. I heard there was something wrong with him, but, I don't know, I hear that about a lot of people that keep hanging around. Rest of the people with him are just his crew. Probably got them along to make him look like he's tough and not worth arguing with."

"Same reason I have you and Conn along," Marty muttered, acknowledging that he was the man most people would feel comfortable arguing with. Marty was the most recently junior of the people in the room so could most easily become everyone else's punchbag if he didn't do a damn good job of protecting himself.

Davey Boyd was one of the biggest distributors of drugs in the country and had been working exclusively for Jamieson for a few years. It had been a while since I'd seen him, back when he was the picture of health. I recognized one of the people he had with him, a tough guy who worked distribution for the Robot. The other two looked like they were there to drink the coffee and make up the numbers.

I could see Bobby Wayne standing near the window, back to it, looking around the room like an autograph hunter. Bobby owned a bunch of warehouses, garages and other useful storage spaces that people like Kevin Currie had urgent need of. Kevin wasn't around, nor was Lafferty himself as far as I could see.

Stuart Crockley, who oversaw the process of cleaning up the money now that John Young was in the clink, was sitting talking animatedly at old Brendan Thorne, who looked after the housing stock the organization owned. Thorne was sitting there not listening to a one-sided conversation that was obviously unimportant given its volume.

There was another little knot of young, tough-looking guys standing off to one side who could have belonged to anyone in the room other than themselves. Take those kids out and you were left with a fine collection of white, middle-aged men to set fire to if you wanted to damage the organization. I stopped myself shaking my head in front of people who might see and take note.

Marty nodded a familiar hello to someone who had just come

into the room and I turned to look down at Billy Patterson. Still looking for all the world like a street thug, Billy did the donkey work running the debt collection side of the business, keeping a lot of tough guys on staff and reporting to Marty. They made an odd and uncomfortable partnership, the tough and quiet Billy and the brash and sneaky Marty, but they were holding it together. They were making damn good money, so of course they were holding it together.

"Hasn't started yet," Marty said quietly.

I was starting to realize just how big a spread this was if Patterson was invited along to be a part of it. This wasn't just the very top guys, guys who might be able to keep the discussion a secret: this was enough people to guarantee that word got out.

"Yeah, I saw a few of them coming up behind me," Billy said.

Took a few more minutes for the last of the senior men to arrive. Matt Harris, who oversaw a bunch of pubs and a couple of clubs, and Damon Walker, who ran an assortment of little businesses for the organization, coming in together. If memory serves me, Taylor "Original' Carlisle was the last to arrive. He was running some boiler-room set-up that John Young had been keen on before he went down, a sharp-tongued bastard with a fake tan and a faker accent and hair that should have been cut months ago.

Kevin Currie had wandered into the room not long before, looking like a man who'd already had a conversation he wasn't happy with. He nodded a hello but didn't stop; there were far more senior people in the room he had to be seen talking to.

The chairs were lined up so that three or four were facing a semicircle of twenty or so, and there was little doubt who was to occupy the few that the many were to face. That was for Lafferty and his people, the ones who were taking charge of the meeting, the current crisis and, they obviously hoped, the senior positions in the organization.

It was only thirty seconds after Original arrived that Jake

"Lonny" Donezak stuck his head round the door, made a head count and disappeared again. I'd met Lonny before, briefly, when I went round to Lafferty's house to have a friendly word in his ear on Peter Jamieson's account. Lonny was the tea boy, but being the tea boy meant he was senior enough to be in the house. Made him a trusted employee, if not quite a right-hand man.

Thirty seconds later and a scowling Angus Lafferty graced us with his presence, trying to look something close to presidential as he walked across the room to the chairs. He was never an impressive spectacle, too short and chunky and close to fifty to make a statement with appearance. I knew he'd been to a few of Marty's parties before the fall as well, which ruled out presidential. But here was a man who had one of the best drug import businesses in the country, a man who had made more money than I could burn through in a lifetime, a man who had managed to drag all these men into this room to listen to him just because he was in a huff. That was impressive.

Lonny was with him, and another man that I didn't recognize until he sat down somewhere behind Lafferty and I got a good look at him. Russell Conrad, his name was. A gunman, freelance as far as I knew, experienced and good at his work. I'd worked with him not that long before. He'd killed Potty Cruickshank, a debt collecting rival of Marty's. He did the killing, I did the disposal. One thing the organization didn't have was a gunman we could reliably call our own, and it seemed like Lafferty was about to solve that.

People gravitated towards seats, Lafferty the first to sit down. Taking the seat that he evidently considered put him at the head of the conversation. Junior guys like me and Ronnie held back, letting Currie and Marty and the rest of the senior men sit nice and close if they so chose. Not all did. I noticed old Thorne sitting near the back, making no effort to hide his boredom. A man who understood that this meeting wasn't for him.

I would have preferred to stay standing, but everyone else sat down and you don't want to be the odd one out. Sitting at the back, watching the farce unfold. Sitting watching what could have been a scene from an unimaginative low-budget movie, because Lafferty was an unimaginative director. He wanted a meeting that would make a statement about his influence, a meeting that everyone would remember. Well, he had that much at least, but no more.

"We all know what happened," Lafferty said with a tone that told the room he'd already rehearsed this, "and what we need to know now is who was responsible and how we punish them. Lee Christie was a good man and a good employee, and all of us here know that the way we defend our people is how we are judged by our people. We let Lee down, but we will get justice for him."

He paused, like he was expecting a murmur of agreement from the room. Some gave it, because they were happy to give what was expected of them, but the rest of us stayed silent. I was there to listen, not to play along.

"I want to know who was responsible, and I think I already know who was," Lafferty went on, looking around him for the agreement he had obviously set up before he got there.

"Word on the street is that this Adrian Barrett was behind it," Original Carlisle piped up in his faux-posh accent.

"That's what I'm hearing, and people are worried about it," Crockley added too quickly. "We need to show people we're making moves."

For one thing, Original Carlisle knew as much about the word on the street as I knew about particle physics. The guy spent his life running cons from behind computers and a bank of telephones, and Crockley wasn't a damn sight better informed. They were reading their lines from the script Lafferty had given them beforehand, and it showed. This whole thing had been set up in advance to make sure Lafferty got exactly what he wanted out of it. That's why an old guy like Thorne, who had seen it all before, was sitting at the back of the room; he knew he didn't have a line to play so he sat there while the pantomime went on and would bugger off home as soon as it was done.

"That's what I've been hearing," Lafferty said, "and I think we have to take action. Now I know Marty has had men working on this, so I would presume that by now they've found something useful."

That was a challenge to Marty: throw your men overboard or stand up to Lafferty in front of a room of senior men. I was thinking that Conn and Mikey should have brought themselves some life jackets.

"They've been looking for a very short while," Marty said, his thin voice puffing out its chest as best it could. "They've been investigating the fact that someone they didn't work with was killed, so it's not as though they've had the best chance at finding the truth here. You'll have had guys investigating your man's death as well, won't you?" Now, he asked it like a friendly question, but this was wee Marty Jones rolling a grenade into the middle of Angus Lafferty's parade.

"Of course," Lafferty said a little stiffly. He should have given Marty a copy of the script if he was going to give him a part. Thought he could knock Marty around, but damn it all if Marty hadn't grown a fully functioning spine in a medically improbable space of time.

"We know it was Barrett though," Original said, trying to pull this back around to the version of events he could most benefit from. "I mean, come on, we do."

"Agreed," Lafferty said, "which is why we have to move. We all know that people think we're weak because Peter is in jail, and it's important that we don't let that carry on. We have to make big moves, and that means making big moves against Barrett. We presumably have people who can make some moves," he said, looking at Marty and Kevin like it was their responsibility to provide. It wasn't; if Lafferty wanted something done then in the good old days he could have gone and fucking well done it himself.

"Of course we do," Marty said, getting a little red in the cheeks with all the defiance that was flowing through him now.

I was ignoring Lafferty at this point, watching Conrad behind him because Conrad's moment in the spotlight was about to arrive. Seemed like Lafferty was about to advertise the new arrival, something you should never do with a gunman, or any newcomer for that matter. In most circumstances it's best to keep your new card hidden up your sleeve for as long as possible.

"Good. I, obviously, have good people to contribute to that. I think it's about time we resolved some of the ongoing issues we've had since the arrests. We've let too many things slide for too long, a failure of leadership that we all must take some responsibility for. I've employed a gunman for the organization, which should have been done a long time ago. I also think it's about time we addressed some other issues that are holding us back. All these things, these weaknesses, are part of what's allowing Barrett to attack us."

There were mutters and nods but the matinee idol was over-egging the role; too much of a performance even for the rest of his cast. If you want to put on a good show then you must maintain focus on a single narrative, and we were going off into subplots that people were bored of.

"We need a reliable weapon supplier," Crockley said.

I noticed Damon Walker rubbing his forehead; saw the little smirk on the Robot's face. Experienced men who understood that this isn't how the business works, or how it's supposed to work. You don't have one weapon supplier, because your gunman should have his own and should be left to deal with his own. A good gunman doesn't want a relationship with a new supplier and a supplier doesn't want to be tied to one organization.

"I agree," Lafferty said quickly, "and to that end I think we should make contact with a good supplier and get him on board. We may have to overpay, but this is something we shouldn't be penny-pinching on."

A couple of morons murmured their agreement while the sensible clung to the most respectful silence they could find. This was setting up a new hire that Lafferty had already decided on and the experienced men in the room who weren't part of the performance were getting a little offended. All these decisions being made in advance by a rump supporting Lafferty was beginning to look like the importer positioning himself as leader.

"I want us to make an offer to Mark Garvey," Lafferty said. "He's well connected, he's reliable, he's close to a number of people inside the organization and he's managed to keep himself out of all the trouble lately. Does anyone have a better suggestion?"

It was a nice move, I'll give him that. After picking out Marty as the dissenting voice Lafferty was now suggesting hiring a man that was a friend of Marty's. Garvey was a friend to anyone with money and connections, but he was closer to Marty than he was to Lafferty as far as I knew. There were, it seemed, no better suggestions.

"Presumably this is the sort of hire that our security consultant can make on our behalf, so we'll leave that in his hands," Lafferty said, the one reference I was going to get. I didn't bother blushing when eyes in the room turned towards me.

"There's the issue of cleaning money as well," Crockley said, an area he had a right to speak about at last. "We have a lot of small businesses on the books that aren't pulling their weight. Too many that are behaving like they're separate from the organization."

Ronnie, sitting next to me, stiffened at that and it took me a little while to remember why. His friend ran a little electronics shop that had been circling the drain despite their best efforts, so Ronnie got them some investment I suggested he should avoid. That, I correctly guessed, was what was on his mind. It was only the

start of what was on Lafferty's. There were a lot of legit little businesses like that. They existed just to give people an explanation for
income and were kept carefully away from any illegal activity. Apparently he wanted that to change.

"Then we need to be much more aggressive about getting them
to cooperate," Lafferty said, his voice rising as he got to the end
of the performance. He wanted to sign off with a good line, bless
him. "We need every part of this organization pulling in the same
direction or what happened to Lee Christie will happen again. We
will continue to be attacked and eventually we will lose the ability to defend ourselves. It's why I wanted everyone here tonight. I
want to know that everyone is pulling in the right direction here."

I don't know what he expected at the end of that—some sort
of triumphant cheer of agreement that he saw in a shitty film one
time. Well, that didn't happen, but he got some agreement from
those who were in on the performance, a few grumbles from those
who weren't and silence from a few others.

"Good," he said, "then we can move forwards with confidence
in our direction."

Doesn't take a genius to work out that Lafferty, having been the
first to sit down, also wanted to be the first to get back up. Center
of attention at the open and close of the play. He was the main act,
the star of the show, and that meant everyone else had to follow
his lead. But he wasn't the first to stand up; Brendan Thorne was.

"We're done then, are we?" Thorne asked wearily, standing up.

There was silence, people looking at Lafferty to see how he
would react to being dismissed. "We are," was all he could manage.

"Right, well, I'll be off."

"In a hurry, Brendan?"

Thorne was already putting his coat back on. "I'm an old man;
I don't have as much time left to piss away as you boys." Now that
was a challenge from an old man without the means to back it up,
just the power of his poisonous tongue.

"Piss away?" someone other than Lafferty asked. I didn't catch who; I was watching Thorne on the other side of the room.

"Aye. Your man here isn't my boss. Peter Jamieson's my boss. If I get a call from him telling me to follow everything you just said then I'll follow everything you just said. If I don't, I won't. See you, boys."

Most of us made sure we didn't look Lafferty in the eye in his moment of fury, but he had a line for those that did.

"Must be past his bedtime," he said with a smile.

That gave the sheep something to laugh at. Dismiss Thorne as a goofy old man with a small role to play in the business, which was, at its heart, true. But he was more than that; he was the voice of the silent men in the room. There was some idle chatter for a couple of minutes, and then the Robot and his little crew made their departure.

I waited around for a little longer, making sure my face was well seen by everyone, and then me and Ronnie left. By God, I was glad to get out of there. I was driving home when I got a text on my phone telling me to head to one of Marty's flats, so I did. The world's a funny place when a meeting with Marty Jones is the best meeting of your evening.

9

You can't chase every rat; you will end up getting lost in the sewers. You catch the ones you can. You keep an eye out for the most rotten of them; you don't get distracted from the bigger picture. But some, Jesus, some of them you just can't stop chasing. It's not a professional thing to admit to, no cop should get sidetracked by a criminal of little importance, but it happens. Someone infests your mind. Might be a victim you just have to help. Might be a criminal you just have to catch. Everything else drops into the background.

For DI Michael Fisher it was Zara Cope. There had been a few others before, there would be others after, but at that time it was her. She'd gotten right under every inch of his skin and he needed to do something about it. Ignoring it made it worse, he had learned that. He wouldn't let it get in the way of his actual work; too much a professional for that. Too aware of the consequences if colleagues noticed his obsession. That meant using whatever passed for spare time in his life to go hunting.

He knew she was back in the city; she had been spotted. Some plod had mentioned it; thought Fisher would find the news amusing. Thought wrong. Nothing about Zara Cope ever amused him. A pretty young woman who picked up dangerous men to get access to their cash. Even they must have known that she didn't care about them, but they stuck around because she was pretty. But that woman was brutally cold. Look at what she did when Winter died.

Fuck's sake, she went into the very room where her lover was lying dead on the bed and recovered drugs and money for herself. Heartless bitch is what she was. It enraged Fisher to think about it. He didn't know where the drugs and money went; a girl like her had too many connections to trace them all. But it went, and when she got out of jail, she disappeared as well. Went south was what he heard, and became another little shit flowing out of the city that he could try to forget about. An obsession happily sidelined.

Then she came back. She had some nerve. She came back to this city, his city, almost certainly looking to make some more money from some other poor sap. There were always plenty to choose from. When she got out of prison he had followed her around, just a little. Keeping an eye on her in his spare time. Didn't have much of that; there was far too much going on at the time. She knew he was watching, he was sure of it. Might have been one of the reasons she left.

He had a justification for this minor obsession, if you care to hear it. The one where he told himself that what he was doing was logical and sound. Zara Cope was a woman who seemed attracted to trouble, and it liked her right back. She would have someone or something on the go, some scheme that any cop would be wise to check out. That was what he told himself. It was almost convincing.

Truth stood pretty far away from that explanation. The truth was that she had pissed Fisher off by telling him the truth. All the lies, all the bullshit she spun when he arrested her after Winter died, that didn't bother him at all. That's a pretty big part of the job. No, it was the one time she told the truth. The time she looked him in the eye and pointed out that he was failing. That was what did it. Stared him down in an interview room and told him a truth that made him feel about three inches tall. Just because he was arresting her and not the person who killed Winter.

Some of that bitterness was gone now. Fisher had put Peter Jamieson and John Young in prison. He had put Shug Francis and a whole bunch of other more minor gangsters behind bars. Not for nearly as long as he wanted or as they deserved, but it was a damn good score. Didn't manage to pick up Calum MacLean after he pointed a gun at Fisher and stole his car, but he hadn't given up on him. He had every right to be proud of what he'd managed to achieve and little right to be sitting in his car across the street from the guesthouse where Zara Cope was staying. It was a busy road and he was exposed, parked across the street. There were trees out the front of the building that obscured the view. But if he hadn't been there, he wouldn't have known who she was with.

People tell you not to get negative and obsessive, but sometimes it's the best damn thing you can do. It's the difference-maker. It was starting to get dark, the streetlights were coming on, and Fisher was watching the entrance to this place. Can't have been more than twenty rooms in that building. Less, probably, although he couldn't see how big it was out the back. She had turned up in the city and it had taken him little more than a day to track her down. Spotted her in the city center, picked up the trail and followed her to Nate Colgan's house. She didn't get in, went back to the guesthouse.

Fisher was happy to sit there watching the building all night, watch for people coming and going. Every one of them was worth watching. Couldn't do that though, because his phone started to ring. DC Ian Davies's name on the screen. A useless, harmless DC, hanging on long enough to retire and claim his barely earned pension. He wouldn't dare phone Fisher off duty unless it was something important.

"Fisher."

"Boss, it's Ian, uh, DC Davies," he said, never confident enough that his superior would remember who he was despite the years they'd spent working together. "Listen, I think you're going to want to come along to see what I'm seeing."

Fisher had no idea what the man was seeing, and less idea why he would want to share the moment with him. "What are you talking about?"

"You know the office building that Angus Lafferty owns?"

That was enough to grab his attention. "Go on."

"I'm in an office down the road from it, other side of the street. We got a message in from uniform saying there were a lot of people of interest turning up at the building."

"What do you mean by a lot of people of interest?"

"Well, a lot of them were in by the time I got here, but Lafferty, Kevin Currie, Marty Jones, a whole bunch of others. Basically everyone you can think of that matters to Peter Jamieson."

"Give me an address and a safe entrance to the building you're watching from."

He hated to leave the guesthouse unwatched, but the problem with personal obsession was that it was personal. He couldn't get anyone else to stand in for him. Took him nearly fifteen minutes to get round to the building Davies was watching from. Parked a street away from that building, ran round to the next street, in through the front door, up two flights of stairs and along to an office at the back. The back of the building looked down onto the street where the entrance to the garage and Lafferty's building sat. They could see the glow of light from first-floor windows, but they didn't have an angle to see into the room.

Davies was sitting on an office chair at the window, looking down into the narrow street. DC Baird was standing by the edge of the window and another man in plain clothes was sitting at the side of the room. He, Fisher assumed, was the one who'd let Davies into the building.

"Well?" Fisher asked.

"Some of them are leaving already. Not sure who the first guy out was—couldn't see him. See, they're going across the alley to the building next door where their cars are parked. Can't get a good look at them in the cars," Davies said.

Fisher was standing in the dark, looking down into the street to see cars leaving in the hope of getting a glimpse of the occupants. Davies had a notepad on his lap and a pen in his hand as he watched the building next to the offices. A trainspotter in the dark.

"Can't have lasted long," Fisher said.

"Less than half an hour between the last one arriving and the first one leaving," Baird said. Took Fisher ages to learn that man's name but he still seemed irrelevant, even in the company of Davies.

"Here's another one," Davies said, as a car emerged from the red-brick building next to the offices.

It pulled slowly onto the street and moved away, a dark saloon with more than one person in it. They couldn't see more than that; the high angle they were at was useless. Getting closer would get them spotted. Fisher sighed loudly.

"Give me some names."

"Well, we don't know them all because a few had arrived before I got here," Davies said. "I saw Marty Jones and I think I saw Billy Patterson as well. Can't be a hundred percent though. Lot of little skinheads around. Definitely saw Kevin Currie arriving, he had someone with him. Think I saw Damon Walker as well, although I wouldn't put my house on it."

Another car emerged from the building as he spoke.

"I think that's Marty Jones's car," Fisher said. He thought it but he wasn't sure. It was the sort of car he had anyway, one of those big four-by-fours that nobody needs on a narrow city street.

A figure crossed from their side of the street up towards the office, walking briskly with his collar pulled up and his head down. He moved with a purpose, striding fast.

"That guy?" DC Baird asked.

"Nobody," Fisher said. He was a man with an intimidating walk and a sense of purpose that didn't belong to him, but that didn't mean he was a criminal. There were plenty of little men walking with that stride in this city, convinced that nobody had anywhere more important to be than they did.

They stayed at that window for another two hours, waiting until they were sure nobody else would leave. Fisher wasn't sure what he was watching. It was big because of the numbers and visibility of it, but that didn't mean it was important. Seemed to him that the most likely explanation was someone making a move within the organization. The internal politics of a struggling beast.

"I have a theory, sir," Davies said as they were walking slowly down the stairs. Baird had stayed behind with the security guard.

Fisher did his best to ignore any theory that managed to fight its way through the gloom of Davies's mind. He thought it best not to encourage him; instead let him reach his longed-for retirement with the least possible fuss. But now and again, you just never know, he might say something useful.

"Go on."

"That Christie guy was working for Lafferty. Suddenly Lafferty is bringing everyone to his offices. If you were Lafferty and you wanted to position yourself as the big cheese, this would be a golden time to do it, right?"

Fisher thought about Lee Christie. Dead in the corridor of a nice enough flat in an area a knowledgeable pro wouldn't use. Too busy. He'd gotten to the flat where it had happened after DS Louise Forbes. A brash young woman, probably because she had to be to keep the rest of them in check. She was short with dark-brown hair always tied back in a short ponytail. A cop he did respect. That he thought had a chance to be great. They didn't know much about the victim, until a uniformed officer Fisher couldn't bring himself to trust anymore linked him to Lafferty. A drug-trade killing. Christie wasn't important to Lafferty, but his death could be used for position.

It wasn't arrogant for Fisher to think that he would have reached that conclusion eventually without anyone's help, but

Davies was right. Things had settled down a bit in the city after the arrests; now would be the time to start positioning yourself for leadership. A smart and ambitious man could gather enough power to make sure that Jamieson had no organization waiting for him when he got out. It could become the Lafferty organization. Bold move. Dangerous move. Public move as well, and using the Christie killing to justify it. This was worth Fisher's ongoing attention. But he was still thinking about Zara Cope.

10

I was one of the last to arrive at the flat above a charity shop on what would be a fairly busy street in the daytime. If any one of the stories I'd heard about Marty Jones was true then I guessed the charity began at home with that shop. I went upstairs and found Marty, Billy Patterson, Mikey, Conn and Ronnie waiting awkwardly for me, and Kevin Currie still to arrive. I nodded hellos to men I'd seen all too recently and stood next to Ronnie beside the door of the living room we were in.

Marty was pacing. Mikey and Conn looked relaxed enough. I got the impression that Patterson didn't see this as being much of his business. But he ran debt collection for the organization, which made this very much his business. He was important, whether he liked it or not. Smart people often didn't want to be important in this industry. Billy always looked like he wasn't bothered about anything in this world. That was a lie. Billy Patterson was hellishly ambitious. He had run his own debt collecting organization before he hooked up with Marty and I was sure he wanted to run his own organization again in the future. Working with Marty was a convenient way of making sure the Jamieson organization didn't wipe him out. Maybe he didn't care much if Marty got hacked down by these events. Maybe he figured it would help him get back out there on his own, free from the deal he made with us in the first place. There were a lot of agendas, even in that little room.

"Just waiting for Kevin to get here," Marty said to no one in particular. Might have been me.

We were in a small living room and the place was crowded. There were two couches in the room, Billy Patterson on one with Mikey on the arm of it. Conn was sitting on the window ledge, which meant the empty space on that couch was for Marty, if he ever decided to sit down. Didn't seem likely to me. The other couch was empty, waiting for Kevin and Ben Carmichael, who was Kevin's second in command. A smart guy, and Kevin trusted him, which was enough. Me and Ronnie just hung around silently by the door for five minutes until Kevin Currie and Ben Carmichael arrived.

They came into the flat; Conn went out into the corridor behind them to lock the front door now that everyone was here. Kevin and Carmichael were smiley and said hello to everyone before they sat on the couch. Kevin knew that he was entitled to the best seat in the house. He carried his authority lightly, but it was always in view. Had to be. As soon as his arse hit the leather, Marty started talking, and wouldn't have stopped if Kevin hadn't thought to interrupt him.

"This is ridiculous. Way fucking beyond ridiculous. I mean, Jesus Christ. You see that dickhead, sitting there running off at the mouth like we were all kids and we had to sit there and listen to it. I mean, come on, what the fuck is this anyway? Is he in charge now, is that it? Are we all just going to trudge along and listen to whatever he's got to say like he's some sort of boss now? Sitting there talking like he was Peter Jamieson, as if Peter fucking Jamieson would have called everyone together like that in the first place. Has this prick never heard of a security risk?"

"All right, Marty," Kevin said, running a hand over his mouth while he considered a response. "I talked to Lafferty beforehand. He had this all planned out well in advance."

"Too fucking right he did," Marty said, his voice a higher pitch than God intended for him. "He's been waiting for a chance like this."

"Maybe, but he's handled it well," Kevin said. "He had managed to get a call with Peter in prison before he arranged the meeting; got Peter's permission to go down this road."

Marty groaned and Billy looked mildly surprised; the rest of us looked like juniors who weren't entitled to a big reaction to a boss's decision.

"He already knows the first move he's going to make as well," Kevin said. "He's found out who Barrett's gunman is and he's going after him as well as Barrett. He's serious about getting revenge for this Christie person."

"No he fucking isn't," Marty said with a hiss. "He's serious about making himself look like he's the big shot in town now, that's what he's serious about. And how the hell did he find out who the gunman is when we haven't got anything to go on?"

"Lafferty's well connected down south. He managed to find out a bit about Barrett's history. Found out that he's a smart mover, used to have his own network down there, a small one but still something. He left the Midlands after trouble. Came up here with his crew, brought along his own gunman with him. Jawad Nasif, the gunman's name is. They call him Nasty, apparently."

"Course they do," Mikey said with a smile.

"So what now?" Marty asked. "I mean, are we just going along with all this? If Peter says yes, then yes, I do it, but this is nuts. This is giving Lafferty the chance to run just about everything until Peter gets out."

"It does, yeah," Kevin said, "and there's not a whole lot we can do about it. Barrett needs to be dealt with and Lafferty's taken the lead in that. What can we do? We have to help the man; it's our own necks on the block if we don't. We do it and we see what plays out."

Marty sighed and Billy folded his arms; nobody else seemed to feel like filling in the silence so I thought I'd take a stab at it and see what damage I could do.

"So he got Jamieson's agreement to hire Conrad?" I asked. My voice rumbled round the room, deep and older-sounding than my years. Sometimes my voice intimidated people on my behalf.

"Yeah," Kevin said.

"And he found out about Barrett's background within a few hours of looking around for it. Has he found out where Barrett or his crew are now?"

"He says not yet," Kevin said, "but he's looking around for them with everything he's got."

"Kicking up a storm, in other words," Billy said. It was a small and ordinary voice, made to sound higher and lighter by the impression mine made. A fact I kind of liked.

"There isn't anyone in the business who isn't going to see his boys stomping around the city," Conn said. "Gonna make sure every bastard knows that he's the man now."

"Advertising it won't get him far," Mikey said.

"He find out anything else about Barrett?" I asked.

"All he told me was that his connections down there knew the name, respected it, didn't know that he was up here."

"So Lafferty doesn't know if Barrett's working for anyone or just decided to come up here on a whim—fancied the weather or something?" I asked.

"You're thinking about Don Park?" Conn asked.

Damn right I was. Everyone was thinking of Don Park and someone needed to say it. Wouldn't be the first time he tried to use a new name to attack us. He'd done it before: picked up a young guy that was looking for a way into the business and used him as a front, attacking us on our own patch to try and take business. Park was smart and a threat, and we needed to talk about that.

"Could be Park," Marty said. "I already talked to a contact I have in MacArthur's organization. Senior contact, mind, no bullshit. MacArthur isn't involved, but that doesn't mean fuck-all for

Don Park. Park's pulling jobs by himself these days, only reporting them to MacArthur when they're done. MacArthur's scared, close to the end of the rope."

Alex MacArthur ran a major organization in the city, bigger than Jamieson's but flabby. MacArthur was old, coughing up a lung every time he took a step, so the story went. Don Park was young and ambitious. He had been a rising star for MacArthur. Now he was morphing into a treacherous successor. The best ones always do.

"We need to find out if Park's involved then," Kevin said. "Doesn't change anything if he is. Priority is finding Barrett and putting an end to him. In that regard we have to back Lafferty unless Peter says otherwise."

We were all a toxic mix of misery, anger and impotence leaving that meeting. Everyone knew that this was Lafferty trying to put himself at the front and marginalize everyone else involved in the running of the organization; there was no secret to that. If you call everyone to a meeting in your office and make demands for their support then you've blown any secret out of the water. But Lafferty was smart enough to wait until he had a damn good reason to claim support, which was why it was important that we got to Barrett before he did. If he could clean up the mess then he would be untouchable, at least until Jamieson came out.

That was the real issue here. Lafferty was playing for leadership until Jamieson got out, but what happened then? Having split leadership was all part of Jamieson's plan to make sure nobody got too big for their boots before he got out. If Lafferty changed the equation then his release became an unpredictable event. Nobody wanted unpredictable. Unpredictable was invariably trouble.

I walked down to my car with Ronnie and we stood on the street for a few minutes, talking. Conn was giving Mikey a lift home.

Billy, Kevin and Carmichael had already gone and Marty was staying in the flat for the night. I think his plan was to get as drunk as possible in there and see if the morning would calm his fury.

"I know it's loose change," Ronnie said to me. "But about the stuff they were saying in the meeting about businesses doing their share ..."

"Uh-huh."

"They're talking about businesses like Owen's shop, aren't they? Small businesses, legit businesses."

I nodded and said, "Yeah, they are. I wouldn't worry too much about it though. There's no way Jamieson's going to let them start harassing small legit businesses into cleaning money through them. He's far too smart for that. He needs some legit businesses to clean money through, but he needs some to just be legit businesses so he can explain income. That doesn't change."

"But if Lafferty's pulling the strings ..."

"If Lafferty's pulling the strings then you and me will end up being hung from them anyway," I said. I wasn't looking to depress the boy, but he had to know where this was going. "If Lafferty gets any amount of real control then it's going to be Lafferty's boys that get to do all the meaningful work. You and me might find work as low-level muscle, debt collection and bullshit like that, but the whole security-consultant cover will go to someone else, someone close to Lafferty. We'll be pushed down the chain or pushed off it altogether."

He sighed loudly, making a show of what a bad thing that might be, but it was as skilled a performance as Lafferty's. I could see that he quite liked the idea of being pushed out of the business, of having to go legit. It would be an escape route back to a safe life.

"How much do the Turners owe Kevin?" I asked, just to drag him back to horrible reality.

"He bought a twenty-grand stake in the shop. He owns it;

they're not paying him back. It's just a minority stake though; I mean, they still run the business."

I looked at him and raised my eyebrows, thinking that I must have taught him a lesson about ownership in the industry by now. Apparently not. "The second they let someone from an organization take a share in their business, they stopped running it. Not like they can do anything to stop Kevin doing whatever he wants with it."

"But Kevin doesn't want to put pressure on them though, does he?" There was naive hope in his voice.

"No, he doesn't," I said, "but I don't know how much that's going to matter. Not if Lafferty gets his way."

It was a suitably horrible way to end the day, so I drove back home. It was late when I got in, pushing past midnight. I checked for messages and breathed out when there were none. There would be plenty coming, I was pretty damn sure. People were starting to make moves that were all about sending messages.

Lafferty had men out there looking for Barrett and this Nasty gunman of his, and that was going to mean blood. You hold yourself up in front of the organization as a man who defends his people and you bloody well better come up with a result. This was a dangerous game for Lafferty too, and that was where I dared to get a little bit hopeful. You take any gamble as big as this and you can lose. We could still knock Lafferty down on his arse. Not to harm him; he was still profitable to the organization. There was a route out of this that kept the status quo. We find Barrett and deal with him and his crew before Lafferty can get Conrad on the job. We make it clear that we handled it for Lafferty and now that he has what he wanted, it's time to play nice. If he gets what he wants from us rather than getting it for himself then it holds him firmly in place. Holds him where Jamieson should want him.

I went to bed with all that shit running through my head, so that's my excuse for not sleeping that night. Three, three and a half hours altogether, perhaps. Yet another night of not sleeping well. Not because of the things I'd seen or done in my life. They ran through my mind when I was awake, not when I was sleeping. I was always waking up growling at the darkness, scared of the things I was yet to do.

11

Being awake early let me get to work early, which just ensured I had even more time to get slowly pissed off with the world. Nobody seemed to know anything at all about Adrian Barrett or Jawad Nasif or any other member of the crew Barrett had brought up with him. They were invisible men, drifting silently through this city.

Nobody would tell me a thing about them, and that got me worried. People tell me things, because they know the cost of silence if I find out that they've been holding back. If they were more scared of Barrett than they were of me then Barrett was a man to worry about. It had to be fear. There were people in this city who knew something about him.

Me and Ronnie stumbled through the morning, powered by bacon rolls and watery tea, clearing as much of our list as we could. Properties where a crew coming in from outside might hide. We were at the point where we had ruled out the idea of the Barrett crew staying in any hotel or B & B that we could think of. Everywhere was too public, too easy for them to be spotted. That meant they had a place or places of their own in the city. Made more sense if you were willing to buy into the idea that they were here for the long haul, and that they had people from the city helping them.

"What now?" Ronnie asked me.

"Now you go pay a visit to Brendan Thorne and have a conversation about housing stock, who has what, that sort of thing."

"And you?"

"And I have a meeting of my own I have to go to."

"Yeah?"

"Yeah," I said, giving him a look that told him the questions ended round about here. He needed to understand that not every meeting I had needed his permission, or even his awareness.

I headed over to the place on George Square Zara had said to meet her. I was nervous about it—no shame in admitting that. I hadn't seen her in so long, didn't want her back in my life, knew she was poison to me, but couldn't stop myself being excited. Being a man of reasonable good sense I then couldn't stop myself from being angry with that excitement.

She was sitting at a little table towards the back of the busy little place when I went in. It was the kind of narrow restaurant designed to make tall and broad men like me look epically clumsy. The tables were all too close together, the chairs were all too big for the little square tables. It was all a good way of making a small place seem busy, but it guaranteed that I bumped into two chairs and stood on some poor woman's handbag on my way to Zara. I already disliked the place by the time I sat down.

Zara was sitting there, looking like a thinner version of the girl I had known. Her cheekbones stood out more; her lips looked a little thinner and her eyes a little bigger. Her hair was the same as I remembered, dark and just past her shoulders. And she was still the same Zara, still beautiful and just a little too obviously dangerous for most.

She was one of the few people I had ever been close to. Properly close, in an emotional sense. I don't have a lot of emotion to spread around, so very few people get a share. I make a point of keeping my distance. Create a sense that I exist a split second and a million miles away from everyone else, that nothing in the world the rest of you live in could intrude on the one I occupy and dominate. I want to be just out of reach, especially for people as dangerous as Zara. And then, for a little while, when she was pregnant with Rebecca, she crossed the gap into my world. That was when we connected, when we really had something special. It had to end though, when she had Rebecca. There's only room for one other person in my world, and from that moment on it would always be our daughter. I pushed Zara back out, and I'd been pushing her further and further away ever since. I thought I'd done a good job of that, until I saw her sitting there waiting for me.

"Nate," she said when I sat down. "You haven't changed a bit."

Not entirely true, but truth was a barrier Zara had long since hurdled over. I was a little greyer, maybe a little broader in the gut than I was last time we met. The lines on my face that had started digging in when I was still in my mid twenties were deeper than ever. But I had a look that aged well, so her lie was at least living on the same street as the truth.

I reached into my pocket and pulled out a slip of paper, passing it across the table to her, beside the bowl of soup she'd ordered. "That's all the details you'll need to empty the account. Got as good a price as possible for what you gave me." I said it cold and businesslike, making sure she got the message early and clear.

She reached out and pulled the paper across the table, glanced at the bank name and the sequence of numbers on it, and put it into her bag. "Thanks. I do appreciate it, Nate. I know you didn't need to help me."

That, right there, was the moment that the last grain of trust between us put on its coat and left the building. Zara being nice and appreciative was not Zara. I looked at her with a stern expression, waiting for her to say something reassuringly sarcastic.

"What?" was all she could come up with.

"Is that it then? Are we done?"

She looked disgusted, a look she wore with the kind of perfection only practice can bring. "You're that desperate to get away from me, huh?"

"I'm busy."

"Sure you are; you always were. Cleaning the blood out of the grooves in your boots, wiping other people's skin off your knuckles. Always so busy. You can't even manage one conversation?"

There she was, the good old Zara I had expected. "If you have nothing else to say then I don't," I told her.

She smiled that wry little smile of hers. "Always the enigma, playing your cards close to your chest. I'd like to know how my daughter has been, seeing as my parents enjoy speaking to me about as much as you do."

"She's fine," I said, then decided it was only decent to say a little more. "She's into photography at the moment, however long that'll last. Enjoying school, but she's smart enough to enjoy it." That was as much as I would commit to saying; anything more and it might feel like an invitation for her to ask more.

In fact, it was about as much of a conversation as she and I needed to have, and I was ready to get up and leave. She could see me glancing at the door, trying to work out a way of saying goodbye that was polite but firm.

"So who are you working for these days?" she asked me, looking down at the table so that we couldn't make eye contact.

That meant that my withering look in response was entirely wasted, which was a shame because it was a good one. The kind that makes tough men squeeze their lips together to prevent another stupid word squeaking out. I said nothing, kept looking at her until she had no choice but to look up to make sure I was still there. When she did I held her eye until she shrugged and looked back down at the table.

"You still want to keep everything to yourself then," she said. "Good to know you haven't changed; still hiding yourself from the world."

"Still hiding myself from you."

She looked up at me and smiled. Sneered, actually, might be

the better word for it. Trying to make it seem like she could never respect a supposed tough guy who hid himself from little old her, but that was bull. Whatever else she thought of me, she thought I was respectably tough. I started to get up, pretty sure that we'd reached the inevitable dead end that any conversation between us always arrived at.

"No interest in me then," she said, raising her voice and sticking a little quiver into the middle of it.

I was on my feet now, looking down at her, looking around at the busy little place and the busy little conversations happening at the other tables. You can always sense with Zara when she's planning to make a little scene, and I could feel it at that point. I'm allergic to scenes, so I sat back down and put an enjoyably sarcastic look on my face.

"Go on then. Tell me all about yourself."

She looked me right in the eye, and then started talking about herself. At last she had a subject she liked. "I was going to come for this money much sooner but when I got out I was paranoid that Michael Fisher was on my tail. I think he was, you know. Following me around, having me watched, making sure that I didn't go and pick up any money. So I couldn't come and get it."

I frowned, trying to work out if Fisher was enough of a dick to waste his time trailing around after Zara. Probably was, but he was supposed to be a good cop and God knows he was busy at the time she got out. He did well to find the time to stalk anyone.

"Good of you to show patience," I said, only semi-sarcastically. If she'd come running to me for the money as soon as she got out she could have brought a determined cop straight to my door, so there was that much to appreciate.

"I went down south," she carried on, ignoring me.

Maybe, just maybe, I wouldn't have had alarms going off at this point if it wasn't Zara Cope sitting opposite me, and if I hadn't sat through a similarly rehearsed conversation the night before. This sounded like something she'd decided she wanted to say before I even turned up.

"Kicked around down there for a while, trying to make a living, doing regular jobs. Wasn't a lot of fun, wasn't much of a life. So I decided to come back, try and start again up here."

"Turning over a new leaf, huh?"

"If you want to look at it that way. Maybe just make the most of my old leaf."

I was sitting there doing my basic maths and I was convinced that the answer was four. It could easily have been a coincidence: man comes north with a crew of his own to try and muscle in on our market, no previous experience of the city, at the same time Zara comes back. A man who looks like he's being guided by someone who knows the scene. Could so easily have been a coincidence. I didn't believe in coincidence.

"Where were you down there?" I asked her. Kept my tone mildly disinterested so that she might just believe that I already knew the answer.

"Birmingham, for a while."

"Why?"

"Why not?"

"Because you could have gone anywhere else."

She shrugged. "Maybe I always figured I'd be coming back here. I kicked around there for a few months, got bored, came back. Now I need to try and find some work, get a life set up that I can live. I'm not asking for help," she said, the opening shot in her asking for help. She said it with such a determined tone, like the truth could hide behind that.

But I knew that her asking for help was false as well, because everything that was coming out of her mouth was wrapped neatly in a lie. She was the link between Barrett and Glasgow. She had to be; it made such obvious sense. She talks to him about the city, about the organizations up here and how one of them is unstable.

She points out that he's a man who ran a drug network already, so he could do it again up here, make some real money. I could already picture her, whispering in his ear, telling him everything he needed to do to impress her, excite her. I remembered those whispers.

"So you're back up on your own?"

"Of course," she said, a little too quick and defensive. "This is all the money I have now, so I'll need to find something."

She could have been fishing for a job, or she could have been fishing for information about the state of the organization, whether it was hiring or not.

"There's work around if you're willing to do it," I said. "Same as it ever was."

Which wasn't entirely true: there were fewer jobs around for a couple of reasons. One was the mess of Jamieson's arrest; that had thrown everything into the air. Every organization shied away from new employees in a time of uncertainty, especially one with Zara's backstory. The other was the fact that there was less money in the world right now. A poor economy serves some parts of the industry well, others badly, so it sort of balances out. In the end you're usually left with fewer new jobs being created. She nodded and looked suitably unconvinced, waiting for me to offer to help find her something.

"You think Fisher's still sniffing around you?" I asked.

She looked at me a little shocked, like this was something she hadn't thought she'd need to worry about now. "I don't think so. Do you think he might be?"

"I didn't think he would have followed you around before, so what do I know?"

There was silence for a few seconds that I should have filled with a second attempt at leaving.

"You heard anything else about Lewis?" she asked.

"Winter? Still dead as far as I know."

She frowned at me and for a second there I thought she was actually hurt. Zara was always a complicated little bundle of lies and emotions; she might have actually cared about that pathetic man of hers.

"Sorry," I said, quietly enough to be able to deny I'd ever said such a word. She knew as much about Winter's killing as I did. Killed by Calum MacLean on the orders of Peter Jamieson; everyone knew that now. MacLean was long gone, and there wasn't going to be any new information leaking out.

"How's business in the city?" she asked, using my newfound discomfort to roll in the riskiest question she had to ask.

If she was connected to Barrett then she would want to know what I knew about the organization, about the city as a whole. I knew a hell of a lot more than her or Barrett or most other people. Anything she could get from me would be gold. Just a hint, something in my tone that said things were good, bad or indifferent. Something that would give them hope for their little plan.

"Business is business," was all I said. She looked at me like she was about to say something clever, but I'd heard enough clever things in my life already so I cut her off. I leaned forwards, getting closer to her than I had in years, a few inches from her face. Close enough to notice that she didn't smell of anything sweet, which was unlike her. "And you're telling me that you came back up the road on your lonesome."

"I did," she said, frowning at my knowing smile, which didn't know as much as it was pretending it did.

"That right? And you're staying on your own now, huh?"

"I didn't say that," she said, because she was smart enough to remember that I'd heard someone in the background of one of her phone calls. A hard woman to trip up.

"You come waltzing back into town with your wee man and his pals in tow and you think I'm not going to even notice that," I said to her, watching her eyes for a reaction.

It was there, I saw a flash of it, but she killed it quickly because there's nothing she wouldn't kill quickly to profit herself. A little bit of shock, a little bit of fear and a little bit of anger. Most people wouldn't have spotted it, but it was a look she'd worn often in our relationship and it was the familiarity that hit me hard.

Nearly hit me too hard. Knocked me backwards into the past, remembering being on the couch next to her and looking into her eyes. Remembering being in bed with her when she was pregnant. The feelings I'd had back then that I didn't recognize and still can't readily identify, but might have been fear. I was scared of being a father, being committed to Zara. And I looked at her now and saw the bags under her eyes and the too heavy makeup, neither of which had been there before, and I realized that for once her fear and anger might not be directed at me.

"I don't know what you're talking about," she said with a scoff that was too late and feeble an arrival to make an impact on this conversation.

"Him and his crew are heading for a spot in a forest somewhere, or up a chimney stack," I told her. "I won't give you a second warning."

"Warning? What warning? I have no idea what you're talking about. You must be paranoid about something, or punch-drunk at last. Probably paranoid. You were always paranoid. You remember how bad you used to get? Standing at the bedroom window, naked as the day you were born, looking out into the night for some bogeyman you thought was after you. I was eight months pregnant at the time and all you cared about were your little power fantasies, the chance to beat someone up. You haven't changed."

She was red in the face by now, but it all sounded like aimless lashing out, trying to pull the conversation away from the subject she feared. She was scared that I knew what little game she was playing. There was some truth in what she said about me being paranoid. That little story about her and me when she was heavily pregnant was partly true, only I wasn't paranoid; we were both in real danger. I had pissed off a man I shouldn't have, but I dealt with it without her understanding how bad things were. If she knew she would have been upset and she was emotional enough already. I was trying to protect her from me.

"Nice little diversion you're throwing me," I said, "but don't think my memory's that bad; I remember what I said a few seconds ago. You and him are here to push your luck, and it's going to end badly."

She got up from the table, looking a little tearful and angry. "Why don't you go to hell, Nate? It's probably the only place you'll ever feel at home." And she careered off through the restaurant, standing on the same black leather handbag I had stood on coming in.

Zara stormed out of the door and out of view. I never considered going after her. Nobody in my line of work was in the habit of chasing after people on busy streets; it would draw too much attention. I let her get suitably far ahead of me and left the place, thinking about what she'd said. She wanted me to go to hell, and I figured that would be a short journey.

12

I could put every other mistake I made that day down to Zara getting inside my head, but that would be cheap. The mistakes I made were mine; trying to put them on someone else is a damn good way of making sure you repeat them.

First job was to call up Kevin and tell him that I'd learned a little something about our friend Adrian Barrett.

"So he basically knows a lot about the place then. I mean, she has connections here, right, so she could put him in touch with useful people?" he asked me.

"Hard to say what her connections are these days. Little above mid-level when Winter was alive, and she's been away a while now."

"But still, it might explain his reason for coming here, might explain where he got the idea to try and muscle in on Glasgow business."

That sounded to me like Kevin was trying to look on the bright side of this. If Zara coaxed Barrett north then there was a better chance that nobody else had, namely Don Park. If we could take Park out of the equation then the puzzle began to look a lot smaller.

"Maybe," I said. "I wouldn't take it for granted though."

I left him chewing on that new info, knowing that the first thing he would try to do was get a tail on Zara. Find her and there was a chance of finding Barrett and ending this thing quickly. Quickly made everyone look good. There was nothing reassuring about

Zara being involved, not to me. She didn't have direct connections to people like Park, that was true, but she didn't need them. Zara was a woman capable of making connections wherever she pleased.

Next person on the call list was Ronnie. I wanted him to come along with me on the next job I had to do that day, a pointless little thing that he might as well watch and learn from.

"Can't, I'm heading out to some farmhouse with Mikey, Conn and some guy called Bee, or BB. They don't think Barrett's crew are there now, but they might have been. Sounds like a wild goose chase, but Marty Jones called me up himself and told me to go along."

He sounded impressed by the fact that Marty had called him up. Tells you how far Marty had come that even smart people were impressed by a call from him these days. BB was Brian Bradley, young muscle that worked for Marty's debt collection business, now run by Billy. Going in heavy with those four, heavier than he needed to for a possible past location. Sounded like a paranoia crew to me, two to do the work and two to check up on the two doing the work. Didn't blame Marty for taking those kinds of precautions. It was going to be that way until we got all this sorted out.

Ronnie being in on that search meant I had to go visit Mark Garvey alone. I wasn't in the mood for people I liked so I sure as hell wasn't in the mood for Mark Garvey. A middle-aged, smarmy gun dealer that we shouldn't have been bringing into the organization in the first place. This would have gone much better if I'd had Ronnie with me, or if I'd managed to slip my brain out of neutral at any point.

He lived in a semi-detached house out towards Cider Hill, an area I only knew because I knew who was buried out there. I parked down the road from his boring little house on the kind of tight residential street that forces you to say hello to your neighbors, and went in through his front garden. Knocked on the door, ignoring the subtlety of the bell, and waited. The door was opened by a woman in her mid to late thirties, blond hair scraped back and a scowl on her face. Wrapped in a bathrobe and looking like a visitor was the last thing she wanted. This, I knew, was Melanie Garvey, wife of Mark.

"I'm looking for your husband."

"Are you now? Well, he's not in."

She didn't know who I was. "My name's Nate Colgan. I'm here to talk shop. You sure he's not in?"

She got a little combative at the sound of my name. "He's not, actually. He went out; I don't know when he'll be back. Shouldn't be long. I think he was making a delivery. You can come in, wait if you want."

If he wasn't going to be long then there was no reason not to go in and wait. She led me through to the kitchen, a spotless, white place that looked like nobody had ever stepped into it before. I wandered to the far end of the room where a dining table was pushed against the back wall and took a seat there. She filled the kettle, put it on, and walked out of the room.

The world would be a much better place if people had the good sense to leave me alone. Let me get on with my work; let me get on with my life. But they can't do that, they just can't. Everyone has to play their own little game and make me a part of it. On another day I would have had the good sense not to get involved.

She came back into the kitchen, still wrapped in the same bathrobe she had been wearing before. Her hair was loose now. Walked right up to me, stood with one of her bare toes pressed against the toe of my boot. She was short; didn't have to look that far down at me sitting there. She pulled open the robe, reached out her hands to either side of my face. For reasons only she would ever understand, she gripped the sides of my head tightly, digging in with her nails, holding my head to look at her naked body. The reasonable sight of a woman in her late thirties who'd never had a kid and worked out a lot.

She reached down and picked my hands from my lap, slipping them round the back of the open robe onto her backside. Seemed like she wanted me to return her pinch, so being a gentleman I obliged. I grabbed, turned her around and shoved her away from me. Not much force, but she was small and her stumble across the kitchen floor wasn't graceful. She stopped in the middle of the floor and looked at me, dressing gown gaping, mouth slightly open, trying to work out what my game was. Was I really not interested, playing hard to get or wanting something rough?

"You go call your man and tell him I'm not looking for gifts or bribes. Tell him to get in here now."

That ended any thought she had of going through with whatever little game her and Garvey had been playing. She should have been grateful. I wasn't a man to dabble with, even when I was in a good mood. She shut her mouth, pulled her robe shut and walked out of the kitchen, indignant. Maybe she just wanted a fling, but I never thought of myself as handsome enough to invite that. This was her and Garvey trying to get me into their debt, the only thing they could use to hook me. If I owe him, then he doesn't have to play by the rules I was about to lay down. I'd seen people like Garvey using tricks as dirty as that before; I figured it had to be what this was and it pissed me off.

I'd only given that a couple of minutes' thought when the front door opened and I heard a man cheerily shouting hello. Mark Garvey, back just when it was slightly too late to catch anyone out. I've already said I don't believe in coincidences, right? She leaves the room, has just enough time to text the husband and tell him he can come in now. Tell him the big lump that he's scared of hasn't bitten the hook and they're going to have to play me straight.

Didn't take a genius to work out that Lafferty had already told him he was getting the job before he suggested him at his meeting, and that Marty would have called him up the night of the meeting to hunt for info. Garvey was playing at being ignorant; all part of the game him and Melanie were enthusiastic amateurs at, with dreams of professionalism. If Garvey had the "security consultant" in his back pocket then he had a chance to break the rules with impunity. Breaking the rules is a profitable business, and I mean double-or-treble-your-money profitable by selling to multiple buyers instead of just us.

He came into the kitchen, made a show of looking surprised to see me, and walked across the room with a smile on his face and his hand outstretched.

"Nate, God, been a good long time since you and me had a chat, huh?"

"I don't remember us ever having a chat."

"Well, no, maybe not." He sat across the table, looking expectantly at me. He wasn't bothered by my attitude.

"The organization's looking for a dealer that'll supply us consistently and exclusively. Do you think you're capable of living up to our standards?" I posed the question as though I doubted his ability, but he ignored that. He was ready to ignore anything to get this deal done.

"Sure I can, yeah. I have the stock and access to much more if needed. I'll always make sure the organization is as well supplied as it can possibly be."

I nodded and didn't say anything else because there was nothing else I trusted myself to say. He was on board, which was what Lafferty wanted, but we both knew he had no place with us. It made no sense to have a gun dealer tied to us, or have our gunmen tied to a single gun dealer. This whole thing was a result of bad leadership. The sort of bad leadership that couldn't last.

"One thing," I said as I got to my feet. "You will be dealing exclusively with us. You will not sell a single piece to a single other person at any point in time. If I find out that you have, I will deal with you the way I deal with anyone who betrays this organization. No warnings, no second chances. It's us and it's no one else. There is nothing you or your wife can possibly do that's going to get me under your thumb, you understand?"

His mouth was a little open, his face a little red. He stood up to try and match me and realized he would have been better sitting down. He looked up at me, working up the best pious impression he could manage.

"You certainly don't have to worry about that sort of thing with me, Nate. I can tell you now, I'm delighted to be working with the organization and I won't sell a single thing to anyone else. Not a thing. You have my word."

I've blown things out my nose that meant more to me than his word, but I nodded anyway. At the very least I'd denied him the opportunity to pretend that he hadn't been warned. He might have been welcomed into the organization by Lafferty and Marty, but he was still on probation with me and there he would stay until I could find an excuse to get rid of him.

There's a sense of relief when you leave a place you wish you'd never gone to, and leaving that house gave me a rush of it. That was a sad little marriage standing on the brink of collapse and I didn't want to get the dirt of it on my clothes. Instead I went home and killed a little time before I called Ronnie.

Couple of hours had ticked away since I'd last called him, so I tried again.

"You back from your farmhouse?"

"Yeah."

"And?" I knew he'd have called if they'd found anything.

"And it was a farmhouse with no one in it. Didn't look like anyone had been living there for a while."

"What's the story of it?"

"Old house, couple of barns, nothing alive in any of them.

House was recently renovated; one of the barns was new. Farmer overspent, went tits up, owned by the bank or someone now. We went round it carefully; place had no signs of being used. None at all."

I trusted Conn and Mikey to make that judgment. An empty place, not scrubbed so clean it becomes suspicious. They would know what signs to look for.

"How did you get on with Garvey?" he asked me.

"Waste of time," I said. "The guy already knew he was going to be working for us; I was just there to make it look official."

"So what now?"

"We keep looking, is what now. Come round and pick me up. We'll go out and look at a few places. You talk to Thorne like I asked?"

"Yeah, he gave me a few addresses, but, I don't know, he didn't seem confident. He reckons there are better ways of putting people up than that."

"Oh?"

"Yeah, caravans and empty buildings that never come on the market. All the places he had for me were places he knew were available recently, but he reckons they'll be somewhere that was never available in the first place. Places we have are too obvious."

I sighed. "I know it's obvious, but we still have to check them. If we don't and it turns out they're there we look ridiculous. This is donkey work. It has to be done and we're not above it. Come round and get me; we'll have a look at some of those addresses he gave you."

I didn't want to be short with the boy, but he was making this harder than it needed to be. Kids like Ronnie always wanted to go looking for the glamorous long shot and ignore the simple, obvious stuff, and I could understand that. It seemed implausible that Barrett would have his crew hidden away in an easy-to-find place, a hotel or a large house available for rent, but that missed another obvious point. Barrett and his crew couldn't stay hidden forever; they needed to come out into the world and be seen on the streets if they wanted to maintain the credibility they'd built so far. There was no need for a clever hiding place when you had no intention of staying hidden.

13

It was after ten o'clock at night. We'd had no joy finding even a hint of Barrett and his crew, so my mood hadn't improved any. The clock was ticking down to the moment when that bunch of English bastards stepped out of the darkness and into the spotlight. That moment was going to be failure for me. The security consultant. Men like Lafferty would accuse me of letting this happen. Goes without saying that the moment they stepped out was the best chance we would get to take a shot at them. A chance to wipe them out. But that didn't matter: it was about perception. The perception would be that I'd failed. That the organization was weak and hadn't dealt with them.

I had just gotten in, gone into the kitchen to get myself something to eat. Hadn't eaten a proper meal all day. My stomach was rumbling and the tiredness was sitting heavily in the back of my head somewhere. I would have relished the chance of a good night's sleep. Not much chance of that anyway. The phone started ringing in the living room.

The mobile number that showed up on the screen was new to me. No record of it in the menu, no record of it in my memory. Some numbers I don't give a name to on the menu screen; don't want other people seeing. I answered.

"Hello, is that Nate Colgan?" A well-educated version of a local accent, all the edges sanded down. I didn't know who I was talking to.

"It is." Of course it was. Who did he think he had called?

"Is now a good time to talk?"

I still didn't know who I was talking to. "As good a time as any."

"This is Charles Simpson. I wanted to make sure that you were at home. Peter would like to have a conversation with you. Will you be at home for the next hour or so?"

"Yes, I will," I said, all of a sudden taking the phone call seriously.

"Excellent. I'll let him know."

Simpson hung up, and left me alone with a bundle of unpleasant thoughts. First thought was about the trouble they were going to, setting this call up. Jamieson would tell someone in the prison, presumably an officer, that he wanted to call me. The officer would alert Simpson, who was Peter's lawyer, and he'd make sure I was available so that Jamieson didn't waste his time. He wouldn't be calling on some prison phone either; he had his own mobile in there.

None of that mattered much. What mattered was that Jamieson was about to call me. First time since I'd become his organization's security consultant. First time since I became his organization's muscle of choice. This was going to be about Lee Christie. Or Angus Lafferty, to be more accurate. Christie now existed only as a pawn in the Lafferty game. This could very easily be a phone call designed to put pressure on me.

Peter Jamieson, the boss, sitting in his grotty wee cell, waiting for clearance to make a phone call to me. It was almost a comic picture. That man, with all his influence, all his money, sitting there waiting for some bent prison officer to tell him he had fifteen uninterrupted minutes to get the call out of the way. Made me feel small, that this guy was still so much more powerful than me. That's the business though. Always was. The walls of a prison don't determine whether you're in charge or not; the people on the outside decide that.

I knew about his cellmate, a guy called Seth Miller. He was one of ours. Had been loosely tied to us when he was on the outside. Got sent down for something that had nothing to do with us, battering a guy in a pub I think. He wasn't much of a criminal, but he was loyal and Jamieson needed someone loyal to share a cell with him. Needed someone who could act as his bodyguard as well. Miller wouldn't be the only one. Jamieson needed as many people as possible looking out for him while he was in Barlinnie. It wouldn't be long before they moved him somewhere softer, and we would have to get an entirely new bunch of people to look out for him.

He was a sitting duck in there. Just needed one arsehole working for a rival to get at him, and he might never come back out. Look at it this way: if we had a bunch of people on his block to look out for him, what were the chances that other organizations had their own people there? So we had a few prisoners taking money from us to play defense for Jamieson. We also had three different officers on the payroll, trying to cover as many shifts as possible. One of them had been on the payroll for ages, long before Jamieson went inside. Another had been an easy pickup. The third had taken some work to persuade. I had been involved in that, before I was officially on the books. Had to go to his house to scare him into it, in the end. Dirty work, but it was effective. That made three prison employees on the books.

The phone started ringing, thank Christ. I had spent too long sitting there, phone on the arm of the chair, waiting for him.

"Nate, this is Peter. This a good time to talk?" Talking a little more quietly than usual. This was a man from whose lips confidence poured with every sentence.

"Yeah, sure."

"Any progress being made with this Christie killing and Barrett?"

This would have been going through his mind since he heard about it. Sitting in a jail cell, trying to work out a strategy for an organization that was always on the other side of the wall. It was a hard way to run a business, even if it wasn't impossible.

"Not much in the way of progress, no. Haven't managed to find Barrett or his crew, although my theory is that they're hiding in plain sight. They have to come into the open anyway to make this push stick, and I figure they'll want to do that soon."

"Do it on their terms?"

"Exactly. They jump into the open before we push them. Hunting them down might not even be the best use of our time. Might be better to focus on shoring things up so when they do emerge we can deal with them better."

"Mm. I think at this point you got to follow the lead Angus gives you."

"Sure."

Wasn't what I hoped to hear from him. Look, everyone questions the wisdom of their superiors. It happens even when the boss is on the outside. Back in his office above the club, giving out orders with his usual charm. When he's inside, that's when it becomes very easy for people to think he's losing his grip. That his judgment's screwed because he can't see what's really happening on the street anymore. Very little he can do to combat that, other than hire guys like me to throw his weight around for him.

Thing about Jamieson was that he was a married man with two kids, a family man. His wife's name was Julia, tidy-looking woman in her late thirties, early forties. They had two kids. Twelve-year-old girl called Scarlett and a fifteen-year-old boy called Jordan. That was irrelevant when he was on the outside. On the outside he had the time to look after his family, hang out with his kids, be the regular husband and father. Now he was on the inside, people would start to wonder. Was he spending all his time in there missing his kids, having dreams about his wife? Was he even thinking about the business at all? Stupid. A man like Jamieson was always going to spend more time thinking about the business, but it was something else for people to consider a weakness.

"What about Angus? How has he been handling all this?" Jamieson asked me.

That question was so fucking loaded. I took a few seconds before I spoke a word. It was the only reason he had called, obviously. I didn't know Jamieson all that well. Had met him a few times, knew plenty about him, but I wasn't close enough to answer that question with total honesty. I wasn't close enough to trust his motives when he asked it.

"Well, I guess he's been handling it how you would expect," was what I said. "He lost a man. He's concerned about how that makes him look, he's lashing out a bit. Feels like he has to take charge of the issue."

"Just this issue?"

"Seems like he's moving towards some sort of leadership role, but that's just how it looks from where I'm standing. I don't know—time might tell a different story."

"What makes you think that now?"

He wasn't making this easy for me. He was trying to cajole me into saying things I didn't want to say. I paused for another few seconds, wasting the credit on his mobile. Him talking in that low tone, making sure his voice didn't carry beyond the cell. Talking loud enough for his cellmate to hear, but knowing that Miller had been told to keep his ears shut during all phone calls. He was putting me in a spot here and that was tough shit on me; I was his employee and he wanted my opinion. I decided to give it to him. Let him have the truth and react however he wanted, even if it meant me disagreeing with things he'd already agreed to. He needed people to tell him that mistakes were being made on the outside.

"He's hiring people that, I don't know, don't seem like good hires. Hiring Garvey I think is a mistake. We shouldn't be tying our man to a single supplier, shouldn't be tying ourselves to Garvey like this. Hiring Russell Conrad I don't know about. Conrad's fine — I have no complaint about him. Worked with him once before; he was fine. It just feels like Lafferty's trying to make decisions that only a leader would make. He wants people to see him as the man in charge."

There wasn't even a second between me stopping and Jamieson starting. "Okay. I want you to do something for me, Nate. I want you to keep both eyes on Angus. You'll be heavily involved in this, I've made sure of that, and you'll need to be careful that Barrett and his mob don't get the better of us. If they're working with Don Park then it could get complicated fast, but I want you to focus on Angus and what he does, keep me up to date with it."

"Sure."

"All right, Nate. It was good talking to you. Any time you need to talk to me, get in touch with Simpson."

That was the end of the conversation. I said goodbye and hung up. Simpson, I was sure, was making a nice little bundle out of being Jamieson's middleman at the moment. Good luck to him. I pictured Jamieson, hiding his mobile, getting into his bunk for the night. It was actually rather sad. Him sitting there, not able to change the world around him like he always had before.

I went and got something to eat. I wasn't going to sleep, not now. My mind was racing. That phone call had cleared a few things up. Made me feel a little bit better about Jamieson and his grasp on power. He knew what Lafferty was playing at. Me keeping my eyes on Lafferty was part of that. Jamieson could see the threat and he wanted me, and probably a whole scrum of others, watching for it as well. Fine, that was a good thing. The boss was aware. But it also meant the threat from Lafferty was real, and that worried me. If Lafferty was making a run at leadership, no matter how half-arsed it was, it was going to weaken us. Can't defend yourself against attacks from other organizations when you're fighting against people inside your own.

That had been one miserable fucking day. Zara, sitting in that restaurant. I hadn't mentioned her to Jamieson, you'll have noticed. Garvey and his wife. What a pair of bloody clowns they were, and now Garvey was inside the organization. Now this call from Jamieson. And I still hadn't found Barrett.

14

One good thing about not sleeping is that I always get an early start. Actually, I should say the only good thing about not sleeping. I was exhausted, and exhaustion was going to push me into making mistakes. This wasn't going to get any better. Not with Zara in the city. Been a long time since I woke up thinking of her. I showered and got myself something to eat, but it was still only half seven.

I called Ronnie. He was my junior, so if I was up then he should be up. The phone rang and rang. I was happy to wait.

"Hello?" Confused that anyone would have the temerity to phone him that early in the morning. His girlfriend, Esther, worked in an office, so I figured she would be getting up soon anyway.

"We need to split up this morning, get the last of that list Thorne gave you done. I'll do the bottom half; you do the top, all right? Give me a call when you're nearly done. If you see anything that looks suspicious, call me straight away. Don't go in anywhere on your own unless you're sure it's clear."

He mumbled something, cleared his throat and said, "Yeah, all right."

"Good," I said, and I hung up.

There was movement in the background of the phone call, his girlfriend getting out of bed presumably. I was a little jealous of him, I'll admit that. My thoughts drifted to Kelly. I could have that. There could be someone rolling out of my bed after early-morning phone calls. It was a pretty thought, but I couldn't have pretty things in my life. You care a damn about a woman then you keep her as far away from this life as possible.

I went back upstairs, used the bathroom. Didn't know when I'd get back home and I wasn't a huge fan of other people's toilets. I did what I always do when I'm upstairs: I took a good look up and down the street from the upstairs window. The street curves, so you can't see all the way along, but you can see far enough. You can see, for example, when there's a car parked across the street, the figure of a man in the driver's seat. The red car was facing away from the house, but he'd have had a view of the front door in his mirror.

I didn't know who it was, not for sure. Someone who wasn't doing a brilliant job of hiding, probably not making much effort. So someone who didn't care if they were seen. Intimidation tactic? Nah, I wasn't buying that. You don't intimidate me by parking down the road from my house, everyone knows that. So someone spying. Someone who wanted to know what I was doing. Maybe someone who wanted to talk to me. Only one way to find out who. Confront the situation.

My car was parked right in front of my house. I got in and started to drive, heading for a house in the middle of the list. I had a key for this one, given to Ronnie by Brendan Thorne. They wouldn't be there, I was sure of it, but I wanted a house I could get into. The red car followed. It was trying to stay back out of view, I could tell that much. Hoping I wouldn't spot it. Maybe it was someone who didn't want to be seen, someone who was just very bad at his job. He was alone, which was a comfort. One on one I fancied my chances against anyone.

The house I was looking for was on a residential street, council houses in bunches of four down either side of the road. I stopped outside it; the red car went past and stopped at the bottom of the street. Out of the car. The rain was falling down on me. Through the wobbly gate and up the chipped and broken front path, through a noticeably shabby garden. Hard to be noticeably shabby on this street. I had already seen that there were no curtains on any of the rooms in the house: this place was empty. I took the front-door key from my pocket, slipped it into the lock and went inside.

I went through to the living room; the place was a mess. Didn't matter to me. I was looking sideways out of the window, watching him come up the front path. DI Fisher. The bastard. He was a good cop, we all knew it. Not all bluff and bullshit like a lot of them. He was no media whore either, performing for the press. Just a guy who wouldn't give up. If he'd been on our side of the fence, he'd have been a very rich man. He looked ruffled, getting soaked in the rain chasing after me. Let him get soaked. I was going to check every room in the house before I opened the front door again. Might as well strike that house off the list while I was at it.

I stomped around upstairs and down, made sure nobody had been in the place for a long time. Then I went and opened the front door. I squared my shoulders and puffed out my chest, made sure I filled the doorframe. Fisher was standing next to the door, back against the wall, trying to avoid the rain. Being a man of this city, his first instinct when faced with someone so big and intimidating was to look for ways to cut me down.

"Mr. Colgan," he said, hoping he was catching me off guard.

I turned and looked at him casually, a bit of a smile that didn't belong on a face like mine. "DI Fisher," I said. "Fancy meeting you here."

"You visiting a friend?" he asked me.

"Not exactly."

"So just what exactly were you doing visiting this empty house first thing in the morning?"

I didn't say anything.

"Shall we go back inside and have a wee look around?" he asked. He was hoping that there was something in there that incriminated me.

The ease with which I turned and unlocked the door again should have told him that there was nothing inside the house for him to get excited about. Took guts for him. A cop walking into an empty house with a man like me. I could have done anything I wanted to him in there. But he knew I was too smart to play silly buggers. I wasn't ever going to attack a cop.

The house was as cold inside as out. No carpets on the floors, not a stick of furniture, rubbish strewn on the bare floors. Fisher walked around the three rooms that constituted the downstairs and found absolutely nothing. Hoping against hope. He knew there would be nothing upstairs, and searching this place wasn't why he was here. Fisher stopped in the kitchen, leaned back against the sink. I stood in the doorway, watching him, waiting for him to take the lead. He was the one following me; he had to speak first.

"So what were you doing here?" he asked me, as a matter of boring routine.

"Not a damn thing," I said, my voice a rumble that sounded more threatening than it meant to. Hopefully he realized that, didn't think I was trying to intimidate him.

"You just happened to have a key."

"I'm thinking of moving, got a key from a friend, had a look."

"Going to put an offer in?" he asked me.

"Don't think so."

That was about as much bullshit as either of us had the appetite for. It was time to get down to the business that had led him to this dump in my wake.

"So you and your lot are looking for Adrian Barrett, is that it?" he asked.

No reaction, not even a flicker. I had been around too long to

give anything away for free. "I would guess a lot of people are looking for him," I said to him. "I should think your mob are looking for
him too."

"You think so? Why would we be looking for him?"

"Man turns up looking to deal drugs on your patch; I would
hope you might take some interest in that."

He nodded a little, but neither of us was thinking about Barrett's
drug deals. "And Lee Christie?" he asked.

"Man gets shot dead, I would think you'd be investigating that
anyway," I said with a barely interested shrug. I wasn't going to
push him on this. Would be nice if the police took Barrett off the
streets for us, but it would be better if we did it ourselves. "If that
leads you to Barrett then that's your business."

"And you wouldn't be surprised if it did?"

"Nothing much surprises me anymore," I said. I think he believed me.

This was waltzing in circles and neither of us were eloquent ver-
bal dancers. I looked at him, watched him stare right back at me,
held his eye until he looked away.

"I know your lot are going to go to war with Barrett and his people, and I want you to think again," he said. He wasn't begging. No
way in hell a man as proud as him would beg, but he was exercis-
ing his right to ask.

One massive thought was crashing to the front of my mind.
"You know where he is, don't you?" I asked. Kept my tone calm,
polite, disinterested.

He nodded. "I know who he's with too."

"Meaning?"

He looked me in the eye and managed to hold it this time. "He
didn't come up the road on his own; he had someone from here to
lead him on. The mother of your child."

I didn't react. It wasn't a challenge for a man with my practice
to stay dead-eyed. I spent the better part of my professional life

making sure my expression didn't betray me, so this was nothing. It wasn't a surprise, let's face it, but I didn't want him knowing I already knew. Never confirm your knowledge to a cop.

"You're sure of that?" I asked.

"I've seen her with him. Seen him without her as well. Him and most of his crew went to a meeting yesterday afternoon; got a good look at them."

There was a terribly stupid question I was obligated to ask. "Where are they?"

He smiled at me and I kept my face hard. "If they were behind the Christie killing then we'll get them," he said, and ignored the doubting expression I shot back in return. "But if you go after Barrett then you know what's going to happen to Zara. She becomes a bargaining chip that he can use against you." I went for a look of dismissal this time. "You think he won't? And you think that when he does you'll just blow it off? She's the mother of your child. How are you going to explain it to your daughter when she finds out? And she will, won't she?"

Maybe a little bit of annoyance crept onto my face at that point, I'll admit it. A little victory for Fisher. I wasn't used to being spoken to that way. Most people had more sense of self-preservation than to challenge me.

"So what do you want from me?" I asked. He hadn't hunted me down to share anything he'd said so far.

"I want you to do what you can to make sure this doesn't end with bodies all over my city. If this turns into something big then Zara is very likely to suffer for that. I don't want that and I don't think you do either. You're no one's halfwit; you know that settling this my way works out much better for you. If Barrett and his men killed Christie, and I think they did, then I can nail the lot of them."

I stood in the doorway, looking down at the floor, thinking it over. Wasn't much to think about: he was asking me to help him avoid serious trouble. It was that rare occasion when Nate Colgan and DI Michael Fisher probably wanted the same thing.

"You won't tell me where they are?"

"You know I won't," he said.

"Then tell me who they are. We know Barrett, we know his gunman, Nasty, but that's it. I can't find out anything that might help you if I don't know who I'm looking for."

This was a wrench for him. Every instinct in his body would be telling him to clam up, say nothing to a thug like me. But he knew I had a better chance of finding out the right info to lock them up than he did, given the corners I could cut. Take any help you can get, because there isn't much going around.

"Adrian Barrett, goes by the nickname Dyne. Jawad Nasif, goes by Nasty. There's another guy, we figure him for Barrett's right-hand man, name of Elliott Parker. Those three are skin tight—been together for years. Parker and Barrett since they were kids, Nasif with them at least since they started getting noticed down south more than a decade ago. These three won't be broken apart. Used to be a fourth member of their group but he's inside on dealing charges, been out of the picture for a couple of years."

"That it?" I asked him. "Just the three of them?"

"They've got another two with them who seem to be muscle. One of them we've ID'd as Keith Henson, twenty-seven, from the Midlands, got a record as long as a basketball player's arm. The other one we haven't pegged yet, but he doesn't seem to be anything more than another grunt. He's not local either, I know that. They'll have brought him up with them. It's a tight group. They've got your little Zara with them; she seems to belong to Barrett himself. There's another girl we haven't identified either; she seems to be with Parker."

"So they have seven bodies at the most, only three with experience at any sort of level?"

He gave me a look that said he didn't like my last sentence. "They have as much as they need," he said.

I gave him a look that was designed to tell him he was wrong. His theory, I can only guess having not asked, was that they only needed the small number to get started; once they had a name here they could start spending some money on hiring locals. That might seem to an outsider like the common-sense way to do it anyway. It wasn't.

A guy like Barrett needed more than the little help he had brought if he wanted to come into a city like this and make a splash. He needed someone established to help him out, point him in all the right directions. One wrong turn and he was buggered. Zara wasn't an experienced guide to the back-streets. If he had a big crew then maybe he could do it himself, maybe. With a crew that small he wasn't here working an angle of his own: he was here to work for someone else. Finding out who had just leapt to the top of my list of favorite pastimes.

"Promise me," Fisher said, "that you won't go racing into some street war with anyone, and I can promise you that Zara Cope gets out of this unscathed."

"Your promises aren't worth any more than mine are," I said. "Neither of us have any control over this. But I'll do what I can to avoid a war."

I turned and walked out of the house, not bothering to lock the door behind me. I needed the confusion to settle so I could work out what all this meant. Got into my car and started driving, not going anywhere in particular. Barrett was working for someone in the city. That meant Barrett stopped being the priority. He mattered, of course he did, but he had just become a little less important. Barrett was being brought in to work this as an outsider, and when it was over he would disappear. The person who hired him, that was the person that mattered.

My phone started ringing as I was driving. I assumed Ronnie. It rang off before I could find a place to park. I wasn't going to get myself pulled over for using the phone while driving, I wasn't that daft. Looked at the screen. There's a wall that you build between your work and the rest of your life. It keeps things separate, keeps the rest of your life safe, you hope. Then someone knocks a hole in the wall. The call was from Zara's mother.

15

It was agreed by all parties, very early on, that Zara's parents were the best people to raise our daughter. Zara couldn't do it. Wouldn't do it, I suppose. She was young; she hadn't wanted a kid in the first place. Dumping Becky on her parents was a way out for her. Told herself she was doing the right thing for the kid. I did the same. I could have taken Becky. I was making more money than Gordon and Mary, Zara's parents. I was older than Zara, wiser to the challenges of parenthood. Might be why I chickened out as well. I tell myself it was because I wanted what was best for my daughter, and living with me could never be the best. She would never be safe. She would grow up in an unreliable, violent environment, and that was totally wrong. But I could have walked away from the business for her. I didn't. I was a coward, scared of the responsibility.

Rebecca came and stayed with me every weekend. Whenever her grandparents went on holiday I had her, and every year we took a short holiday together as well. I was a big part of her life. A safe part. It was as much as I was able to be.

When I saw the name on the screen, I felt nervous. First time in all this. Wasn't nervous about Lee Christie getting knocked off, or Barrett and his lot. I was annoyed about a lot of things, wary, but this call had me scared. What if Zara had been in touch with her parents? Had been in touch with Rebecca? Becky never talked about her mother, didn't ever seem interested, but that would change if Zara was on the scene. It could change things dramatically. I called back.

"Hi Mary. You were calling? I was on the road, couldn't answer." I tried to sound casual and hoped she'd sound the same.

"Oh, I'm sorry, Nate. Is now a bad time for you?" She sounded her usual self.

"No, go on."

"I'm needing a favor from you, Nate. Becky's off school today; she was sick in the morning. It's nothing serious, just a bug. Problem is that Gordon has a doctor's appointment at twelve. Normally we'd put her with our neighbor, but she asked if I would call you first."

"You drop her off at my place; I'd love to have her for lunch. You can pick her up when you're done."

"Oh thanks, Nate. You're a godsend."

"How is Gordon?"

She lowered her voice. "Well, he's managing to stay on top of it; this is just a check-up. It's not easy though."

There was something wrong with Gordon's heart. Not in the way there was something wrong with mine. He had a condition and every time I spoke to Mary she was more concerned about it. The way she was talking, there was a chance Gordon didn't have an awful lot longer in this world. Maybe she was exaggerating; she did that a lot. But he had stopped driving nearly a year ago, so she had to drive him everywhere. That was why he couldn't go to the doctor's on his own.

Didn't bother me that I'd miss a couple of hours' work to be with Becky. She was worth putting a little burden onto other people for. At the time I figured that was the reason I had gone and hired Ronnie. Thought about that as I drove home. Why had I hired the boy? Was it really so that I could spend more time with Becky? Or because I knew working full-time for Jamieson would give me more work?

They arrived at about half eleven. I saw them coming, opened the front door. I smiled down at Becky; she was pale and sickly-looking.

"They made me hold a plastic bag in front of me in the car in case I puked on the way over," she said. She was as indignant as any nine-year-old girl can be.

"And did you?"

"No!"

Mary and Gordon came in behind her. Gordon looked thin and fragile like he always did. Mary was prim and small, but there was still a hint of her daughter's look in her.

"She was sick in the morning," Mary said, Becky tutting as she took off her coat and went through to the living room. "We won't be long, an hour and a half at the most."

"Take all the time you need," I told them.

They didn't ask about my work. They knew. A conspiracy of silence. They had known when Zara and me met that I was trouble, and I'm sure they'd wanted her as far away from me as possible. I can't imagine they were thrilled at the thought of their pretty little daughter having a child with me either. But they made the best of a bad situation. As they drifted away from Zara, they stayed close to me. They weren't in contact with Zara now at all, but I was doing my best to be the son-in-law they never had.

"So, you want something for lunch?" I asked Becky when they were gone.

She frowned. "I don't know."

Sometimes she knew exactly what she wanted, and woe betide the person who tried to make the decision for her. Other times she couldn't possibly make up her mind, and you had to step in. This was the latter, and that meant she was hungry but worried about throwing up again.

"Something light. I'll make you some toast; you can nibble at it."

It was perfectly mundane. Perfectly being the key word. Making her some toast while she flicked through the channels on the TV and landed on what was optimistically referred to as a music channel. It was ordinary. It would probably be a boring, everyday occurrence for most parents. She ate a little of the toast I gave her.

"Are you not working today?" she asked me.

She's a smart little girl, my Becky. She knew, or at least had a sense of, what that question meant. She didn't know what I did for a living. Not exactly. Myself and her grandparents had agreed to try and protect her from the truth of it. But she had an idea. She seemed to sense that I was involved in something people didn't talk about, that it might be something dangerous. Maybe she was young enough to think that was glamorous, exciting.

It was a conversation I was dreading. The moment she asked me to explain why I did what I did. I spent so much of my time with her trying desperately to be a good person. Trying to be a father that she could be proud of. If she ever truly understood what sort of person I was, what I did to others for money, then she might hate me.

"Well, I was at work, first thing in the morning, when you were still bent over the toilet bowl."

"Dad!"

"Then your granny called me up and said that she was looking for someone to keep you under control for a couple of hours so I said I'd love to. Just for a couple of hours though, I'll go back to work in the afternoon. How are you feeling now?"

Trying to change the subject, move her away from talking about work. She said she was feeling a little better and left it at that. She didn't much like me moving the subject along without her permission. She knew what I was doing.

"How's the photography coming along?" I asked her. I'd gotten her a digital camera for Christmas; it had become her new obsession. Taking photos and then messing around with them on the computer at home. Her grandparents insisted the computer be in the living room where they could see what she was up to. She threw a wobbly about that; I put my foot down. One of those occasions where I could be the bad guy because they had to live with her all day and I only had her at weekends. No way was I letting her have a computer in her room, not at her age. Not after some of the stories I'd heard.

"It's going okay. I got some good shots last week."

"You should email them to me."

"I will," she said, glad that I was showing an interest but trying to hide it because she wanted to seem terribly cool.

The phone rang. I got up and went out to the hall with it. Another number that I didn't recognize. All these calls from strangers, never anything but bad news.

"Hello, Nate. This is Paul Greig."

Let me tell you something about Paul Greig. He used to be PC Paul Greig. He was so fucking bent that even the crooks he was working for couldn't trust him. One of the most unreliable pieces of shit that ever woke up in this city. A skinny little guy, scar down his face, always looking for a way to make a quick buck. He got caught though. Got rumbled during the fallout from Jamieson's arrest, booted out of the police. They should have prosecuted him but they didn't want the bad publicity. Made it seem like he hadn't done anything illegal, made it seem like he was departing the service on good terms. That was bullshit. They knew he was more a criminal than most of us.

"What do you want?"

"I have a business proposition. I have information that you will want to pay good money for."

This was what he was up to now. Selling info, working as a middleman, as much a criminal as when he had a uniform on. "You think I'm going to trust anything you give me? You think I'm going to put money in your pocket?" I was keeping my voice down. Becky was in the next room. I could hear the music from the TV, hoping it covered my voice.

"I'm a man with information that you need."

"No, that's what you think you are; that doesn't mean you think right."

"I don't want to get into an argument with you here, Nate."

"I doubt that you do."

"Let me tell you a little bit of it, just to whet your appetite. You can decide if it's something you're interested in."

"So, tell me."

"I have information that could very well lead to you finding Adrian Barrett. That's what you're working on, right? Trying to find Barrett. The whole city knows it. I can tell you someone who's been working with him. It's…interesting. We'll meet, you pay me, I give you the info."

"How much?"

"Five hundred. Come along to Alessandro's in the town. You know it?"

"I do."

"Three o'clock."

He hung up. I went back into the living room; Becky was just sitting down on the couch when I did. Now, she could have been anywhere before she was sitting down again, but I was sure she'd been listening at the door. I was too busy trying to remember my side of the conversation to tell her off. Trying to remember if I'd said anything incriminating. She didn't ask who had been on the phone.

We passed the next twenty minutes with less conversation than before. She could see that I was in a bit of a mood about something. I didn't want to say anything in case my bad mood crept out into the room and spoiled things. Whatever shite Greig was going to throw at me, it certainly wasn't Becky's fault.

By the time Gordon and Mary came back to pick her up, I had calmed right down. I was goofing around with her, joking about the music and the music videos. Telling her it was no wonder she was sick, that rubbish made me sick as well. When I was her age

I was into wrestling, which I tried to persuade her was a noble entertainment experience. This got more laughs. She was in good spirits by the time she left.

"I'll see you at the weekend," I told her, kissing the top of her head as she left. I meant it, at the time, but I had no idea what kind of weekend was waiting for me.

16

The first thing I needed was five hundred quid. This wasn't a charitable effort so I wasn't going to spend my own money. Having a fund ready for people like me to dip into should have been done at the start, and as far as I was aware it hadn't been done yet. There were a minimum of four of us working on this: me, Ronnie, Conn and Mikey. That was four guys motoring around the city, looking for trouble. There were costs to that, and nobody had done anything to cover them.

I went round to Currie's warehouse, knowing he'd be there. He was a creature of habit, happy to be reachable, always presenting himself as a man with nothing to hide. That was going to change. The more influence within the organization he had, the more he had to lose. Wouldn't be long before he started to mix up the routine, make himself a little bit harder to find.

Biggest reason I was concerned about going there was because there was a chance of bumping into Kelly. She worked out of the warehouse in Hillington, making sure the dodgy goods that passed through the place went to the right people. A time might come when I was willing to think about a relationship with her, but this wasn't it. That time would be a time of peace.

I pulled into the yard, made sure I parked out of the way. The warehouse was busy, always packed with stuff. This was Kevin's kingdom, where he ruled with dazzling brilliance. There was nobody in the city who got more gear shifted in and out without detection than him. Any kind of knock-off you wanted, he had it.

That took a lot of skill, a lot of organization. There were people who underestimated Kevin. He was pleasant and cheerful and he didn't get involved in much violent stuff so they thought he was a bit soft. You don't run a business like Kevin's if you're soft.

I didn't see her as I went in, walked through the warehouse and into the office at the back. Kevin was in there alone, sheets of loose paper in front of him. The thought of what mathematical gymnastics he had to perform to keep all his deals looking presentable hurt my brain.

"Nate, what's up? You're looking serious."

I think that might have been a joke at the expense of my always serious demeanor, but I'm not sure. "We have a very minor issue we need to resolve quickly," I told him. "I need money for something, buying info. Five hundred quid. We should have a pot for stuff like that and we don't."

"Damn it, of course. Should have had that from day one, shouldn't we? Right, I can sort that out right away. Don't you worry about it." He pulled open the bottom drawer of the desk and pulled out a large wad of cash. There must have been a couple of grand there. He counted off five hundred, talking as he did. "Would have had this set up much earlier if we'd been handling it for ourselves. With this being one of Lafferty's men, I don't know, I suppose we were waiting for each other to sort out the details like this. Here, that's five hundred. You want an envelope for it?"

"Please."

He pulled a white envelope from the middle drawer and put the money into it. "From now on, if you need any cash for anything at all, get in touch with Ben. I'll make sure he has a fund, so there'll always be some cash there. Within reason, of course," he said with a smile, handing me the envelope. Ben was Ben Carmichael, his right-hand man. "This info we're buying?"

"Has potential. I'll wait and see though. Could lead us to Barrett in the best-case scenario. Not a source I'm willing to trust just yet," I said, shrugging my shoulders.

Kevin didn't need any more detail than that. Not yet. The only thing that was necessary for him to know was that I was buying info and he was paying. If there was anything to update him with later on I would. Better for him to know as little as possible at that point; you never know what you'll later need to deny.

As I was driving out of the warehouse I saw her. She was in her car, coming back from somewhere. We passed on the road, Kelly waved to me and I raised a hand. I didn't want to encourage her, not too much. We had met in ugly circumstances and that would always hang over us. My work was dangerous, and would be dangerous for her if she got too close. I kept saying that to myself, trying to persuade myself.

The traffic wasn't too bad on the way in but it took me a while to find somewhere to park. I was a few minutes late going into the cafe, a nice enough place if you like that sort of thing. There were plenty of people around, and that was deliberate. Paul Greig didn't want to meet me in private. He needed the security that a room full of witnesses brought. Didn't have his uniform to hide behind anymore. He was at a table close to the door, an oversized cup in front of him. The tables were low, the chairs were large, cushioned things with arms on them. I guess it was supposed to feel like twenty people had just turned up in your living room. I dropped my weight into a chair and looked the skinny bastard in the eye.

"You have the money?"

"You have the info?"

"I know how to find Adrian Barrett. I know someone he's been working with in the city. This person will know where he is, although you might have to persuade him to tell you."

"Fine," I said.

Persuading people to tell me things was a big part of my job description. I reached into my pocket and came out with the envelope. Looked like a thin little thing, too thin to buy anything of value. I passed it across the table to Greig and he slipped it into his pocket without bothering to look inside. Maybe he trusted me to give him the right amount; more likely he didn't want me seeing his mistrust. Also didn't want any of his helpful witnesses seeing the envelope and wondering what was inside. Sort of thing nosy people remember. Once the envelope was out of sight, done subtly by both of us because we've both done this sort of thing before, it was time for some information to change hands.

"Remember when I tell you this that I'm just the messenger and that I have nothing to gain from telling you something that isn't true," he said. Being dramatic.

"Get on with it."

"Barrett's right-hand man is a guy called Elliott Parker. He was in the city before Barrett, I think. If my information's correct then Barrett only turned up in the last couple of weeks and Parker's been here longer than that, setting things up. One thing they needed was a girl. A lure, among other things. Now I didn't know about this at the time, wish I had; would have taken the info to you sooner, or to Lafferty anyway. I heard they got the girl from Adam Jones, manager of Heavenly. You know Heavenly?"

"Know of it."

"Well, the manager there, twin brother to your friend Marty, keeps women on his books for the little parties he throws and he handed one over to Parker. They had some sort of arrangement, some sort of deal that paid Jones good money. He handed over the girl and this morning I found out that she was seen leaving Heavenly with Lee Christie on her arm the night before he was killed."

"This info is rock solid?"

"As close to guaranteed as any info you're ever going to get. I know the girl was working for Parker, whether she wanted to or not. Young local girl, probably didn't realize what she was getting into, so I wouldn't want any of this coming down on her. But Parker was the set-up man, here before his boss came north. He got the girl, got her into this, and they must have used her for the lure on Christie. Now, I can't guarantee that she was the lure, but that seems to make sense to me: Christie was the kind to fall for it from what I hear. Brain in his boxers. I'm also hearing that Parker's still in touch with Jones. Jones thinks he's going to get the girl back and has told at least one person that he knows where they're staying."

"Anything else?"

"Well, I think you've got your money's worth if you ask me, but there is one other thing. Again, I'm just the messenger here, so keep that in mind. I've heard that when Barrett came north there was someone with him, a woman. Now, I think this woman might be the reason he's here, might be the person that—"

"I know Zara's with him."

"Ah, right, well, took the wind right out of my sails there. That's all I've got for now then, but I'll assume you'd like me to keep in touch with my contacts, keep trying to find out anything that might be useful to you."

"You can assume that."

We were done. I got up and left the cafe. Left Greig with his giant cappuccino and his little world of secrets and bribes. Perhaps his info was correct, and that was fine, but it was more complicated than that. You had to trust the information that he was giving you, that it was given with straightforward intent. Wouldn't be a new tactic for someone to feed false information. Wouldn't be Greig himself. He knew what the price would be if he was deliberately misleading me with this. But someone could give the false info to him with a straight face and allow him to pass it on in good faith.

Honest or not, it was explosive. It was a suggestion that the twin brother of Marty Jones was helping Adrian Barrett and his crew. A suggestion that he was still involved with them, still talking to them. That implicated Marty. It was the kind of information that an enemy of the organization would be happy to provide. The sort of thing that all of us within the organization had to handle with great care.

I got in the car and drove straight back to the warehouse. Whatever the truth of it, Kevin needed to know this. Needed to find out before Lafferty did, because Lafferty wasn't likely to take a careful approach. I parked and went in. Kelly was standing talking to someone in the warehouse, a notepad in her hand. She saw me but I didn't stop, marched straight in and went into Kevin's office. He was alone, still going through his papers.

"Nate, you okay?"

Apparently I looked more serious than ever. "You need to find out where Marty Jones is."

17

They must have known as soon as we came through the door that there was going to be trouble. The kind of trouble none of them were looking for. One thing everyone in the business knows: you have less chance of seeing it coming when your own people start turning on you. Your enemies are the ones you face; your friends can sneak right up on you.

They were in a posh-looking office on the second floor of a building in Blythswood Square. The place had had a "To let" sign outside it for as long as I could remember. It would fetch good money in the right market. It wasn't the sort of place you would associate with Marty Jones, but that was probably the point. This was his off-the-radar office. A classy three-story building with a pretty view of the green square.

It had taken Kevin all of three minutes to find them, which was impressive. I was talking to Ben Carmichael in the warehouse while Kevin put the call in. I had already called Ronnie, told him to drop what he was doing and get his arse round to join us. Kevin came out of the office as Ronnie screeched all too dramatically into the yard.

"He's having some powwow with Billy Patterson, Conn Griffiths and Mikey Summers," he said, a little bit of concern on his face.

I nodded. I wasn't going to commit to saying that Conn and Mikey weren't involved. I trusted them, sure, but that meant nothing. They were Billy Patterson's people; he was the one who had employed them. Their loyalties didn't lie with me or with Kevin.

Ben drove us round there. I did some violent maths. Four of us and four of them. Marty's not a fighter in any meaningful sense, so you take him out. Same goes for Kevin, with bells on. So it's three on three. But I didn't fancy Ben's chances in a fight with Billy Patterson. Billy knew his way around a right hook. So it was three on two, in their favor. One of our two was Ronnie, the least experienced of all of us. I didn't expect this to turn into a fight, too many smart heads, but you still work out your odds. Ours told me we had to make sure this didn't get physical.

Kevin went in first. The front door was unlocked; there were other offices operating in the building. We went up the stairs and into Marty's, not bothering to knock. The place was immaculate, all new furniture and fitted carpet. The four of them were sitting round a table near the tall window, only Marty looking like he belonged. They were having themselves a conversation that stopped as soon as the door opened. Uninvited guests kill a good conversation. They might have been more relaxed if it was just Kevin, but I made sure I was second through the door, setting a tone. Ronnie and Ben followed me in, closed the door, still not a word spoken. No attempt at jovial hellos. They must have had an idea what was coming.

"Kevin," Marty said. You could hear the nerves in his voice already; he knew that not planned equals not good. "What's up?"

Kevin moved across to the table the four of them were sitting around, looking down at Marty. He didn't look angry because he makes a point of not looking angry, but you could tell. The way he moved, the way he was watching Marty. Everyone in that room was wary now.

"We found out that Barrett used a local girl as the lure for Christie," Kevin said. "The girl was, I don't know, a party girl, a hooker, I suppose."

"Not one of mine," Marty said, and you could hear how sure he was. Marty kept his girls on a short leash and cut them loose if they struggled. If it was one of his, he would know.

"No, not one of yours. One of your brother's."

There was silence in the room, people glancing around and making eye contact with each other. Everyone in that room knew everyone else in that room, just about. Maybe not Ronnie, but the rest of us had crossed paths. Everyone was looking to everyone else for answers.

"Adam?" Marty said.

"Yeah, Adam. He provided a girl to Barrett for the lure, and it's been suggested that he's bragging about being involved and knowing where Barrett and his crew are."

Didn't take more than three seconds for Marty to put two and two together. We all used to think he was dumb, just a party boy with the women and little else. Got involved in a bunch of other businesses that he couldn't make stick and went back to the women. But he was smart. Made his role in debt collection stick, managed to make himself the biggest debt collector in the city within a year. His failures had given him experience to learn from.

"I know you think that if he was involved then I must know about it but that's horseshit, if you don't mind me saying," Marty said to him. There was this force in every word he spoke that let you know how pissed off he was.

"You had no idea that your own twin brother was working with Barrett?" Currie asked him. Keeping his tone conciliatory, like he wanted to believe.

It was the tone Currie used that mattered, not what he said. Sounded like he already knew Marty didn't know, like he had too much respect for Marty to believe anything else. Showed how far Marty had come in a short space of time that his brother's stupidity couldn't dent him. It's become a cliché about Marty, how people are suddenly forced to respect his work. Marty's brother was a twat but that still didn't mean Marty was.

"We might be twins but we're not fucking Siamese twins. I don't know everything he does, although I bloody wish I did. Fuck's sake." He paused for a bit, glancing at me before he said anything. "Have you been round to see him yet?"

Kevin knew what that was. That was Marty terrified that we'd already dealt with his brother before we came to confront him. Fearing that his brother was a splatter on a floor somewhere and that nothing he could do now would change that. That's why he looked at me. But that wasn't plausible. Not when there was still a chance that we might get something out of Marty first.

This was a two-man conversation with an audience of six. Billy, Conn and Mikey sitting at the table, watching the back and forth. Me, Ronnie and Ben standing behind Kevin, literally and figuratively. Glancing occasionally at each other, making sure nobody was making any stupid moves, reaching into a pocket or anything like that. It needed to be tense to make sure Marty understood how serious this was. It was damaging though. It scratched at our unity.

"We haven't been anywhere near him," Kevin said, "but we're on our way. Your brother has some very serious questions to answer."

"You're too fucking right he does," Marty said, standing up behind the table, "and I'm going to ask them. The bastard. All of us, we'll all go. He'll be at the club at this hour."

"He is," I said. One phone call from Kevin in the car on the way over had confirmed that. Another of his unnamed contacts.

Marty looked at Kevin, nodded, but you could see he was unnerved by how much we knew. He felt outgunned. He was hoping that him leading the questioning could make the questions a little less physical. Me saying that I knew where his brother was extinguished that hope.

Marty was making a show of his decisiveness, putting on his jacket and getting ready to march down to his car and go round to see his brother. In the seconds he took to do it, I looked at Billy Patterson, made eye contact. I nodded, he nodded back, letting me know that he understood what was going to happen next. That was reassuring.

There was no way Kevin wanted Marty going off on his own, or just going off with his own people around him. That would have given him the chance to warn his brother. I wanted to split the two parties up for the drive to the club. I wanted to be in the car with Marty. Billy seemed fine with that, willing to be one of the people who went with Kevin instead to force the split.

We all traipsed down the stairs and out onto the street. It was lovely out there, in the late afternoon sun. Sort of place I'd have been happy to work if I was ever capable of holding down a desk job. The cars were parked on the street in front of the building. Turned out we were parked right up behind Marty's.

"We'll just take the two cars," Kevin said casually.

That was as much as he was going to say. Kevin wasn't going to force Marty to get in the car with me, wasn't going to give out any orders. So far everything was being done at Marty's behest. He wanted to go talk to his brother so we were going to talk to his brother. His demand, his terms. That wasn't going to change, not as long as he wanted the same things we did.

We did it as subtly as we could. Billy gravitated over to Kevin's car and got in the back with him. I walked over to Marty's car and got in the back beside him. He didn't look thrilled to see me, but he didn't say anything. Conn was already dropping into the driver's seat of Marty's car, Mikey getting into the passenger side. That left Ronnie and Ben no choice but to get in with Kevin and Billy. A three-to-one split.

It was a good chance for Kevin to have a conversation with Billy Patterson. Billy was closer to Marty on a day-to-day basis than we were; he might have a few interesting answers. He was in a better position to confirm or deny Marty being involved with Barrett.

"This info about Adam," Marty said to me. "You're sure about it?" Interesting that he correctly assumed I was the one who had found this info.

"Sure as I can be. Only one way to be certain."

18

Heavenly was a dump. It was cheap, it had a reputation as a place you could have a wild time, so it got people in the doors. But it was a dump. Could have been something special — the front looked like some classic theatre — if it wasn't so grotty and badly maintained. We parked across the street and marched in, a conspicuous collection of mobile trouble.

Marty went in first because nobody was more determined to lead the way than Marty. This wasn't just about him confronting his brother; it was about him being seen to take this more seriously than anyone else on God's green earth. Didn't matter how outraged you were, Marty would have found a way of trumping you. Nobody was going to look more innocent than him. He stormed in, the rest of us having to up our pace to keep up.

There were three people in the place and I recognized them all. They were a shabby wee combination of low-ranking criminality. Adam Jones was standing behind the bar. He was the manager of this place. That was his official job title anyway; what he told the taxman. The truth was that he ran private, after-hours parties from this place, something him and Marty had been doing for a while. He was also, apparently, edging his way into Marty's business of renting out women that he assumed belonged to him. It was grim, what they did. Finding desperate women and pushing them into prostitution. Paid some with drugs alone. I don't doubt some of the women made the decision for themselves, kept control of what they were doing. There were plenty who didn't.

There were two men sitting on the other side of the bar, closer to us. One of them was Aaron MacLennan, a tall, narrow guy with a mouth that took up most of his face. He was in his mid thirties, and he'd been around the business almost as long as I had. He was, not to be too technical, shite at everything. I'd never known him to make a good job of anything he'd done in the business, and I knew he'd been inside at least twice. If he was working for Adam Jones, then Adam Jones wasn't running much of a racket.

The other guy was Neil Fraser. A big lump of dumb muscle. He'd been stabbed the year before, if I remember my dates correctly. Not stabbed hard enough, because he was still polluting the city with his presence. He was a big guy, and that was where his skill ended. He was stupid. He was loud. He wasn't a good fighter. He was short-tempered. He used to work for us, the Jamieson organization. When Jamieson went down, the unreliable were the first to hit the dole queue. Seemed like he was now plying his trade for Adam Jones. Intimidating wee girls for money. That was his level.

We went in looking angry, and the eight of us could conjure up a pretty furious picture. Adam was trying to play it cool, with the bar and his two mates acting as shield. Fraser looked as dopey as ever, like he didn't understand. MacLennan knew. He looked like his rectum had exploded, now trying to shrink himself painfully into his bar stool.

"Marty, what can I do for you?" Adam said to his brother. Still trying to play it casual, but he wasn't much of a player. He so desperately wanted to be lord of the manor. He looked at Neil Fraser and smiled a bit, and Fraser, being as sharp as a brick, smiled back.

Marty was scowling. Now, days gone by I had seen Marty scowling and it looked petulant. He looked like a kid about to throw a tantrum. Not now. This scowl was dangerous. It was the sort of scowl that said he had seven men with him and Adam had two and fuck anyone who counted differently.

He stood there, halfway between the entrance and the bar, looking at his brother. "Adrian Barrett, you provided a girl for him." Said it quiet, trying to keep his temper in check. Smart leaders don't lose their temper.

"Never met Adrian Barrett," Adam said, giving a wee glance sideways to MacLennan as though he was being the smartest guy in the world.

"You met his right-hand man, Elliott Parker. You provided him with a girl to use. I hear you know where they're staying. Tell me."

The smile on Adam's face got a lot less sure of itself. He glanced at MacLennan and Fraser but they were now extremely busy looking at the floor. They knew that this wasn't some brotherly confrontation; this was business. This was way beyond their pay scale, and it scared the crap out of the pair of them. A few sentences in and Adam didn't have any backup left.

"Why don't you take a seat and we can talk about this?" he said, after pausing for a few seconds. He looked across at the little tables and chairs on the other side of the dance floor against the back wall of the club.

"Why don't you tell me where the fuck they are?" Marty said through tight lips. That temper was bubbling away.

"I didn't meet anyone called Parker," Adam said. "I provided girls for some people. That's part of what I do, brother. None of them was called Parker. We can talk about who —'

"Quit dicking around," Marty shouted at the top of his voice. The shout bounced around the empty dance floor. Everyone tensed a little. Mikey and Ronnie took a step forwards, ready for the fight that usually trotted along following a shout.

Adam put a hand up like he wanted to say something, trying to take the edge off this. Anything he said at that point would have set Marty off. I saw it, and Kevin did too. That's why Kevin took a few steps forwards, putting himself halfway between Marty and the bar. He was asserting control.

"We know that you provided someone for Parker. We know that you've since told people that you know where they are. Tell us where they are, Adam; this doesn't have to turn nasty."

Kevin Currie is an impressive man if you know who he is, what he does. By that I mean what he really does, the sort of risks he handles, the tough decisions he makes. If you don't know, don't understand the detail, then you might think he's a soft little middle-aged man who sells knock-off DVDs and cigarettes. You might make a grave error. Adam Jones laughed at him. Stood behind the bar and snorted. Looked at Marty as though Marty was the only one he would deal with.

As soon as he laughed, Kevin turned around. With his back to Adam, he nodded at me and Conn. That was our signal; we didn't need to be told what happened next. Conn, Mikey and Ronnie moved quickly across to the bar, covering MacLennan and Fraser. They fenced them in, didn't do anything else. Didn't need to. Neither of them was going to try and fight back. Adam stood behind the bar, looking at them, waiting for them to do something. Waiting for someone to throw the first punch. He looked disappointed with his own two. Shows how dumb he was if he thought either of them was loyal enough to fight us on his behalf.

Adam was watching this when he should have been watching me. I had hung back about half a second, let the other three get in front of me and take their positions. They provided a barrier between me and the bar, one that I could swing behind as I made my way towards Adam Jones. He saw me when it was too late to do anything; I was almost in front of him. He looked nervous, obviously thought about running, but tried standing his ground. Admirable tactic, if you've got what it takes to back it up. The bar between us wasn't going to help him, and the sudden widening of his eyes when he realized he was my target told me he knew it. That was my reputation, leaping ahead of me and screaming my name.

The one thing he did was look behind me, presumably at Marty. Just time for a glance across, where his twin was standing with Kevin, Ben and Billy. Perhaps hoping that Marty would say something. People always think that it's just scare tactics, that the worst thing possible can't possibly happen to them. If ever Marty was going to step in and make sure that the worst didn't happen, that was the moment. But Marty stayed silent. He was the last person in the world that was going to step in and help Adam now.

Move fast. Don't give a person time to react. Try and do something they can't possibly expect, so that you stun them, even just for a couple of seconds. Those couple of seconds, when they're trying to work out what's going on, are the couple of seconds where you take total control. I got to the bar and reached my arms right across it. He saw them coming, both arms shooting out towards him. He would have thought I was going for the front of his clothes to grab him, or even his throat. I wasn't. I grabbed him by the ears. Didn't have a great grip, but I didn't need one; he was happy to do all the work for me. I yanked him towards me and he very nearly leapfrogged that bar. To the untrained eye it might look like I dragged him across, but I was just holding on. He leapt like a man scared of losing his ears.

He was whimpering, sliding across the top of the bar and dropping heavily onto his knees on the other side. I had to lean down to hold on, gripping the ears as tight as I could. Don't stop. Don't give him a second to think about what's happening. Don't let him fight back. I glanced sideways as I started to pull him across the floor. Marty was watching, a grim look on his face, Kevin and Ben staying expressionless beside him. Billy had moved back to the door, making sure nobody came in to break up the party. Adam was still on his knees, trying to get up. He was shuffling and stumbling in the direction I was leading, trying to get up. He stumbled and I pulled at him, my grip slipping from one of his ears. He shouted something but I didn't care what, I wasn't going to stop. Keep dragging. Keep a hold of those ears. Never give him a chance.

We'd gone ten, fifteen feet, him whining beside me as I leant down and dragged him. Aiming for the tables and chairs where he had suggested talking when we first came in. He was going to get his chat, and his location of choice. Just wasn't going to make the journey the way he had intended. I stopped at the first table; no point making more work for myself than I needed to. I lifted him up and he wasn't expecting it; I could feel his ears stretch and strain. The boy screamed, loud and frightened. If nothing that had happened before then had told his two pals that he wasn't in charge here anymore, that did it. That one scream, terrified and weak.

He was up on his feet, whether he realized it or not. His eyes were shut when I shoved him into the chair. He went down harder than I expected, eyes still shut. The chair rocked back a little when he hit it, not nearly far enough to tip over. Didn't matter to him. He had lost all sense. Ears burning, eyes watering and shut, he didn't know what was happening. He must have thought he was going to tip backwards because he suddenly lurched forwards, trying to protect himself. Both hands reached out, flat onto the table, making sure he was secure. He grabbed the edge of the table with one hand, like that was the protection he needed.

No security. Never let them settle. Keep them uncertain. I placed my feet and punched him hard in the mouth. Aiming for the mouth, making sure that he had another part of his head to worry about. Knocked him sideways off the chair. Adam landed hard on his side with a gasp, a little blood coming quickly onto his lips. His eyes were shut, like he was happy to just lie there. Playing dead maybe. Seen people doing it before, pretending to be unconscious in the hope of buying time. I wasn't selling. There was a pain in my right hand but I ignored it. Doesn't matter how many skulls you hit, there's still a little shoot of pain. I took a step towards him and bent down, grabbing him by the shoulders of his shirt and lifting him up. He wasn't heavy, and he didn't resist. I shoved him back into the chair where he sat lifeless, head tilted forwards, mouth shut. Waiting for the next terrible thing to happen to him. Assuming that something even worse was coming and knowing there was nothing he could do to stop it. He was beaten. He was ready to be questioned.

No one said anything. I stood silently and waited for whoever wanted to ask some questions to come forward. Adam sat in the chair, trying to pull himself together. His eyes were still shut. He started to open them but they were watery and I don't think he was seeing much. His hands were in his lap. He raised one to his mouth, touched the blood. No teeth came away. He put them up to his ears and, to his obvious surprise and relief, found they were exactly where he had left them. He rubbed them and blinked heavily, trying to clear his eyes. Still silence around us, nobody stepping forward to take the lead from me.

I looked over my shoulder, a way of hurrying the rest of them along. Adam was about to remember where he was and what was happening to him, and that was going to make him harder to question. Ronnie, Conn and Mikey were still standing by the bar, babysitting Fraser and MacLennan. Everything that had gone on and those two hadn't moved a fucking inch. Told me everything about that pair. I could do anything to their supposed pal and they wouldn't even raise a voice, let alone a challenge. Nobody would expect them to start a fight when they were so significantly outnumbered, but they hadn't even suggested backing off a little. They weren't even looking at Adam. They were looking down at the floor. Ashamed of themselves. Kevin and Ben hadn't moved. Billy was still over by the door. Marty had. He'd come just a little closer.

Now he was walking across to us, stopping beside me. People like Marty often stood beside people like me for the sake of looking tough, threatening. Not this time. He stopped as close to his brother as he could get, and that meant beside me. Marty didn't look angry anymore. It was out of his system because he'd already seen his brother being punished. He still looked pissed off, but the worst of it was gone. He looked down at Adam.

"Tell me where he is," he said. There was sadness in his voice.

Adam said something in response that sounded a lot like fuck off. It was a mumble though, and as soon as he started to speak, little trickles of blood made their way out of his mouth. He started to mumble, barely coherent. The word brother was in there, presumably aimed at Marty. Some plea, or some castigation. Could have been either, wasn't possible to tell. The words were slurred, getting louder, more blood and spit coming out. Then he was shouting, Lord knows what. He was trying to look at Marty. Then looked past him and started shouting at someone back there. Again, no idea who he was talking to or what he was saying.

"Tell me," Marty said, and this time he wasn't shouting or angry. This time he sounded desperate.

It was that desperate tone that changed the mood. The shouting and spitting had been Adam's attempt at defiance, his last attempt at being a tough guy. The beating I'd given him might have defeated him, but he was still clinging on to a shred of self-respect. That tone Marty used, that was what really scared him. Adam looked up at him through red eyes. His mouth hung open. His expression changed.

"I don't know exactly," he said, not shouting inaudibly like a fucking retard this time. He was quiet, looking down at the floor. "I know ..." he said, and paused to spit out some blood. Some hit the floor, some dribbled down his chin and onto his shirt. "I know they were using a couple of different places. I know where those places are. I don't know which one they're using. I'll tell you them, the ones I know."

Marty knelt down beside him and he started to mumble again.

Sounded like vague descriptions rather than actual addresses, but he was providing just enough detail for us to know where to go. This was progress. Marty was leaning in close; I could see that Adam had accidentally spat some blood onto Marty's shoulder. One of the descriptions was of a house that I didn't recognize, the other was of a dive of a hotel that I thought we'd already looked into.

"They're moving, see," Adam mumbled. "Going back and forth and stuff, so nobody can pin them down. The hotel. That's the one they're at now, I think. Just went."

Marty stood up and looked round at Kevin. I walked with Marty over to where Kevin was standing. We talked in whispers; no need to share this with Adam and his two hapless companions.

"I'll hit the hotel," I said in a low grumble. "Take someone with me. Billy, let's say. You two and Ronnie go to the house and check it. Less likely to be anything there."

Kevin nodded. "Conn and Mikey?"

"Someone needs to stay here and make sure that none of these three put a call out or do anything else stupid."

Kevin nodded again. It meant us going in light to the hotel. Me and Billy Patterson didn't add up to much of a crew, but it was enough to start with. The first task was just to make sure that they were there.

Being the man in charge, it was Kevin who walked casually across to Adam and looked down at him. Even left alone he hadn't tried to get up. I very much doubt he'd have managed to run for it, even if he had been inclined to try.

"Some of the boys are going to stay behind, and we're going to check these addresses you've given us. If it turns out the addresses are bullshit, I'll call them up, and we'll finish what we started here," Kevin said to him, that casual tone all the time.

I went over to Ronnie and told him he was leaving. Told Conn and Mikey to sit tight and wait for the call. Told Billy he was coming with me; Ben Carmichael could watch the door instead. Me and Billy headed for the hotel; Ronnie, Kevin and Marty for the house. I could have taken Ronnie to the hotel, but there was still a small question mark over Marty. Billy was one of Marty's people. Billy and Marty alone with Kevin wasn't something I could risk yet. Out into the street, me and Billy getting into Kevin's car and heading straight for the hotel.

19

Hotel was a rather lofty term for the place in Pollokshields we were heading for. It was getting dark, there was traffic crossing the river. Billy Patterson seemed less than thrilled to be in my company but that was just too bad. He was a tough nut, was Billy. A good man to have along on a job like this.

"We sure they won't be carrying?" he asked me as we got close.

I shrugged. "Not important. We're not looking for a fight; we're just confirming they're there. We do that, and we get a team together, properly armed, and we deal with it."

"Deal with it?"

I just glanced at him. Billy ran a debt collection business; Billy knew what deal with it meant. Billy had dealt with stuff like this before.

I found a place to park along the street. The entrance to the place was small; hard to spot that it was even a hotel. Five stories, sandstone, on a fairly busy street. If we had to clean them out of there, it was going to be an issue. There were cars parked on either side of the road, a hairdresser's, a cafe and a corner shop taking up the ground floors of neighboring buildings. We weren't getting in and out without being seen.

"Let's go," I said.

In the front door and up the steps to reception. Reception constituted a desk in the hallway. This wasn't a place that tried to trick you into thinking you were getting luxury; it wore its earthiness on its sleeve. As did the fat, bald guy behind the desk.

"We'd like to see who's staying here, please," I said to him. Kept it dry, not quite threatening but not far off.

He looked up at me and twisted his mouth. "You're not cops."

"I know."

"So why am I showing you anything then?"

Billy chuckled. "You really want to say no to this guy?" he asked, glancing up at me.

"I don't have any guests people like you would be looking for."

I smiled. "You have no idea what we're looking for. Let me see."

The frown on his round face was as much opposition as he could raise. He nodded for me to come round the other side of the desk and he got his list of recent arrivals up on the screen of his computer for me.

"That pair are about a hundred years old each," he told me, pointing to a couple who had checked in the day before. "Look like either one of them could drop any second. As long as they don't do it here."

There were two that might be interesting. One on the first floor, one on the fourth. Two young men had booked two single rooms on the first floor; a couple had a room on the fourth.

"You check one eight and one nine; I'm going up to four eleven," I told Billy.

We left the fat guy behind the desk shaking his head. We took the stairs, Billy peeling off at the first floor. I bounded up as fast as I could, not wanting to waste any time. My phone was in my pocket, waiting for a call from Ronnie about the house Adam had mentioned. They should be there by now, checking the place out.

It was bloody boiling in that hotel. There were old, fat radiators in the corridors, belching out more heat than I needed after running up those stairs. I was in a long corridor, white walls and white doors on either side of me. A single door at the far end of the corridor. Room four eleven. I walked down towards it.

There were a few feet between me and the door when I started to slow. Listening for any sound coming from the room. Any clue. I heard someone talking, a loud female voice. Couldn't hear what it was saying. Then a shout.

"Nate. Help me, Nate. Nate."

I recognized her. Years apart, but the sound of her voice was still so familiar. It was Zara shouting. I knew, deep in the back of my mind, that there was something strange about the way she was shouting. Something that wasn't quite her. But I didn't stop to think about that. Zara was shouting for my help and she was going to get it. Something deeper within me, something that I'd worked so hard for so long to crush, welled up again. When the shouts became muffled, I acted.

Shoulder to the door, firm but with a short shove. There was a crack, and I dipped back and hit it a second time, same as before. The door seemed to crumple inward, smashing round the lock and breaking on the hinges. It was open and I was in.

The room was dark, the thick curtains drawn. Too hot. Adrian Barrett sitting on the end of the bed, legs crossed, facing the door. There was a laptop beside him on the bed, giving out the only light. He had been watching something. Watching me, coming into the hotel and up to the room. A set-up. He was in T-shirt and jeans, a long, thin face and hair cut close at the sides. None of that was what stood out with him. What stood out was the small handgun resting on his lap, pointing listlessly towards Zara.

She was lying on the bed, sitting up against the headboard. Headboard was a filthy thing; you could see the round stains where other people's dirty heads had rested against it too long. The pillow beside her, that she had been shouting into, was yellowed. Even in the light from the laptop and the little creeping in from the corridor I could see that. It was Zara, just not the one I'd known.

She was naked, sitting up, the blanket covering her bottom half. Made to look vulnerable. The man with the gun, showing me what control he had over the mother of my child. Using her like that. Her eyes were half closed, her mouth was half open. She had a small smile on her face. Laughing and stretching out so that her ribs showed. She was never that thin before. Never. Laughing hard and then falling silent, like she was asleep. Looking away from me, which I was glad of.

I looked away from Zara, looked back at Barrett. He had his hand on the gun but he wasn't gripping it. He was making it look casual. I had about two seconds to work out what this was. Not an attempt to kill me. You don't drug your lure if you need to make a quick exit. He might well have other people nearby, in the next room. I could be in for a beating. They might use a knife. It's how I'd have done it, if I was going to kill someone in that hotel room, but the broken door complicated things. So this was a warning. Or a dickish attempt at delivering a message. It took a lot of effort to make sure that I had no expression on my face.

"You knew I was coming," I said. Kept my voice low.

Barrett didn't respond to that. If he admitted this was a set-up then he'd be inviting me to punish those involved. Starting with Adam Jones, the man who had given me this address. So he wouldn't confirm it, but he didn't need to.

"I want you to deliver a message," he said to me.

I raised my eyebrows just a little, whether he could see it or not. "Do you now?" I said.

He started talking more quickly, obviously trying to hurry this up. He knew Billy was downstairs; he was concerned about the change in tone if I had backup. "Tell your bosses that they need to hand over their suppliers and distributors to me. If they don't, I'll pick them all off like I did with Christie. They don't have long."

I said nothing for a few seconds, still standing in the doorway. The light was behind me and I knew it made me look huge.

"That all you want?" I asked sarcastically.

"Tell them," he said. "Tell them or people die." Barrett raised the gun slightly and pointed it at Zara properly. Letting me know that I wasn't the one whose life was running out of road. Not even other Jamieson employees. The first person to go would be Zara. Fisher had asked me how I would explain that to Becky. How the hell would I deal with it myself?

It was a stupid demand. Moronic message. Tell them to hand over everything they have to some nobody who just turned up. They would laugh at the message, but he knew that. The real message wasn't in what he said. It was the way he was doing it. Showing me that they had Zara and could frighten me with that. Showing the city that they could go toe to toe with Nate Colgan.

"I'll tell them," I said quietly.

Zara moved, rolled onto her side, facing me. Her eyes were shut, but she mumbled something. I don't know what. I stood there looking at her. The blanket was down to her knees now. I've always considered myself a smart man. Always thought that I could handle any situation, no matter how tough. I've done grim things, pushed myself beyond the boundaries I thought I had. Here was this smart, tough guy, standing there watching her sleep. Watching her naked body. Knowing that the business didn't matter, doing the right thing for Jamieson didn't matter. I was going to do the right thing for her.

"Go on then," he said, hurrying me up.

His tactic was obvious. Get me out of the building and then get himself and Zara out before I had the chance to come back with a crew. This wasn't where they were staying. Whether they'd fed the information to Adam Jones without him realizing or not, this was all fake. They set up cameras here; waited for someone from the organization to turn up. They knew I was working this, but they got lucky that it was me who went to their room. Whoever it was, they had a girl to point a gun at. A girl everyone knew mattered to me. If it had been Ronnie or Billy or Conn, didn't matter. They'd all have known not to push it with Zara there, in that state.

I turned and walked out of the room, walked quickly down the corridor. Didn't run. Nobody's ever going to see me run away from them, not in this fucking life. I strode, purposeful. When I reached the stairs I started moving quickly. There was a half-chance, and we had to be seen to make a stab at it. Get Billy, get a crew together, get them round to the hotel.

Billy was back at reception. He nodded to me. "Anything? Because I got nothing."

"Come on," I said, walking past him and out of the front door.

There was a young man standing at the bottom of the steps. He watched me walk down, smiled at me. Actually had the nerve to smile at me. He was Barrett's man, watching to make sure we left. Shit. That blew part of the plan away. Meant we had to actually leave, to put some distance between us and the hotel while we called round the rest of them. They would be gone by the time we got back. Of course they would.

"The fuck's going on?" Billy demanded as we got into the car. He knew better than to ask in the street.

"Barrett was there. Had Zara and a gun. A message, demanding we hand over the drug business to him. Whole thing was a fucking set-up."

"Fucking Adam Jones," he said with a hiss. Then, "What are we going to do about it?"

"Let everyone know, get a team here, see if we can catch them, spot them going. Something." Truth was there was little we could do that didn't put Zara at more risk than I was willing to accept.

20

Adrian Barrett knew he had about five minutes before Colgan came back with a crew, armed to the teeth. He ran out of the open door, knocked on the room next door on the right side of the corridor and went back in to Zara. He slapped her a couple of times, made her put on a T-shirt and jeans and shoes. He had to do most of the work; her responses were slow and unhelpful.

Elliott Parker, Jawad "Nasty" Nasif and Gary Aldridge were next door, awaiting further instructions. They moved as soon as they heard the knock, knowing they were up against the clock. Elliott went first to get his cameras back. One at the other end of the corridor, another downstairs near reception. Nasty went ahead with Parker; Aldridge helped Barrett lead Zara unsteadily downstairs.

Once they were out on the street they saw Keith Henson. Sitting in the driver's seat of the van, window down, the same smile he'd offered Nate still on his face.

"They went off, didn't leave anyone behind." Said loudly and into the street. That got a frown from the more experienced men. They all piled quickly into the van and headed back to the hotel in Mount Florida. There was a lot of work still to do.

Back at the hotel and packing up everything they had. Leaving nothing behind, no trace. The owner knew the cost of admitting they'd been there. The van was filled, everybody in, even the terrified girl that they should have gotten rid of. Another complication. Elliott getting attached to a girl that shouldn't now be anywhere near them.

One last safe house, that was what Barrett kept telling himself. One more move, a couple more days and they could all get in the van and go back home. That was all he was thinking about. Sitting in the front of the van, dreaming of getting his old life back down south. Take some good money home with him. Start again. The last time he'd had a network of his own it had fallen apart. Left Ricky Saunders, the other member of their quartet, in jail. Left him, Elliott and Nasty with nothing. Barrett started using more than he had before. Then he met Zara. The first bit of good luck. Now they were this close to being able to start again. This close.

"Drop me at the other safe house," Nasty said. "I'm meeting a gun dealer, getting rid of that gun and getting a clean one. Come back and pick me up."

"Make it quick. They'll be looking for us now," Barrett told him. "Crawling all over the city."

"I know."

They dropped Nasty off, Henson telling him he'd be straight back after dropping the rest at the new safe house. Nasty watched the van pulling away, watched its lights disappear round the corner so that only the street lamps were left to brighten the darkness. All he could hear were his own footsteps. The residential street reminded him of the one he'd grown up on.

He knew as soon as he opened the front door, shoving the key back into his pocket, that the gun dealer was there ahead of him. That instinct, when you know someone's nearby just before you see or hear them. The house was dark, but the dealer was hardly going to light it up. There was still some warmth from the last time some of the group had been there, a newspaper on the stand at the bottom of the stairs. They'd used this place and the hotel for the first stage of the job. The stage that lasted from arrival until first direct contact with the Jamieson organization. The second stage, the final stage, would see them holed up in a small safe house in the north of the city that wasn't anywhere near large enough for a group their size.

"I'm in here," a male voice called out from the living room.

He had seen Nasty coming up the front path. The gunman went into the living room, unwilling to switch on the light given that the room looked out onto the road. There had been nobody out there when he was coming in, but that didn't give him an excuse to get sloppy. He could see the middle-aged man standing by the fireplace, on his own, which was a basic part of the relationship between any gun dealer and any gun buyer. Both parties should always be alone when a deal is being done. Common sense to ensure that both sides are kept as calm as possible when guns are around.

"Just the one?" the dealer asked. There was disappointment in his voice.

"For now," Nasty said. Keeping up the pretense that he was going to stick around long enough to be a repeat buyer. They'd been pretending that to everyone they met. Only those in the group, and their employer, knew they were only here for the short term.

"Here you go," the dealer said, passing the padded envelope with a single handgun inside.

Nasty took it and handed over the old one, wrapped in a plastic bag. Used on Christie and now waved at Colgan. Too risky to still have around. He opened the envelope, saw that the dealer had provided exactly what had been asked for. He reached into his pocket to pay him.

The dealer paused for a second while he waited to see what Nasty pulled out, worried for his safety. When he saw the wallet he relaxed and said, "Don't worry, it's paid for."

Didn't take a lot of brainpower to work out that Nasty's employer had made sure the gun was paid for in advance, ensuring that he had every opportunity to do the job well. That was reassuring, reaffirmed the idea that this would be finished soon.

"You can head off," he told the dealer. "I'm waiting to be picked up."

"Right, fair enough," the man said, nodding a little goodbye as he went.

Even if he hadn't been waiting for someone to come back and pick him up in the van he would have let the dealer go first. It was the right and proper way of doing these things. The person who comes first will typically have the right to leave first, although if one person is noticeably senior then you might let them come and go as they please. Being the customer doesn't give you the right to treat the seller in any way you want. Nasty had always believed it was important to make sure your dealer felt that you were giving them as much respect as possible. That relationship is vital, and for it to really prosper you need the dealer to respect you, even like you if possible, even when you have no intention of using them again.

He was alone in that house, a semi-detached in a residential area that probably wouldn't be empty for very long. It was officially on the market, although whoever owned it was under strict orders not to let anyone view it until they were finished using it. A glance around the living room with its wooden flooring and striking fireplace told him that if they didn't price it stupidly it would move quickly. He wandered over to the large bay window and looked out into the street. There was nobody there, no movement now that the dealer had gotten in his car and driven away. It was a strange thing, but he felt safe being in that house on his own in the dark. Much safer than he felt when he was around Dyne and the boys.

Dyne and Elliott had been hanging around with each other since they were in primary school. It was Elliott who had given Barrett his nickname. Nasty had joined up with them when he was eighteen and they were both twenty and they were all looking for a way into the underworld. Ricky Saunders was the fourth member of the crew, joining them a couple of years later. Ricky was tough but a risk-taker and he was eighteen months into a six-year stretch when they went to Glasgow. That original group of four had found a way into the business because, between them, there wasn't much they weren't willing to do for money.

Nasty was always the killer, whether it was knives or guns or, on one occasion, his hands. He was willing to kill for the right price. Elliott was the schemer, the one who liked to plot things out and had the ambition to make big moves. He was always a little creepy, sometimes a little unreliable in the way he behaved towards others, especially women, but he was smart. Ricky was the muscle, the extra-tough guy who didn't know where to draw the line. Dyne, he was the leader because he was a force of nature. When Dyne got going, things got done, and that was why they made their reputation and their money. People knew that if they hired those four for a job it would get done, that they were good value for what they routinely delivered.

Like any group with ambition, they outgrew being other people's weapons. It was only natural when they saw the amount of money their employers were making from the things they did. All they needed was the structure of an organization to support the ambitions they had. So they tried to build something of their own in Birmingham, and did a damn good job in the early days. Not damn good enough though, because there are always other people who think they can take what you've built. Others who think you should just be happy to make the money you were making serving them. They got knocked down, had their business ripped apart by the wolves they had been feeding in the past and ended up with little more than the shirts on their back.

It damaged them all. Dyne took it hardest. Losing his network, losing Ricky. He went off the rails, wallowing in it. Nasty and Elliott let him get on with it for a while: plenty time to pull him out of it later. Then he met Zara Cope at a party somewhere. The rest didn't like her but Dyne was smitten. She became more than just a girlfriend; she became a part of the group. Whispering in his ear that he should make another run at setting up his own organization; all he needed was the money to get a head start. That, she said, had been what he'd done wrong the first time: didn't have enough cash to hire the people he needed to protect them through the tricky first couple of years. All of which was fine advice, a little obvious even, but where were they going to get the sort of money they needed? Didn't take long before she came back with an answer, telling them that the money was waiting in Glasgow.

The job was perfectly decent, sort of thing they'd have done in a flash if it was back home. Only the change of scenery and the fact Zara had suggested it unnerved Nasty and Elliott. They didn't like how much she was influencing him, although she was clever about it and did her best to look vulnerable whenever anyone was watching. Nasty just didn't feel safe as part of the group anymore, and that was the first time he had felt that in nearly a dozen years together.

There was something about looking out into a strange street in the late evening that got him all wistful about the past. Something a man of his experience shouldn't have been doing. It wouldn't take long before the van came back. Another five or ten minutes maybe, so he took the time to wander through the house and make sure they hadn't left anything behind that would let the world know who had been here. The main thing was making sure there was nothing to tell people where they had gone next. Not likely, but it was professional to check. The two meatheads they had brought up for help weren't to be relied upon to do the basics like check for identifying material.

Nasty moved slowly along the corridor and into the kitchen, realizing as he did that he was hungry. It was only because he was in the kitchen that his stomach started to growl; he could easily have waited until he got to the new safe house where the cupboards would be full to bursting. But no, his gut was his master, and he walked slowly over to the fridge and pulled the door open to see if there was anything inside. He was sure there had been an open packet of sliced ham in there last time he was here and the memory of it lured him to the fridge before he'd taken a proper look around the room.

He must have been in the kitchen waiting for Nasty, had stayed in there throughout the meeting with the dealer. He'd have come in the back, and he didn't want to shoot in any of the rooms that faced out onto the street. That was the problem of an empty house for sale: the curtains were always open or nonexistent and any flash of light was going to get people thinking if they saw it. The dealer must have let him in. That was Nasty's last thought as the bullet crashed in through the back of his skull and he fell forwards, slumping against the fridge and onto the floor.

He didn't hear his killer step silently out of the back door. Nobody heard or saw that man. It was another fifteen minutes before Henson returned, alone, with the van. He sat outside the house, on the street, assuming Nasty would come out. He didn't. Shouldn't be sitting out there, people able to see the van's number. He needed to hurry Nasty along. Got out, went up to the front door, found it unlocked. Inside and into the living room, but there was nobody there. Through to the kitchen.

Didn't really need a light to see what had happened here. Henson put the light on anyway. Nasty was lying face down, blood running off his neck and down onto the floor. Henson glanced round the room. Just a glance. Making sure he couldn't see who had pulled the trigger. That gave him the confidence to walk across to Nasty and pick up the package with the gun in it. Then his confidence deserted him. He ran out of the room, swinging out a hand and switching off the light as he went. Out of the house and into the van, pulling quickly away.

Drove fast, faster than a man keeping his head down should. Ran into the new safe house, panting, the padded envelope in his hand. Barrett and Elliott were sitting at the kitchen table when he barged in.

"He's dead, Nasty's dead." He stopped to pant. "I went back for him and he didn't come out. Fucking hell. I went in and I found him dead in the kitchen. Someone had shot him, right through the back of the head. Bang, right through the fucking head."

Aldridge came through from another room; someone was coming down the stairs. Zara was standing in the doorway before anyone spoke.

"Anyone there?" Elliott asked.

"Just Nasty. He was dead in the kitchen. I didn't check the whole fucking house. Couldn't. Come off it. I wasn't armed."

"What's that?" Barrett said, pointing at the envelope.

"It's the gun," Henson told him. "The one that Nasty went to buy, I suppose. It was lying on the floor beside him. And there was blood, and, fuck, I don't know."

"So you were armed. You could have checked."

"Dyne," Elliott said. This was no time to argue about something that couldn't be changed. Their friend was dead. Gone. Something Elliott couldn't even contemplate right now.

"Right, fine," Barrett said, shaking his head. A pause of a few seconds, everyone in the cramped kitchen watching him. Waiting for his leadership to direct them. "He had the gun, so the seller was there. Gave him the gun."

"Can't have been the seller then," Zara said from the door.

Elliott turned and frowned at her. It was her who had brought them up here and now Nasty was dead because of it. She should be keeping her damned mouth shut. The seller leaving the gun didn't mean anything.

"Do we go back, get the body?" Aldridge asked.

"No," Barrett said quickly. "There was a gunshot. The cops could be there already. The van's been there twice, can't go again. We leave him there. And we can't stay here."

"Hold on," Elliott said.

"No, we can't stay here. Someone knows. Someone fucking knows, Elliott. They knew he was going to be there and they popped him. They know where we are. They fucking know."

"You don't know that," Elliott told him. Voices were being raised. The prospect of moving again.

"We have another house we can use. We use it."

Elliott shook his head. Moving again. On the run. Going to a house that was to be used in emergencies, that hadn't been properly scouted. None of them even knew where it was, except maybe Zara.

"You want to argue about this?" Barrett asked him. Steely, making it clear what the end result of an argument would be.

"Let's get everything back into the van," Elliott said to Henson and Aldridge. "I'll get the girl."

"Fuck's sake," Barrett shouted. Wasn't clear if that was directed at Elliott wanting to take the girl with them again or whether it was directed at the situation in general.

Elliott didn't wait to find out. He went quickly upstairs, taking the key to her room out of his pocket. Jessica was still wearing the same dress she had been wearing all week, since they killed Christie. She'd been able to take showers, to stay clean, but she had a drawn look about her now. Elliott smiled, trying to be reassuring.

"Come on," he said, "we're moving again."

People were moving loudly downstairs; from the doorway Elliott could hear Zara doing a lot of talking. Talking to Barrett, calming him down. Might actually be doing some good for once.

"Where are we going?" Jess asked, stopping herself before she added the word "now." Elliott wouldn't want to be reminded that they were making a second move in an hour, that they were obviously running from something.

"Somewhere safer," he told her, stepping into the room and smiling. "Don't you worry, Jess. I'll look after you."

He enjoyed how scared she looked when he said it. The way her eyes widened when he walked over and took her by the arm, leading her out of the room. No need to make sure that she had left nothing behind; she had nothing to leave.

Jess had thought so much about escaping in the last few days. Four days since they killed Lee Christie. She kept telling herself that it wasn't her fault. She thought about jumping out of the window, but she would have broken her legs. She could have shouted into the street, but they'd have heard her downstairs and punished her. There was no way out. Not unless they let her out. She knew they wouldn't, no matter what sweet words Elliott spoke. They would kill her rather than let her go.

Most of their belongings had never made it out of the bags, so they were back in the van already. Aldridge and Henson were in the van; Barrett and Zara were waiting for Elliott and the girl. Barrett gave her a dirty look. The plan had been to get rid of her. Nasty would have done it. Now he was gone, and Elliott was determined to hold on to this pretty little treasure. Even hinting that he might take her back down south with them when they went. Fucking crazy.

She noticed that the one they called Nasty wasn't there. Nobody was talking about him. There was a strange atmosphere, the kind that only came when something bad had happened.

"I need to use the toilet," Jess said quietly.

"At the next house. Won't take long," Elliott told her, gripping her arm and leading her out to the van.

Barrett locked the house; he and Zara were the last into the back of the van. Sitting on the narrow benches on either side. Zara sitting opposite Jess, making sure she didn't make eye contact with her. Zara had never spoken to the girl, never given her a speck of hope. They had needed Jess for this job to work properly. Zara's job.

Henson drove, Aldridge in the passenger seat giving him

directions. Neither of them seemed to know where they were going, but from the back of the van you could hear street names
being repeated. They were going slowly, Henson more concerned
about not getting lost than getting there quickly. They were going
north and east to Shettleston, Zara knew. Going to a house that
none of them had even checked to make sure was safe. Dyne had
panicked, leading them further away from the certainty this job
had so far contained.

The van slowed to a crawl, pulling over to the side of the road.
In the back they could hardly see anything.

"Can't park here," Aldridge said.

"What's going on?" Barrett said, grumpy. His nerves were running, giving him energy he needed to shift.

"There's no garage or anything," Henson said back over his
shoulder. "We'll have to park out on the street."

"We can't park out on the street," Barrett said, his Birmingham
accent getting thicker with fear. "They'll be looking for the van.
Fucking hell, park somewhere else. Find somewhere near. Fuck."

Jess watched Zara put her hand on Barrett's. He turned and
frowned at her, but he didn't take his hand away. The two in the
front were mumbling, Henson leaning across to look at the map.

"What's that?"

"Church."

"That's just round there, back that way. That'll have a car park."

Aldridge looked over his shoulder to Barrett, sensing he needed
the boss's permission. "There's a church back down the road and
round the corner. We can park the van there, walk up to the
house."

"Fine. Just fucking do it, will you?"

They swung the van round in the street, something else to draw
attention, and moved slowly back down to the junction. The
church was on the right-hand side, plenty of parking around it.
Henson slowed to a crawl, looking for a spot they could use that

would draw the least attention. It wasn't clear to him what was going to happen now. Finish the job. That was the obvious bit. If Dyne didn't intend to finish the job then they would be on the motorway right now. Could they finish it without Nasty? Wasn't up to Henson to ask.

"Park it there, at the edge," Aldridge said.

They stopped at the back of the small car park at the side of the church, against a wall and underneath some trees. It was as far out of view as they could get. Two days, max. That's what they'd been saying. Finish the job in two days. So if nobody complained about the van being there in that time, it would be fine.

Everyone got out, taking all the bags with them. They wouldn't come back for a second trip. Zara led the way. She knew where the house was; she had the back door key in her pocket. Out of the churchyard and down to the corner, left along the street. The whitewashed houses were in bunches of two. Up steps to get to them all. Zara found theirs.

Elliott was walking with a bag slung over one shoulder and the other hand gripping Jess's arm. He didn't like this house. It faced down an adjoining street; it was too far from the van; they had no idea who was in the houses around them. They should have stayed where they were. They all filed round the back and into the house. Cold and unfurnished. No wonder it was emergencies only.

"Get her out of my sight," Barrett said, turning to glance at Jess.

Elliott led her through the kitchen and into the corridor.

"I still need the toilet," she told him quietly.

They went upstairs; he pushed open a couple of doors and found the bathroom. Pushed her in and stepped in after her. She stood and looked at him. He smiled.

Henson and Aldridge put the bags in the corridor and started searching the house, happy to leave Zara and Barrett alone in the kitchen. Barrett stood by the sink, eyes shut, trying to process it all. Nasty was dead. They were under attack. Someone had known where Nasty was going to be and when. None of them were safe. Not in this city. They should get out. Just cut and run. They had gotten half the money up front. Take it and run, and if their employer sent people after them then so be it. Survive crossing this bridge before you worry about the next one. He felt Zara's hand on his shoulder. He opened his eyes, turned and looked at her. His girl.

"Hey, listen, we're nearly done," she said to him, looking up into his eyes. "I know this is hard. I know it. Losing Nasty like that. It's hard, and it's shocking and it makes you want to run from everything. Two days, and that's it. Two days and we're out of here, you and me. Back down south, and we can build something amazing together. Two more days."

She hugged him tight, and he felt better. Two days. They didn't need Nasty for what was left. He could do this.

21

I got the call early from Kevin himself; they had been tipped off by one of their police contacts. Jawad "Nasty" Nasif had been found dead in a house that was up for sale. Bullet to the back of the head was what they had been told; someone sneaking up on him in the kitchen of this house and leaving the body behind. I put the phone down and got out of bed, sat there thinking about what this was going to mean. I didn't like it, which is strange given that it got rid of the gunman of our threat. But it didn't add up to something I could be happy with, coming hours after I had encountered Adrian Barrett in that hotel room.

That meeting was on my mind; what we had done after it was on my mind as well. We had gone back with a full crew, armed and ready to bring them down, but they were long gone, of course. We tried to find out where they had gone but the staff in the hotel knew nothing. Their ignorance was genuine, not bought and paid for. We had the message to pass on, but it wasn't a message anyone was going to pay any attention to. It was passed to Lafferty given that it was his import business that was partly under threat, and I understood that, despite being a small man, he had hit the roof.

"He was shouting about you, Nate," Kevin had told me. "He couldn't accept that you had walked away from Barrett when you had him right in front of you."

"He had a fucking gun on his lap. What did he want me to do?"

"I don't know. Nothing I suppose. He'll calm down; he's just bricking it right now. He thought this was going to be his chance to step up to the top and he isn't dealing with it, not as easily as he thought he could."

Now that Nasty was dead it was inevitable that people were going to point the finger at us, particularly if they knew that Barrett had confronted us the previous night. Everyone would be thinking about that, expecting Barrett to retaliate. Maybe Barrett was already planning to retaliate. He probably thought it was us that had moved against his gunman because, let's face it, that was the most logical conclusion to jump to.

"We're sure Lafferty didn't make this move?" I asked Currie when he called.

"As sure as we can be," he said, and his tone didn't aim for reassuring. "I might not place a high regard on his tactical prowess, but I don't think he would try and pull this. Killing the gunman doesn't wipe them out, he has to know that. Just pisses them off. The way Lafferty's thinking, he would only make a move against Barrett or against all of them. He is getting nervous."

"But not nervous enough for this?"

There was a pause while Currie considered it. "Christ, I don't know. I don't think so, that's as much as I can say."

Which left a lot of questions that we needed to find the answer to just as much as Barrett did. Was this someone else muscling in on the act? Maybe another dealer or supplier that they'd threatened. Or was this their employer, let's assume they had one, trying to get rid of them because he felt their work was done? Or, and this was the most likely one, was this a falling-out among the group that ended with them getting rid of their own gunman? All of those questions hinged on it not being Lafferty.

I got up, showered and called Ronnie, told him what had happened and that we should expect a response. I warned him to be on the lookout in case anyone tried to target him. He seemed a little shocked by that suggestion, maybe a little dismissive even. I warned him a second time, made sure he understood.

"If Barrett thinks that we made a move against him then he will make a move against us. He has to. Doesn't have to be against Lafferty or Currie or one of the top guys. As long as he can show people that he can still hit us without his gunman then he gets his message across. You and me, guys out on the street, we're all at risk."

I hoped that got the point across to him and sat down to work out what I was going to do next. In a sense this didn't change a lot. We still needed to know where Barrett was if we were going to deal with him quickly, and we needed to prepare for him and his little mob when they stepped out into the open. His mob being littler than expected didn't matter. We also needed to know who, if anyone, was backing them. But still, our enemies had lost their gunman and we were no further forwards thanks to it. We didn't know where they were and there didn't seem to be any obvious way of finding out. That, right there, was why I was leaning towards Barrett being the killer of his own gunman. Couldn't work out who else benefited much.

The safe house was interesting. Needed to find out if it had been checked, but if it was for sale then it probably had. So maybe that wasn't their safe house, just a place for, what, doing deals? Storage? Something like that. Didn't change the fact that after an attack they were bound to have moved. Bound to have. That meant the squad of them all moving at the same time, because they couldn't plan to go earlier if they didn't know the attack was coming. Even if Barrett was behind it they couldn't have moved earlier without alerting Nasty to the fact that something was going down.

That was exactly as far as I had gotten when my doorbell rang. I didn't like that, a Friday morning and someone ringing my doorbell without warning. If it was someone from work, Ronnie or Mikey or someone like that, they would have called first. There's an etiquette that says you don't turn up on someone's doorstep without giving fair warning. If it's an emergency, fine, but I didn't want an emergency ringing my doorbell either. I opened the door to something worse than an emergency. I opened the door to DI Michael Fisher.

I nodded for him to come in, seeing that he was angry and feeling my own anger beginning to boil. I wasn't his contact and he wasn't mine. I don't know what our relationship was at that point. Didn't matter—if you're looking for info or influence you do not turn up on someone's doorstep, not when you're a cop and certainly not when you're a high-profile cop. He was putting my life as well as my career in danger by being there. I ushered him through to the living room and we stood looking at each other, just a few feet apart, me looking down at him. Always impressed me, how little guys like him managed to look tough using only naked fury.

"Was it your lot?" he said. "It bloody was, wasn't it?"

"No, it bloody was not," I said, growling because I was trying to stop myself from shouting. He had no business being here just because he was in a huff about the Nasty killing.

"You know about it though."

"Course I do. I heard half an hour ago. But I'd be as interested as you are to find out who was behind it."

"Oh, would you?" he said, raising his voice and trying to sound sarcastic. He sounded a little frantic to me. "So I tell you who's in his crew and a day later one of them is found dead."

"We already knew all about Nasif. I didn't need that from you. We couldn't find them and we still can't. You were the one who knew where they were."

There was something in that glance he gave me that set alarm bells ringing. It was guilt, that's what it was. There was a guilty look in his eyes.

"You didn't know where they were," I said.

"I did," he said, snapping at me, "but I don't now. I went round to the hotel they were at and they'd moved; I haven't picked them up yet. The house we found Nasif in? I didn't know they were using that place, if they even were. Seemed like that house had been used by someone, so, I don't know, must have been them."

He fell silent and I let him. It was a good thing for him to calm down a little before I tried to prize any other info out of him. I felt a little sorry for him, which was ridiculous. He might just have been the last person in the whole damn city that I should have had any sympathy for. The guy was trying to stop bloodshed, and I could respect that. It mattered to him.

"And there was nothing to ID the killer?"

"No," he said with a shrug, "there was nothing there. There was no weapon found anywhere in the area, nothing that we can grab onto yet. Might be, still early, but I doubt it. I think the guy was a pro. I think he was the kind of pro that an organization like yours might employ."

"Maybe he wasn't a pro," I suggested. "Maybe he was known to the victim. That would let him get close, make sure the job was as clean as possible."

He thought about it but I could see that he wasn't buying it. "His own lot don't benefit from it, not in any way I can see. Your lot, you're the ones who benefit most from it; that's why I suspect you."

I said nothing to that because I'd told him how wrong he was and he didn't need to hear it again. "I want to stop this as much as you do," I told him, whether he believed me or not. "We're all at risk here, and more people will be dead before this is all over. I don't want that. I'm still trying to find Barrett, and if I do, I give you my word I will try to make sure that it ends peacefully. I'll try to make sure that it ends with Barrett in your hands and not mine."

He looked at me like he believed me, perhaps because I was being honest. I could see his discomfort, partly because he was talking to me and I wasn't the sort of person he wanted to talk to. But there was something else there. I think he was a little bit panicked by what was happening. He had made a huge score with

Jamieson and Young, Shug Francis and all the other smaller fish he put away. He was the star pig in the pen, but now he was watching an incident coming down the tracks that he couldn't stop. He needed my help.

"You get me Barrett," he said, "and I'll get you Zara Cope. She's tied to Barrett, but I'll make sure he doesn't drag her down with him."

I nodded because there was nothing I wanted to say to him about Zara. My thoughts about her were my business and certainly not some cop's, but I wanted her out of that mess and he was the man who could make that happen. The thought of her, lying on that bed, drugged to the eyeballs, laughing because she'd tricked me. It wasn't her. Not the Zara that I had known back in the good old days. This one was a skinny, wasted, pathetic version of the sharp and determined woman I had known. It was the sharp and determined woman that I needed to rescue and then keep the hell away from me.

22

The morning had been an unscheduled meeting with Fisher. Around lunchtime I got a call from Ronnie. He was supposed to be working on finding out where Barrett and his people had gone. Same thing I should have been working on, but my mind was starting to drift off into other areas. We were beyond the point where Barrett working for himself was plausible. He was working for someone, and I needed to figure out who. The call from Ronnie told me he had a lead on who had employed them, that I needed to get round to his mate Owen Turner's shop.

I hadn't been there before, but I knew where it was. I'd heard all about it from Ronnie. His mate had a store selling technology, mostly high-end stuff. It sounded like the sort of stuff nerds and show-offs would buy, but they had a good spot in the city center. Had its problems though. Bad economy made selling high-end stuff hard, and their shop wasn't the swankiest place. A cramped little space with narrow aisles and poor lighting, but they were planning to change all that. Going to renovate the place with the money they got from Kevin Currie for a cut of the business. That was their hope, anyway. A young couple, living on hope. Owen and Trisha Turner. Tish, Ronnie had called her. I remembered that. Remember names; remember why the people behind them matter.

Didn't manage to get parked anywhere near the place, so it was a short walk up to the shop on the corner. It didn't look like a young person's shop from the outside, that was the problem.

Needed paintwork and a sign, needed a better window display. Can't remember what that shop was before they had it.

Inside wasn't a lot better. Too much stuff in too small an area. No room for people to wander round, browsing. That's what I figured a place like that needed. Get people in to look and maybe they buy something. Or maybe they see something they want to save up for. Or maybe they see something they tell a friend about and the friend comes in to buy. Walking up the narrow aisle to the counter, tall and broad, I felt closed in. It needed change.

There was a young woman standing behind the counter. Late twenties, dark curly hair, pretty enough. Had a hint of the hippy about her with a nose ring. Anyway, I assumed she was Tish.

"I'm looking for Ronnie. He about?"

She looked at me. She must have been a good judge of character because she didn't like the look of me.

"Hold on," she said with a wary nod and disappeared into a back room.

She emerged after twenty seconds, Ronnie sticking his head out of the door after her.

"Come through," he said. She said nothing, watching me walk round the back of the counter and through the door to the storeroom.

This place was cramped as well. Boxes of everything stacked against three walls, including against the fire door. The only wall that wasn't covered with boxes had a small sink and worktop with a microwave and a kettle on it. There was a table in the middle of the room, Ronnie taking his seat at it. Owen was already there, dark hair down to his shoulders, a beard that belonged to an older man.

"Take a seat. Owen has something to show you," Ronnie said.

I sat in between the two of them and looked at Owen. He had his mobile phone in his hand, twisting it back and forth nervously. He looked at me like he wasn't sure he was supposed to speak, then leapt into a sentence.

"I got a video of them on my phone. Not much, cos you can't see the ones that came in," he started, and I stopped him.

"Start at the beginning," I told him. "Tell me everything. I want details."

The problem with people is that they always want to tell you what they think is interesting. They skip straight to the punchline, and you don't get the detail. That's where the Devil is, and we were looking for him.

"Right, well, it happened this morning. I was in the shop, everything normal, quiet. Sold a tablet in the morning, so that was something. And then these two guys came in. They came up to the counter."

"Describe them."

"Right, yeah. They were both twenties, I guess late twenties. Casual, but well dressed. One of them, the one who did the talking, he was the smaller of the two. I figure he was, I guess, the more senior. Sometimes you can just tell, you know?"

"Sure," I said, nodding my head. He was nervous; he didn't like the way his day was panning out.

"So they both came up to the counter, and the smaller one...Well, he was smaller than the other guy, but the other guy wasn't that big. I mean, not as big as you, for example. He asked if I was Owen Turner. Seemed casual, nice enough. I didn't really think about how he knew my name. Only afterwards I realized that should have got me, you know, suspicious. When I asked him what I could do for him, he said that I could recognize that Kevin Currie no longer owns his share of the business. I played dumb, you know," he said, looking to me for a nod.

"No one was supposed to know about Kevin owning a share," I said, nudging him along.

"Exactly. He said I had to recognize that Adrian Barrett now owns that share of the shop. I had no idea; I never even heard of this Barrett guy before. Said that if I acknowledged that now things could work out very well for me. I just told him that Kevin Currie owned a share of the business, that it was a legit business and that he needed to speak to Kevin Currie about it. He laughed at me, told me that the Jamieson organization was dying and Adrian Barrett was the guy who was going to kill it. Said that Barrett was the coming power and I needed to think carefully about whose side I was on. I told him to leave."

I nodded. The guy didn't like talking this much, not to me. I was familiar with that. People are waiting for me to lose my temper, for me to do something terribly scary. The more they say, the more chance of saying something that upsets me.

"Did they have an accent?"

"Local," he said quickly. "Definitely local."

"Tell him what happened next, Owen," Ronnie said quietly, doing his bit to push his friend over the finish line.

"Yeah, right. Well, they went out, and for the first few seconds I was just glad to see them gone, you know. Then I thought, well, fuck them, who are they coming into my shop and saying all that. So I went out, stood in the doorway. I could see the car they were getting into; they had parked down the street. There was other people in the car too. It came up to the corner, and, you know how there's traffic lights there? They had to stop for a few seconds, then pulled away. As they were coming up to the lights I got my phone out, videoed them."

He held up the phone, glanced between me and Ronnie to see if now was the time for him to play it. Ronnie nodded and he played us the video. It was wobbly, showed a blue saloon car moving up the street to the corner.

"Didn't get either of the two that came into the shop: one was driving and the other was sitting behind the driver's seat. You can see the other two passengers though."

The car stopped at the lights, the phone pointed at them. The angle wasn't great, but it was enough. I recognized him straight away.

"Take it back a little," Ronnie said. "Pause it where the car's right alongside you. That's a better shot."

I already knew, but I was willing to get a better look and make my ninety-nine percent certainty a round hundred.

"There," Owen said, passing the phone to me.

A dinky wee thing, too small a screen for my fingers to manipulate it. He'd paused it as the car pulled alongside him, as the passenger in the back of the car glanced his way. All fake tan and stupid hair. Taylor "Original" Carlisle. One of Lafferty's little pets.

The silence in the room was broken by Ronnie. "It is, isn't it?" he asked me. Not mentioning the name in front of Owen Turner.

"Could you leave us for a few minutes, Owen," I said to him. Being polite, but I wasn't asking.

"Sure, yeah," he said, and he got out of that chair like it was on fire. He went out into the shop to help his wife and to get away from me.

"It's Original, isn't it?" Ronnie asked me. "I called you as soon as he showed it to me. It's him, and he was here, talking about Barrett being the new power in the city."

"Fuck's sake," I said, looking down at the table. I had worked out how bad this could be and I was already working out all the possible ways this could go next. There were a lot of directions that all led deeper into the shit. I picked up the phone and looked at it again. "It's Original Carlisle all right. Fuck."

We had to work out what this meant, who we could trust and who we couldn't. Original was a right-hand man to Lafferty. Him being involved in this could mean a whole bunch of things, but jumping to conclusions tended to be akin to jumping off a cliff. It could mean that Lafferty was working with Barrett. It could mean that Original was stabbing his own boss in the back and helping Barrett. It could mean that Lafferty was testing us out, trying to work out if people were loyal to him by being a dick about it, provoke us and see how we reacted. It could mean something else entirely that didn't leap to mind at the time. We had to know which of those it was before we made any sort of move. Knowledge is power. Go into battle as the dumber of two armies and you have a right good chance of being taught a lesson.

"What do we do?" Ronnie asked me quietly.

I didn't like people talking when I was considering things. I think that was down to the fact that I much preferred to work alone. Always had. Spent years avoiding getting tied to anyone, working for different employers and always working alone. That was my reputation. Lone wolf. Hire Nate Colgan and you don't have to hire anyone else. Ronnie was the first person I'd ever brought under my wing. A nice kid with no history of violence. A strange choice.

"I don't know. We have to tread very carefully with this and not go accusing Lafferty of anything until we know for sure. But it isn't good, whatever it is. We can put to bed any idea that Barrett is up here on his own."

"Maybe Barrett's got Original working for him."

"No," I said, shaking my head. "Not unless there's someone else, someone senior. Original wouldn't walk away from what he has for the risk of a start-up."

"Doesn't mean that he's working for Lafferty though. That would mean Lafferty ordering the killing of Lee Christie."

"The guy who was feeding info to Mikey and Conn, yeah. Would be a ballsy move for Lafferty, but a fucking messy one as well. Doesn't add up to his style, either way. He could be spinning a lot of plates though; might not just be Barrett he has. Fuck, might not even be Lafferty. Could be Don Park. Could be any bastard. Gets to Original, uses him to help organize all this. Creating weaknesses from within the organization. Once we start turning on each other we're doing our enemies' job for them. I don't know."

I was wrestling with a giant alligator of a problem. If the guilty party could be anyone then who do you go to with this information? How do we solve the problem when we don't know who's on our side and who isn't? "Trust no one" is a fine principle if you're working alone. I was an organization man now, the security consultant, no less. This was my problem and I had to share it with someone, but I was buggered if I knew who.

"We need to get to Original," Ronnie said suddenly, surprising himself with his certainty. "If not Original then someone close enough to Lafferty to give us the truth."

I straightened up, thinking about it. He was right, I knew it. He must have been spending too much time around me when he came up with it that bloody quick, but I knew it was the right way to go. We track down Original or some other senior figure and we get the information we need from them by any means necessary. It was sadly obvious. It would cause ructions. You don't go questioning a senior man without causing offense to someone or other, but someone or other was just going to have to put up with it. The organization came first.

I started nodding, thinking about candidates. Trying to come up with a name that would cause the fewest problems. Had to be senior, close to Lafferty. Had to be someone that would have useful knowledge, not just some hanger-on. Someone I could talk forcefully to without them pissing their pants. There was someone. A person I'd been thinking about chatting with since my early-morning visit from DI Fisher.

"That's true. There's someone I want to talk to. I been thinking about it all day. The Nasty killing. That was professional, and I've been thinking about who might have carried it out. I can't work out why, but I have an idea for who. He'll be able to give us some answers."

23

Ronnie was standing watch from a garden across the street. If he saw our target coming home early, he would ring my mobile, which was on vibrate. I was round the back of the house, sneaking up to the back door with Vernon Bell. Vernon was a little old guy in his sixties, English-born but been working Glasgow for a good forty years. He would once have been called a burglar, but there wasn't much call for breaking into houses these days. Most of his work was for professional organizations, breaking into offices and storage facilities. A boring old house was a rare challenge for him.

He only said yes because he knew I was working for the Jamieson organization now. If I was on my own he would have politely declined the risk. I watched him kneeling down by the back door; couldn't see what he was doing to the lock. Made a scratching noise for the first ten or twenty seconds, silent thereafter. There was a little island of hair on his otherwise bald head, tilting sideways as he worked. He hadn't said a word since we got out of the car.

Took him about three minutes. He straightened up, nodded to me, and walked out of the garden. It was his car we'd come in; he would drive home and I would be left to find my own way. He didn't need to hang around. From what I understood of it, getting into the house involved breaking the lock to open the door, and then fixing it with the door open. Something like that anyway. It wasn't a skill of mine. The door was ajar and had been for the last couple of minutes while Vernon worked at it.

I went inside and closed it. Walked through the downstairs of the house, took a quick look upstairs as well. Nobody there. Nothing of obvious interest, but I knew there wouldn't be. A small terraced house, a man living on his own, careful about his work. He was hardly going to leave incriminating evidence lying on the bedside table, was he? I wasn't wearing gloves or a balaclava. I was here for a conversation, nothing more. Just a conversation on my terms. It was nothing the police needed to worry about.

I went back downstairs and into the dark living room. Nothing much to do until he got back. Sat in the chair beside the table with the lamp on it, facing the doorless arch to the corridor. A good spot. Made sure the lamp was plugged in. Would make a neatly dramatic scene.

We knew he'd be out; Ronnie had been watching the house from across the street for a few hours. We didn't know how long he'd be gone. I was sitting in that chair for forty fucking minutes, waiting for him. The phone in my pocket rumbled, then went still. Ronnie had seen him arrive back. I'd heard the car pull up in the street. Heard the car door closing. There was nothing out there for him to be suspicious of. He wouldn't see Ronnie. He hadn't been followed. His front door wasn't tampered with, and his back door didn't look like it had been. He came into the house, blissfully unaware.

It was silent, perfect. He walked a couple of steps from the front door until he was in view of the arch. That was when I clicked on the lamp. Russell Conrad. Gunman. Our gunman, now. The sudden burst of light from the living room caused him to spin and stare at me. Nearly caused me to spin in the chair. The man must have had a hundred-watt bulb in that fucking lamp. He looked frightened, which was a good thing.

"Come in and sit down," I said to him. Said in a way that made it clear he didn't get a second option to dither over.

He moved slowly, but he moved. He walked into the living room and took a seat on the couch, looking across at me with the kind of look his victims might have specialized in. Confused, horrified and very suddenly aware that something bad was nearby.

I let him get comfortable, took a few seconds before I spoke. "You killed Jawad Nasif."

"Nasty? Yeah, I killed him last night. That was the order. If you wanted to know about the job then you should have gone to Lafferty. You got no right coming to me the day after a job; you know how risky that is."

It was convincingly said. Gave me pause, another little puzzle to twist around in my hands. That reaction, quick, honest and defiant, made it seem like Conrad didn't know what he'd done wrong.

"I think I'd rather talk to you about it. You don't mind talking to me about it, do you?"

"We're on the same side of this, aren't we?"

"We might be," I said slowly. "That's the very thing I'm trying to work out."

He frowned and grimaced. He didn't like the sound of anything I was saying. He was new to the organization, and that made him vulnerable. If he was on the wrong side of an argument that he didn't even know was happening then he was in peril. He had reason to be concerned.

"Well, you tell me what you want to know and I'll tell you anything I'm able to. As far as I'm aware we're on the same side here."

"How did Lafferty find out where Nasty was going to be?"

"I don't know," he said. The casual shrug of a man who only needs to know where his victims are, not how they were found. "He called me up, told me he wanted it done, said that he thought Nasty was going to be at that location but that there was a tight window because he was only visiting the place, not staying there. He gave me the location, told me to get there early. I did. Went in through a downstairs toilet window that some idiot had left open. Went into the kitchen and waited because the kitchen was at the back of the house. The front looked out onto the street and there were no curtains in the place so I didn't want the gun flashing there. I heard him come in; he was in the living room for a while. I don't know why—I didn't go through the house to check if there was anything there. Cleaning up, maybe. He came into the kitchen, went to the fridge, I shot him. That was it. I figure he was going to stay there the night or something, separate from the others. I don't know."

My face was stone. There was nothing he could have said that would have elicited a reaction from me in that room. What he was saying tallied with what I knew about the killing, which wasn't nearly enough.

"Do you think Lafferty lured him there?" I asked.

"He might have, I suppose. Good for him if he did; we got rid of their gunman. Isn't that a good thing? Am I missing something here, Nate?"

Russell Conrad was a long-term, high-caliber gunman. You don't get to be that if you aren't a reasonably smart person. You don't reach thirty-six, which he was at the time, with a dozen years' experience in the business, which he had, without above-average intelligence. He could have been acting. His surprise wasn't enough to gain trust.

"Was there any mention of Barrett in this job?"

"No, just the gunman, nobody else. If they knew where Barrett was then they'd have gone after him, wouldn't they?"

Without a pause I asked, "Did you kill Lee Christie?"

"No, I did not," he said quickly and confidently. "Nasty killed Lee Christie, didn't he? That's my understanding of it anyway. Why would you think that I...Wait a second, Nate, what the hell are you getting at here? You're pitching an idea I don't much like the sound of. You're saying that Nasty might not have killed Christie?"

"I'm saying he probably did," I told him: emphasis on *probably.*

"But you're nodding and winking towards Lafferty right now, aren't you? That's what this is about. You're saying he killed his own man, used Barrett and his crew as patsies. Now, what? You think he's picking off Barrett's crew so that they can't drop him in it?"

I might have been surprised at him reaching that conclusion so speedily if I didn't already know how smart he was.

"What do you think?" I asked him.

He sighed and looked me straight in the eye. "I think we got a big problem here, Nate. I don't much appreciate you breaking into my house and scaring the shite out of me, but we'll put that aside. I've done worse. I just had a conversation with Lafferty, not more than an hour ago, and you were mentioned in it. Look, I don't want this turning into a war, but I think it's going to. I want to be on the right side of this. I'm trying to make a living and nothing more. I just got in the door with this organization, and I had no idea the way things were shaping up when I did. I thought Lafferty hiring me had everyone's support; otherwise I'd have walked away. But this, this thing, this job, it's all going to hell. We've both been around a lot; we've both seen the crazy shite that people pull. I think that's happening now."

"Why?"

"Because in the meeting I had with Lafferty just now he was pointing the finger at Marty Jones and Kevin Currie. He said that they used Marty's brother to get them a girl that would lure Christie to where they killed him. He thinks they're using Barrett as a front to push him out and take control of the drug business for themselves. Once they have that they can take the whole organization before Jamieson gets out. He pointed the finger at you, Nate. He thinks you're leading the charge—that's why Currie hired you. Leading the battle at street level. You're supposed to be my next target."

I still didn't change my deadpan expression, although it took a little more effort this time. "That right?"

"He's more afraid of you than he is of Barrett now. With Nasty out of the way he thinks he's dealt with the worst of Barrett. But you? You he's terrified of."

"Did you believe what he had to tell you?"

He shook his head a little, frowning. "I don't know. He was talking about Currie and Marty and blaming them for everything under the sun. Sounded, I don't know, a little much. But I don't know either of them, and I don't know you well. I haven't been on the inside of this organization or this job. I only know you by reputation, and that doesn't help you much in this case, no offense."

I shrugged that off. My reputation was the uniform of my business. Sometimes it fell out of fashion. "Could Lafferty be faking all this? Could it be that he's the one working with Barrett, trying to give himself an excuse to take over the organization? Doesn't that seem plausible right now?"

"None of it seems plausible to me right now," he said with a shake of the head. "I will say this: if this organization is in the process of eating itself alive then we both picked a hell of a time to join up."

Almost smiled at that one. He wasn't the only one who had signed up without bothering to check the small print. "True, but if we're going to sort this out then there's a chance that we both come out of it well, don't you think? We just need to be on the right side of the argument."

He could see where this was going. "What are you suggesting?" he asked, already knowing the answer.

"What I'm saying is that right now you're standing on the wrong side of the fence, and you need to hop across. We'll make sure you don't rip off a bollock on the barbed wire as you jump. If you get caught on the wrong side of the fence, you won't work for this organization again. Might not work in this city again."

"I only ever said yes to working for Lafferty because he had

Jamieson's clearance. Way I saw it, I was working for Jamieson, and when he got out of the jail I would be answering to him. If keeping on working for Jamieson means working against Lafferty then I work against Lafferty. You have a plan, I take it?"

I nodded very slowly. "I'm getting towards that point, yeah."

I stood up and he did the same. I was much taller than him, looked down on him. I wasn't trying to intimidate him because there was no point. He was a gunman, he had done awful things that even I hadn't done, but it was worth gazing down to see if he would wilt a little. There are plenty of men in this business, in this city, who are as big and tough as me and know how to throw a punch. There are plenty of brave men, plenty of psychos, plenty of men who can handle themselves in a fight. No gunman would be intimidated by any of them, because most of them didn't have the balls to do the things that Conrad had already done in his life. But that reputation of mine, that made it worth looking down on a man you knew had worked in the darkness as well. That reputation had been hard earned by acts that created the indefinable little element of fear in others that separate the truly dangerous from the merely wild or nasty.

"Whatever the plan is, there's a high likelihood it's going to require a gunman," I told the gunman in front of me. "I need to call some people together, get this sorted out. I'll call you soon, let you know."

He nodded, didn't say anything. That was as much as either of us needed to say to the other. I left the house by the front door, out onto the street. The car was parked on the next street along, far enough out of sight to make sure he didn't spot it. Ronnie had his orders. Wait for me to leave, then get back to the car without ever being visible to the front of Conrad's house. The gunman could guess how we'd worked it, but there was no fun in making it easy for him. Took Ronnie a couple of minutes to get back to the car.

"So?" he asked.

"So you know how we took the piss out of Lafferty for his get-together?"

"Yeah."

"We need to arrange a get-together of our own."

24

Barrett was still in a panic. Someone had shot his best mate and taken away the comfort blanket of having his own gunman. Zara sat next to him on the bed. They'd been in the emergency safe house for almost a day, and the nerves were only getting worse. He was shaking. It was hardly his first experience of death, but him and Elliott and Nasty had been together for so long, it was like losing a limb this time.

"We should get out now," he said. "This place is gonna kill us if we don't get out."

"Calm down," Zara told him, and put an arm around him. That was mostly to stop him going for the little stash he had in the drawer at the bottom of the wardrobe. She wanted him to keep a cool head for what she was going to suggest next. "Listen to me, Dyne, you can still finish this. We have half the money, but we can get the other half. We get back down south and we build something fantastic down there. Listen to me, babe; we're this close, this close." She was holding his face in her hands at that point.

"We're also that far from being wiped the fuck out," he said quietly. There were times with Barrett when he was walking right on the very edge, ready to fall off into a depression that would have taken him out of Zara's control.

Her control. She thought she had him under total control, but things were moving too fast for her to steer now. In that hotel room, acting as a lure for Nate. When Barrett had that gun in his hand, when he was making her inject so that he could present her to Nate…Zara didn't even remember it, not really. There was a misty memory of shouting for Nate, but she didn't remember Nate being there. What she knew about it was what Barrett told her afterwards. It had worked perfectly, apparently, right up until the moment Nasty took a bullet to the back of the head.

He deserved it. She had no sympathy for Nasty, no matter how much he meant to the others. There was something alarmingly cold about him. Nasty killed a bunch of people and he couldn't have cared less about it. Zara used to hear him talking shop with Barrett and Elliott, and Nasty didn't have a compassionate bone in his body. The guy was just empty. Perhaps not as bad as Elliott, in some ways. Elliott got off on making people uncomfortable and hurting people who couldn't fight back. He was the sort of kid who would pull the legs off spiders, where Nasty would just stamp on them and go looking for more. Dyne was the most decent of the three of them, and he was a borderline junkie desperate to become a big-time gangster.

"Listen to me, Dyne," she said to him. "You have to set up a meeting. Go meet with him, tell him what happened to Nasty and demand some proper protection. This late in the day he has to give it to you. We're this close to finishing the job, so he has to help you out. If this fails—listen to me, Dyne," she said harshly when he tried to turn his head away from her. "I need you to listen to this. You call him up, you set up a meeting. You go there and you tell him that in light of losing your only gunman you're going to need some extra backup from him to finish this. He'll give it to you, Dyne, he will. He hasn't got a choice. If this fails then he doesn't get a second chance. You're all he's got, his one chance. So you go to him and you get the protection you need and we'll get through this. A couple of days from now we'll be long gone from here and we'll have a hundred grand to get us off the ground. Think about that, Dyne. Think about it."

He started to nod sadly, still thinking about how long two days could be instead of thinking how big a hundred grand could be. He just wanted out, and she didn't blame him, but her plan was never going to work if his bottle crashed.

She sat on the bed and listened to him making the call, demanding a meeting and sounding coherent and angry. He was playing his little part well and that helped Zara a lot. If she could get him and Elliott out of the house then she could get rid of one little problem they had been lumbered with. A bonus opportunity. Then she was close to finishing what she had come here to do.

"You get a meeting?" she asked him, knowing he had.

"In half an hour, so I got to move it. I'll take Elliott and one of the boys. Shouldn't take long. He had already heard about Nasty; he said he would come up with something to help. We should get this sorted out, then we can finish this fucking thing off."

He had some of his swagger back, some of the old fire that had attracted her to him. He was going to need every scorching drop of it. He was going to a meeting with a jackal and if he got out of it with the shirt on his back then he'd be doing well. But that jackal would give him enough to reassure him, just for a little while. A little while was long enough for Zara.

The three of them left almost straight away, Barrett, Elliott and Aldridge. That left the house to Zara, Keith Henson and the girl locked in the bedroom upstairs. Zara went into the kitchen, where Henson was scrolling through betting odds on his phone.

"I'm going to write up a shopping list; you'll need to go and get some stuff for us," she told him.

He looked at her with a frown. He didn't know how he should speak to Zara. She was Dyne's girl, and that meant he had to treat her with respect, but he stupidly thought that even dumb muscle like him was worth more than the boss's girl.

"I ain't doing shopping. I ain't here to do shopping."

"We need food, Keith," she told him, looking for a pen. "Do you want to go the next two days without anything to eat? Do you want to go the next two days without wiping your arse or brushing your teeth? Neither do I. This place isn't stocked properly. I'm writing a list and you can go and pick some stuff up. Find a supermarket that's still open. We don't need much, not for a couple of days," she said offhandedly as she started scrawling a list for him.

"I don't have transport," he said smugly.

"Get a taxi."

"Then people will know where I am."

"Yes, but they still won't have a fucking clue who you are. I'm known here, I can't go. Nobody knows you." Nobody in your own back yard knows you, she thought. Henson and Aldridge had been cheap muscle and nothing else.

"What about the girl?"

"We can't send her, for God's sake."

"No, I mean I have to watch her. That's why I was left behind."

Zara sighed. "She's locked in a room. I'm pretty sure I can handle her, but we need food and we need toiletries or the next two days are going to be hell on earth."

She kept on writing and he put his phone away, grumbling under his breath at having to do something as menial as shopping. This was a guy who spent his working life acting as chauffeur, bodyguard and all-round grunt for much smarter people and he was bothered about having to get some food, something that actually mattered. He was bothered because a woman was telling him to do it and his tiny brain couldn't handle that. Zara finished the list and handed it to him. She'd written a number for a taxi company at the top.

"Money," he said, so she went upstairs and got some for him.

He seemed happy once he had the cash in his hand, which told her that he was going to ignore the sensible list he'd been given and just buy whatever junk and booze he wanted to pass the next two days gorging on. Fine, whatever, she just needed to shift his dopey arse out of the house as quickly as possible. That meeting might not last long. He called the cab and wandered out into the street, Zara watching at a window to make sure he was really gone. Now it was time for her to make a phone call to a different taxi company. She gave them the address, told them to be there in five minutes or they'd get to hear all about her displeasure.

Then she went upstairs with a key in her hand and stood outside the bedroom door. Took a deep breath before she unlocked it, because she had no idea who the girl was or what sort of person she was going to be. The fact that she had allowed Elliott to push her around the night before didn't mean anything; Elliott pushed some very strong and very smart people around when he was in the mood. She could have been dangerous, or she could have been so dumb as to be impossible to move. She could have been anything, but of course she was just a very ordinary young woman who had been lied to and controlled by bastards with weapons and no morals. There were plenty of them around.

Zara unlocked the door and went inside. Jess was standing at the window, looking out into the street.

"They've all gone," Zara said to her. "If you're thinking of making a run for it then now would be the time."

Jess looked at her, not sure what to think. She didn't trust Zara; this could be some kind of trap. Get her to run so that you have an excuse to punish her. She had only ever seen Zara hanging around with the one they all called Dyne, the leader of the very people she was praying she could escape from. Zara got it; she knew she'd have felt the same if the roles were reversed.

"You want to go?" Zara asked her, pushing her. Speaking harshly because she needed to hurry this up. The meeting Barrett and Elliott had gone to had been arranged in a hurry and was going to involve telling someone powerful things he didn't want to hear. It wasn't likely to drag on. Give the bad news, get some reassurance, get out. Zara had already wasted more than fifteen minutes trying to get rid of the Brain of Britain.

"Yes," Jess said, and then looked at Zara curiously. "Are you going to run too?"

Zara smiled at her. "No, I'm not finished here, not yet. There's more that I have to do, but you are finished here. There's no reason for them to keep you, and they won't want you going out into the city knowing what you know. You need to get away, you understand me? You need to go now."

Jess started nodding. Kill her or take her with them, those were the equally grim options Elliott and his pals would be considering. But she couldn't shake the feeling that the woman in the doorway was every bit as bad as the men who had put her here.

"Is this a trick?"

"No, it's not a trick. People are starting to die," Zara told her, speaking with what sounded like frustration. The frustration of a woman who was seeing her master plan spin just out of reach. "Once the dying starts, it tends not to stop until someone strong enough to stop it puts their foot down. I'm hoping I know who that person is, but I know it's not me and I seriously doubt it's you. There's no reason for you to end up even more a victim of this than you already are."

Jess started nodding; she could feel the tears starting to form and she was starting to shake. She was so close to getting out. When Zara spoke again it was in her most domineering voice, an attempt to get Jess back on track. Shove those tears back where they came from and smarten up. She still needed to keep her head together; being out of the house didn't mean being out of danger.

"Listen to me," Zara said. "There's a taxi coming here in about two minutes' time; it'll take you wherever you tell it to take you. Do you have somewhere safe to go?"

Jess paused and thought about it for far longer than was reassuring. "I can go to my grandparents', I suppose."

"Right," Zara said, assuming that Elliott and his fellow super-creep Adam Jones didn't know where her grandparents lived and wouldn't have the time to work it out, "you go there. Now, when you get there, you don't tell anyone where you were or what happened, okay? Not for a few days. Not until Monday anyway. Can you do that for me?"

"Yes, I can," Jess said, nodding and still crying, which just annoyed Zara to see. She wanted the girl to be forgettable-looking to the taxi driver and anyone else who might see her on the way out of the house. "Right, come downstairs. We'll wait for the taxi."

Zara locked the door behind them as they left the room. Jess never once asked her what she was going to say happened, how Zara was going to get herself out of trouble for rescuing her. It had occurred to Jess; it worried her a little, but not nearly as much as the chance of Zara changing her mind. She didn't want to mention the possibility of reprisals against Zara in case she ended up back in her room before the taxi came. Zara didn't want her thanks anyway; Jess blubbing on her shoulder and saying what a good person she was would have been too much to take. It was Zara's idea to come up to Glasgow and work this plan. It was Zara's idea to use a lure on Christie. If it wasn't for her, Jess would never have been in that mess anyway. That was Zara's thinking. One of the two reasons for doing this. The other being the damage it would do to the group.

The taxi came and Zara walked Jess down to it, put her in the back and returned to the house without looking back. As soon as she had closed the taxi door behind her, Jess had curled up into a ball with her feet up on the seats, looking scared and vulnerable and annoyingly memorable. She was gone though, and that was a positive that Zara could cling to. It was also another possible hurdle to her own intentions she had removed.

Dumb-Ass got back from his shopping trip before the crew arrived back from the meeting. That helped Zara a lot. She was at the front window, watching for any of them turning up, and saw him pull up in the taxi, getting out with all his shopping. She ran upstairs to the bathroom and locked herself in. Gave it a couple of minutes, heard him moving around in the kitchen, putting things away. She flushed the toilet, washed her hands and walked loudly back downstairs, wiping her hands on her jeans.

"You get it all?" she asked him, knowing that he hadn't.

"Some of it," Henson said. "Got what we need anyway."

She could see the two twelve-packs of lager that she hadn't put on her list and wondered what else he had bought as an alternative to food, but she didn't much care. Zara helped him put it all away in the cupboards and didn't complain too much about the stuff he'd failed to get. He'd bought some junk, so she took a packet of crisps and can of Coke and told him to take it up to the girl; she hadn't been fed that evening.

Zara stood in the kitchen and waited, listening. Whatever took him so long, probably eating the crisps, it was nearly five minutes before he came running downstairs, shouting that she wasn't in the room.

"What do you mean, she's not in the room?" Zara shouted.

"I mean I unlocked the door and went in and she ain't there, is what I mean. She must have got out."

"She can't have gotten out," Zara told him, sounding certain. "She was locked in that room; there's no way she could have gotten out. Is the window shut? Did you check the wardrobe? Is there a cupboard in the room?"

His eyes widened; he spun round and sprinted back upstairs. Zara ran after him, changing her plan as she went. The original plan had been to pretend that Jess must have somehow disappeared when Zara was in the toilet, maybe pretend that she must have found a key in the room or something stupid like that. Now she had a much better plan and her dim-witted shopper was generously going to take all the blame on Zara's behalf. She reached the corridor and ran into the room. There was a wardrobe, she knew that already, and no cupboard. Henson had the wardrobe door open and was looking blankly inside at nothing at all.

They were both silent for a few seconds. She looked back at the door. "When you came running downstairs just now, did you leave that door open?"

"Yeah," he said with a shrug, already on the defensive.

"For God's sake," Zara said with a sigh.

"What?"

"What? She hid in the wardrobe and then you went running down the stairs and left the door open for her is what. Come on, she can't have gotten far."

She sent him out the back on the grounds that Jess would probably have gone that way if she'd been on foot. Zara went round to the front and walked up and down the street, and the street facing the house, pretending to look for her. By the time she went back to the house she could hear voices: Barrett and Elliott both shouting at Henson the shopper. They were calling him every name under the sun, which suited Zara just fine.

25

Organizing a meeting wasn't hard. People seemed to be getting used to dropping everything and turning up on command. Actually, this one was easier, because this one was about the first one. This one had fewer people attending, and they all had a vested interest in being there. That's how you call a meeting.

The first person to get on board was Kevin, and once he was willing to turn up, everyone was. He and Ben would be there, Marty Jones, Conn Griffiths and Mikey Summers. And me and Ronnie, of course. We were going to meet at Marty's place out by the airport, a decent spot where we could come and go without drawing too much attention. This wasn't like Lafferty's meeting. We weren't sending any messages with this.

I picked up Ronnie. He got into the car, looking quite excited. He was growing into the job, becoming the sort of employee I thought he would. It's always a judgment call when you hire someone, especially when they're someone from the outside. He was smart and he could be tough, but there was always a question mark over his commitment. I had, basically, bullied him into taking the job in the first place, something I hadn't forgotten about.

"You think we'll start making moves tonight?" he asked me. There was enthusiasm in the question, like he wanted to get out there and do some work. Also sounded a little like a wee boy wanting to know if he was going to get to stay up past his bedtime. Reminded me how inexperienced he was.

"Not tonight," I told him. "Next forty-eight hours, but not

tonight. Tonight is about making sure we have the right people on board to make moves." I'd have made moves if I thought I could get permission, mind you. Lafferty was pointing guns in my direction; I wanted this done as soon as possible. Wouldn't get clearance for it though, not yet.

That enthusiasm Ronnie had, I didn't like it. Maybe it was because I was used to working with experienced guys. I had been lucky when I first came into the business, working with people like Gully Fitzgerald. Old hands who taught you well. On the few occasions when I did work with someone, it was usually someone experienced. Now I had someone to mold, to make into the kind of sidekick I wanted. I didn't want an enthusiastic sidekick. I wanted someone who was as cynical as me. Cynical of the business and all the people in it, me included.

We drove round and picked up Russell Conrad. If this went according to the plan I had, he was going to play a big part in what happened next. He had a right to be there, hear about it.

"The others know I'm going to be there?" Conrad asked, sitting in the back of my nondescript car.

"Some do," I told him. "The rest will be fine about it as long as you don't give them a reason not to be."

He didn't say anything. He was a brave man, Russell Conrad. Getting into the back of my car with me and Ronnie for company. Going to a meeting that would be populated by Kevin Currie's people. It was a risk, not to be taken lightly. The sort of risk that occasionally ended with someone being killed. Conrad wanted to be on the right side of events. Wanted to see the bullet going away from him at the end, not towards him.

Marty had gotten there first; made sure the place was unlocked. Conn's car was there as well, which meant him and Mikey had beaten us to the meeting. I didn't see Kevin's. We went inside; they were in the office to the left of the foyer this time.

We said polite hellos, hands were shaken. Conrad immediately dropped back into a corner. He was the odd man out and he was busy showing it. He should have made more of an effort, gotten involved in conversations, tried to be casual. Wasn't his fault. There weren't many gunmen who were talkers. A solitary, weird bunch, on the whole.

"No sign of Kevin yet," Conn said, trying to make sure the atmosphere didn't get too chilly.

Conn made small talk with Ronnie, asking him about himself. Marty butted in because there's never been a conversation Marty Jones didn't think he could improve. Talked to Ronnie, talked to Conn, made a few jokes with Mikey and me. The pretense was those three getting to know Ronnie a wee bit better, making sure he knew them properly. The truth was that they were desperately trying to stop Conrad turning the rest of us to ice. He was still over in the corner by the door, silent.

It was a blessing when Kevin Currie and Ben Carmichael turned up, fifteen minutes late and not needing to apologize for it because Kevin was the boss. You could, technically, make an argument to say Marty was his equal these days, but Kevin had taken charge of this.

The office on this side was pretty much the same as the office on the other side, cupboards and units against the side walls and not much else. Marty had found a few chairs from somewhere though, and some of the group were taking the weight off. Bright lights from strips on the ceiling, big windows with no blinds so all the light could be seen outside. Wasn't as subtle as I would have wanted it to be, but it wasn't me who got to decide these things.

Some guys were sitting on the units, some were standing up. I always stood up if I could because that was always the way you wanted to be if things got violent. Trust me, if you're somewhere that things might kick off, you want to be on your feet from the start. The guy on his arse when it starts is going to be the guy on his arse when it finishes. Currie and Marty were sitting down, so was Carmichael. On this occasion, so was I. It went against my instinct, but I was a man with something to say and if you're going to open your mouth, you look better doing it sitting down. People don't like having to look up to you when you talk. Ronnie, Conn and Mikey kept standing. So did Conrad.

"Okay, Nate, this was your call. Give it to us," Currie said, looking at me.

The best way to approach anything like this was to be a straightforward bastard. Hit them with everything I had. "I've come to a conclusion about what's really going on here. I think Lafferty hired Barrett and his crew to come up and put pressure on the organization so that he can take control. The hit on Christie gave him the excuse to take control in the short term. I think he's going to point the finger at the two of you." I was saying this to Currie and Marty. My impression was that it didn't shock Kevin so much, just saddened him. Confirmed something he had already suspected.

"Us? What do you mean, us?" Marty said with his voice going squeaky. Reaching for the high notes the way it did when he was all nervous and worked up.

"He's going to accuse you of trying to wipe out his business so you can take control of the organization. That gives him the excuse to wipe out you two and take control for himself. He'll say he was pre-empting you, defending himself, protecting Peter Jamieson's share of the business from you. By the time Jamieson gets out, this'll be Lafferty's organization."

I could see that Marty was going to start bouncing off the fucking walls. That was the kind of guy he was, his basic nature that he couldn't quite suppress. Sure enough he had matured, but he still threw some massive wobblies when he wasn't getting his own way; he was just smart enough not to throw them in front of senior men. Conn had told me about one or two of them, Marty letting off steam on things that didn't matter, holding it together for things that did. I thought he was about to lose it in front of us all, but Kevin spoke before he got the chance.

"How sure are you, Nate? Not that I don't have faith in your work, you know I do, but, Jesus, we have to be a hundred percent before we do anything about an accusation like that."

This wasn't Kevin questioning my judgment, I knew that. I had seen the look on his face when I pitched the theory. He had to be certain, and he had to be seen to be certain. Make sure everyone here saw him question me, saw him leave no stone unturned before he went after Lafferty. That had to be a last resort. I nodded and then looked round at Conrad, who was lurking behind me. Telling him this was his moment to shine. Conrad started talking.

"Lafferty's been talking about how it was you two who organized the whole thing. Said that you wanted control of the organization, and that you had to be stopped. He said it to me; I wouldn't be surprised if he said it to other people as well. He wants that story to get out. He, uh…He told me that he wanted me to line up Nate as my next target, because Nate's running things on the ground for you two."

Marty was muttering under his breath now. Kevin was just shaking his head. None of them had trusted Lafferty. He had been the hardest one to keep on a leash when Jamieson went down. The one who doubted the organization's ability to survive. I had helped to persuade him at the time. Regretted that now. If he'd walked, he wouldn't have been trying to push the rest of us over the edge. Neither Kevin nor Marty liked him anyway, that was obvious. They didn't like the way he'd tried to take control of events just because Christie had been his man. I hadn't said it, but it was obvious the reason he'd chosen Christie instead of someone else to spark this was because Christie was feeding info to Conn and Mikey. Killing two birds with one stone.

The place fell silent after Conrad spoke. He had brought the idea of me being killed into the conversation. Had confirmed the suspicion that Angus Lafferty had us all in his sights. It was Currie that spoke first.

"We have to move quickly, put a stop to this. You have a plan," he said to me. He was saying it rather than asking. He already knew. We wouldn't all be sitting there if I didn't have something more concrete to offer than this. I could have taken this to Kevin alone if what had been said so far was all that needed to be said.

"I think we need to focus on Lafferty and forget about Barrett," I said. "Barrett's just an employee; he's only here as long as Lafferty's paying him to be here. I have an idea that puts Barrett in the police's hands: let them deal with him. They have enough on him to lock him away for a good spell. He's not the priority here; him and his crew are nothing to us. They killed one of Lafferty's men and then Lafferty had one of their lot killed. He wants them wiped out so that he has a guarantee of silence. Probably save himself some money into the bargain. We need to deal with Lafferty and it needs to be in the next couple of days. I think we have to remove Lafferty completely; anything less than that and we've got a long-running headache."

I glanced around at all of them, looking for instant reactions before they had time to think about it. Kevin didn't look surprised and Marty looked pleased. Ronnie and Mikey were expressionless, assuming that this had little to do with them. Conn was concerned, but he often was. Conrad was the one that mattered most. I could see that he didn't look happy because he was the one that was going to have to go kill Lafferty. That was a monster fucking job, and Conrad knew it. You kill a guy like Lafferty and it follows you around for a long, long time. He looked worried about it, but what could he do? Lafferty had employed him but he was working for Jamieson and this was the right thing to do for Jamieson. Kevin kept up his newfound habit of breaking silences.

"I know this needs to be done quickly," he said, "but before we make a move that serious against a man like Lafferty I think we need to clear it with Jamieson. Set things up, fine, because I think Jamieson will give the all-clear, given the situation. Set it up, but we don't make a move until I have clearance."

Nobody was gonna argue with that; it was common sense. Nobody would ever sit there and say no, don't bother asking Peter Jamieson, the boss of the whole damn thing. It was the reason I had told Ronnie we wouldn't be moving that night. So everyone nodded along and Currie looked back at me.

"Go ahead and set up what needs to be set up, use who you need to use. I'll trust your judgment to run this," he said, nodding firmly. That was as much to assert my authority to everyone else in the room as it was to reassure me. "As soon as I have the all-clear, I'll let you know and we can solve this. It'll be a relief to put it behind us."

He stood up and nodded goodbyes to everyone else. Kevin and Carmichael left first and the rest of us had to stand around to give him a head start. Marty making small talk because he was always the king of that. I hated it; I wasn't in the mood for talking.

Me, Ronnie and Conrad went next. Marty would have to stay until last, the man with the keys. We had given Kevin a near ten-minute head start, which was enough to be polite. The car was silent on the drive back to Conrad's house. As soon as we had dropped him off and driven away, Ronnie started talking nervously.

"This is pretty huge, isn't it?" he asked.

It was the biggest thing I'd ever been a part of by a good long way. It was big enough to intimidate me, but I wasn't going to terrify him with that.

"Yeah, it is," was all I said. Sometimes saying little can be even worse.

26

Zara Cope. The first step in the most daunting job of my life was calling her up. Nothing was going to be easy about this. If I'd been home that first time she came round to visit then she would never have written her number down for me. I might still have had it on my phone, but it would have been hard to resist the temptation to delete it. A person I didn't want to speak to again. Get rid of it to remove the temptation. Crush sentiment before it crushes you. But I had it on the piece of paper she'd put through my letter box. Still sitting in the drawer of the little table beside my chair in the living room. A reminder of her handwriting. Sentimental.

I put it off until the afternoon. Made a phone call in the early morning to ask Becky's grandparents if they could keep her this weekend. Her grandmother understood when I said I had to work. Understood enough not to ask any questions. I didn't mention that one of the jobs was meeting her daughter. She didn't put Becky on the phone, which I appreciated. I didn't want to have to hear disappointment in her voice. The one person whose disappointment mattered. Then I went back to finding reasons not to call Zara.

Found a million little excuses that together didn't add up to much. I just didn't want to talk to her. Didn't want to be in her company. Didn't want her being the center of this job. This was just the set-up; I could afford to waste time on it. The following morning and I still hadn't had clearance from Kevin. That would come when he got a talk with Jamieson, and that would happen only when Jamieson's schedule allowed.

Took me until after midday to dial the number.

"Hi, Nate," she said, before I'd even opened my mouth. She sounded pleased that I had called.

"We need to meet," I told her, in that dead tone I use when I want to make sure that you can't possibly work out what I'm thinking. It's a tone I use a lot, and used a lot around Zara back in the day. She would have recognized it, and, sharp as she was, would have known what it meant. It meant I had something to hide.

"I suppose we could meet," she said to me in that stupid way people talk when they want a nearby third person to know what's being said. It was done for my benefit; there was no need for her to exaggerate like that just for Barrett or whoever else was nearby. It was her way of letting me know that someone was nearby and listening to what we were saying. Her way of telling me this might not be a secure line.

"Right," I said, trying to let her know I'd understood. "How about we meet the same place we did before?" I would keep this as brief and quick as possible; give only the very basic details needed to get her there. If that bastard Barrett was listening then I wasn't going to give him anything.

"Sure," she said enthusiastically. "When?"

"Soon as possible," I told her. "Can you get there in an hour?"

"Yeah, I can be there in an hour."

And now I was nervous. She was maybe the only person who could do that to me, and she had to be right at the fucking center of this thing. It could only be her. Clearing her out of the city when this was over was the priority for me. I couldn't have her tormenting me like this again.

I didn't get parked anywhere near the square. Didn't matter. I was deliberately early. I wasn't going to go in there, trample on handbags and skulk up to a table at the back to wait for her. Sitting there at a wee table, looking like the incredible sulk. Waiting for her to turn up, Barrett and his crew at her back. There was a bench in the square where I could sit and watch the entrance. Wasn't a good view, too far away, but I'd know her when I saw her, and I'd know if she was alone. I wanted to see if she was dropped off by Barrett or one of his crew, and where they went when she was in the restaurant. Paranoia, my old friend.

A taxi pulled up near the restaurant. Zara got out. She was alone. The taxi went off; no other car stopped nearby. I watched her go in, bang on time. I got up and wandered slowly across to the restaurant, crossing the street and looking carefully for anything that would give my suspicions justification. Nothing. No one, to be more exact. No Barrett, no muscle, no anyone lurking on the street, looking out for me. She'd done well to get this far alone.

She was sitting at the back of the restaurant. No makeup, hair scraped back. She was wearing a baggy jumper, shapeless thing. It wasn't because she wasn't making an effort that I felt sad. In the past, in our past, she didn't need to make an effort. Zara was film-star gorgeous without even bothering. What made me sad was that she was thin. Aged far more than made sense for the time that had passed since she left the city. Seeing her here the first time had told me there was something wrong. Seeing her in the hotel had shown me what. This was where I started fixing things.

There were no handbags on the floor this time; they must have seen me coming. I walked slowly, trying to look inconspicuous. Hard thing to do when you're six foot three, broad and cursed with a permanent scowl. We had reached that point with a job when you plan for every possible failure. If someone here sees me, tells a police contact about me meeting Zara. Tells Lafferty. Tells anyone. Start behaving like everyone's your enemy.

"You rang," Zara said with a little smile as I sat down opposite her.

I didn't like sitting with my back to the door, but that was the price of arriving second. I looked at her, at the tightness in that smile. Whatever scam she was working, whatever she had gotten herself into, it was time to make for the exits.

"This is nearly finished," I said to her. Keep it short. "I'm ending this, probably tomorrow. Tomorrow night, it'll be, more likely than not. I want to know where Barrett and his crew will be tomorrow night."

She didn't even stop to think about it. It was, I knew, the reason she was here. If Zara was working an angle, then she was close to the endgame and needed out. I was prepared to hold the door open for her. If she was stuck in something bigger than she could handle then the same applied. Incidentally, I didn't for one moment believe it was the latter of those two. Zara's never been stuck.

"I can give you the address of the house he's using. I'll make sure he's still there, and you can go pick them off."

I shook my head. Didn't like the way she was leaping to the bloodiest outcome. "No, I'm not going to do that. I'm going to get you all arrested instead."

"Excuse me?"

"I have a deal in place. You'll be let go; the rest of them will get some solid time. Should do, anyway, if they don't screw it up in court. But you'll get off the hook. You'll be swept up with the rest of them and then let go."

Her mouth was a little open; she couldn't find the words to throw out that would let her shut it. She couldn't believe what she was hearing. "What are you talking about? What happened to you? Are you working for the cops now? What is this?" She was stunned, hence the string of stupid questions.

"I'm not working for the cops. Barrett isn't the big score here, so I'm turning him over to PC Plod in exchange for you getting off the hook. There's a bigger target that I'm going after. But that's none of your business. You just need to make sure that Barrett is in the right place for the cops to get him and his lot with the minimum fuss. Will you give me the address of the safe house you're in?"

I already knew that she wasn't going to argue with me. Zara wasn't in any position where she could argue with me about anything, so she was always going to play along. But she was simmering. Partly with me, but I think mostly with herself. She had thought this was going to be predictable, that it would pan out the way she planned. That was naive of her. Zara had forgotten that this business was capable of surprising you at every turn. No job ever went down the road someone mapped for it.

"Yeah, I'll write it down." She rooted in her bag for a pen and paper.

She wrote it out, telling me about the layout of the house, what it was like inside, what view there was from front and back. She warned me that you could see right down the adjacent street and right along the street the house was on, so they would have to move fast to catch Barrett's boys by surprise.

"You can't do anything that might tip him off," I said. "You have to sit tight in there with him. Accept being arrested; trust me that you'll get out."

She nodded; Zara wasn't stupid enough to do anything that rocked the sinking boat. The way this was shaping up, she was still going to get out of it with whatever score she had her eye on.

"You be careful as well, whatever it is you're doing," she told me. Sounded like she meant it. We were both getting treacherously wistful.

"I will," I nodded, looking away from her. Careful was never part of my job description, and it was a million miles away from this gig. "Tell your man that he and I will have a meeting the day after tomorrow. Make sure he stays at the safe house until then. You'll be raided tomorrow night."

"Sounds like fun," she said with a shrug. This wasn't what she wanted, but I couldn't let myself care. Nothing was going to deter me from finishing the job I'd started with Lafferty. The world would bend to my will.

I nodded and reached out a hand; put it on top of Zara's. I didn't know what I was doing, what I was going to say. I couldn't leave without saying something. "Look after yourself," I said. Pathetic. "When this is done, go somewhere safe, get yourself clean, get yourself healthy." I got up and walked carefully out.

From anyone else it would have been an insignificant gesture, but she understood what it meant from me. Even when we were together, when she was pregnant with my child, gestures like that were rare. I can't be a touchy-feely kind of guy, can't express concern or pleasure or anything else I can avoid expressing. It's not that I won't, it's that I can't. I made no effort to be comforting or helpful, and when a little concern found its way out of me it meant something. Zara knew me well enough to know that it mattered.

I hope it reassured her. That was the most important thing about it. It showed Zara that I still cared about her enough to arrange a deal with the cops to make sure that she didn't suffer for the arrest that she had coming. And boy, did she have it coming.

There was nobody outside that I needed to worry about. Time to concentrate on getting Zara out of my head. There was a dark little corner where she lurked, agitating me. Pulling at my memories of her, reminding me that I wouldn't have Becky without her. She was the only person in the world to whom I owed anything. At least, the only person I felt any obligation to repay. Now I needed to get professional. Angus Lafferty. A target big enough and complicated enough for me to blank out the rest of humanity. I had never done a job like it, and I had enough scope to botch it without distractions. Zara was Fisher's now.

27

They say you can live without water longer than you can without sleep. Water was easy to come by. I tried to work it out, came to the conclusion that I'd gotten about nine hours' sleep in four days. It was enough to keep me alive, but not much more than that. Don't go into the biggest job of your life tired. That's my great advice. You'll be more emotional, suffer poorer judgment. That assumes my judgment could get any worse.

There was a dream I had as a kid, a recurring nightmare I suppose. I would always picture it like I was looking at a screen. There was a square on the screen, and I knew I was looking at it from above. At the top of the square as I looked at it was me, a small boy, standing there. At the bottom of the square was a large man, moving slowly round the corner to the side of the square. He crept slowly along; I don't remember ever seeing his legs move. I stood at the top of the square and I knew he was coming for me, I knew that he was going to do me serious harm, but I didn't move. I stood there knowing I should run, and he moved up the side of the square towards the corner at the top. It always panicked me, and I always woke before he reached the corner, this terrifying man.

Funny, I hadn't remembered the dream for years until that evening. Trying to get a little sleep and failing. I was relieved when my phone went and Kevin told me to come round to his office for a chat. Being sluggish on a job was better, by a slim margin, than being sluggish at home. At least I'd be doing something.

It was nighttime at the warehouse in Hillington. The place

seemed almost empty; there was little to no chance of bumping into Kelly. One blessing. I wasn't up to the task of dealing with any more complications. I feel like I've used that word a lot telling this story. It was a world made up of one complication after another at the time. I went through to the office at the back. There was a light on, Kevin waiting for me.

"I managed to speak to Peter about an hour ago," he told me as I sat down across the desk from him. "We discussed your plan and he eventually came round to the idea. Dealing with Lafferty he agrees with, of course. That needs to be dealt with and he likes your idea. It's the bit about leaving Barrett for the police he's not too thrilled about. He thinks Barrett has damaged us, and been seen to damage us, more importantly, and he reckons we need to be seen hitting back. But in the end he agreed to go along with your plan. If it had been anyone else I don't think he'd have gone for it, but he seems to put a lot of trust in you, Nate."

I nodded at that, taking it like it was no big deal to me. It wasn't, really; you have to accept other people's reactions with ease. You can't stop the opinions of others; just try to shape them to your desires. That's not going to be done by leaping out of your chair the first time they say something. Most people would be impressed by the idea of Peter Jamieson putting that much trust in them. There's a caveat, as there so often is, which is that if Jamieson really objected to the plan he would put his foot down and leave us all in no doubt. The fact that he was letting other people make the call told me that he wasn't enormously concerned about Barrett anymore, that Lafferty was the one that really mattered to him. I understood that.

"I'm going to set up Barrett and his crew tonight, try and make sure that it's carried out tomorrow night when I'm working the Lafferty job."

"And the Lafferty job?"

"I know how I want to do it. I know how it needs to be done. It could get messy, I suppose."

I said it matter-of-fact. Maybe made it sound like I didn't much care about the violence I was about to be a part of. That wasn't the case. There were others who didn't seem terribly concerned by the jobs they were given, no matter how difficult or violent. Mikey Summers was a notable nonchalant; he never seemed concerned. With men like Mikey it was because they were conditioned to the violence, or perhaps because they simply didn't understand the scale of what they were up against. I understood it perfectly well. There was a part of me missing, I think. The part that tells the rest of you to pull back from something that's too much to handle. I had no such reflex, no little voice telling me this was something I ought to be afraid of.

I mention that only because it must have been my tone that prompted Kevin to ask what he asked next. A question he shouldn't have asked.

"Are you nervous, at all?"

I looked at him like he'd asked a question that was a long way beneath him. He should have known better. "No," was all I said, but not in a dismissive way. I said it with a forceful certainty that he might just have found convincing.

"You have everything you need?"

"I think so," I said, a little less sure about that. "If there's anything or anyone else I need then I'll be in touch about it, but I doubt it. I'll be off the grid for a lot of tomorrow, me and Ronnie both. Emergency contact only."

"Sure," he said as I got up.

I had decided to end this meeting. Time was running out on me; I had another meeting I had to make happen that night. I'm not sure how impressed Kevin was with me standing up. I was the junior man; it wasn't up to me to decide when the meeting ended. He had called me here, wanting to tell me face to face I had the go-ahead from Jamieson. He wanted to see my reaction. I'd take a guess that he wanted to convince himself I was up to the job. Little bit insulting, but I was muscle, and muscle didn't usually handle something this big. This would be led by the gunman, or by someone senior like Kevin himself. Would have been Jamieson, if he wasn't in Barlinnie. It was rare for a man of my position to lead this sort of job, so I was asserting my own authority. Kevin didn't seem to care.

"Good luck," was all he said to me as I pulled open the door to go out. I glanced back and nodded.

It wasn't a perfect plan, and letting Barrett and his people keep on breathing afterwards was something that Jamieson apparently recoiled from, but it was shaping up to be the best plan available. If we'd hit Barrett and his people as well as Lafferty then it would have become impossible for us to cover the job up. Keep it small, keep it simple. Letting the police deal with Barrett gave them something to play with while we went after Lafferty.

I wasn't in a great mood leaving his office. Kevin Currie wasn't really cut out for leadership. He could lead his own part of the business, the counterfeiting operation. He knew it inside out, he was good at it and he'd worked out how to do it without getting himself caught or killed. What he was doing at that point, stepping up to help fill the gap that Jamieson's imprisonment had created, put a pressure on him that he'd never experienced before. Something I wasn't convinced Kevin Currie had been built to withstand. He didn't have the stomach for it that Jamieson did. That man could make decisions that ended the life of another person without batting a stress-free eyelid. Jamieson was as good a leader as I had seen, and that was the standard Kevin was to be judged by.

It was obvious from the way he looked at me, talked to me, that he still wasn't comfortable having me around. I was Jamieson's hire, not his. Kevin had worked with dangerous people before, and he had ordered them to do dangerous things, but they were his dangerous people. When his only responsibility was the counterfeiting business, everyone he worked with was a person he had hired. He scouted them, made sure they were the right person for the job, someone that he could be comfortable working with. Now he was working with people that others had hired. People who did things he would never normally ask a person to do. People he could never feel comfortable with. People like me.

One of the people he'd scouted and hired was Kelly. She was there. Coming into the warehouse as I was walking to my car. I couldn't ignore her, couldn't be that much of a bastard. She smiled at me and came over.

"Good to see you, Nate," she said. "How you been?"

It had only been a few days since she was at my house. "Good, yeah. Busy." Hardly the most polite way of talking to the girl.

"Right, well, I won't keep you," she said. Kelly did an excellent line in hurt feelings, looking away like she was trying to hide it. A pretty girl, pouting like that, I bet it had an effect.

Problem for Kelly was, every time I looked at her I saw two things. The first was the dead body of Tom Childs. He had been her man, and I had stuffed his corpse into a suitcase in a grotty room of the St. John Hotel and taken it for disposal. The second thing I saw was Zara. The last woman I had pulled close to me. I was still trying to shake her off.

"Maybe next week, when things have slowed down, I'll give you a call," I said. Surprised myself, saying it. Hadn't intended to. It wasn't because she was pouting; I'm not that easily won over. It was the picture in my head of Nate Colgan, the fat old man decades hence, sitting on his own in that dingy house of mine. Alone. Always alone.

"I'd like that," she said, and headed into the warehouse.

She'd like it. Someone happy at the prospect of me giving them a call. I heard that rarely enough that I was actually feeling positive when I went to the car. The next person I met could easily change all that.

28

I'd known where he lived for years. Not with any intention of doing something with the information, let me say. Knowing DI Michael Fisher's address didn't mean anything. It was a little piece of information that was interesting but unusable. There's almost no circumstance in which you could use it. Almost none. You can't go round and harm him. He's a cop. Maybe, if a cop is dangerous enough to you and corrupt enough that he won't report you, you can try a little intimidation. But that's still a maybe. A last resort. A normal cop, in normal circumstances, is off the table.

It's not a respect for the law, although you probably already guessed that. It's a fear of what the law will do when they think you're targeting them. You can commit crimes, and of course the police will come after you. That's them doing their jobs. You target a cop and that's personal. No organization wants to get into a personal fight with the police. Only the desperate, the stupid and the detached from reality ever do.

So I knew where he lived. Had never done anything with the information until now. I was sitting in my car, across the road from his house, watching. There were no lights on. I had no idea what hours he was working. It took a while of sitting there, I don't know how long, before his red Renault pulled up in the little driveway in front of the house. He got out and went in without looking around. Interesting. Something I'd always wondered about cops. Did they take the same sort of precautions people like me did? I never once went into my house without first taking a look up and down the street. Always playing safe. Don't need to play at it when you're a cop.

A light went on upstairs. He lived alone, Fisher. He had been married before, a long time ago I think, but it hadn't produced any kids. I never heard any rumors about him having girlfriends. People in the industry know Fisher, watch him. Watch him like a fucking hawk since he put Jamieson and the rest away. A man once respected but underestimated, now feared.

I don't know why I sat there and watched. I could have gone up to the door and knocked, gotten the conversation out of the way. It wasn't a fear of what I had to say, or a fear of him refusing the offer I was going to put on the table. There's an instinct you get. Takes a lot of time, a lot of work, before you have it. Ronnie, at that point, wouldn't have had it. I have no doubt he'd have marched straight up to the door and tried to finish this as fast as possible. My instinct was telling me to give him some time. Let him get settled in the house before you disturb him. Don't let him know that you've been outside watching, which he will if you knock as soon as he goes in. That'll unnerve him; make him wonder if he can trust you.

My watch told me it was after midnight as I walked up the front path. That would spook him. I was guessing he didn't get a whole lot of visitors, and none at all at this hour. There was a risk in me being here. Same risk that I criticized him for taking when he turned up on my doorstep. Someone sees us and they make assumptions. They think that I'm giving the police information. I was, and I didn't want the world jumping to that entirely accurate conclusion.

I knocked on the door and waited. Took about thirty seconds for him to open up. Stood there looking at me, not saying anything. He was wearing jeans and a T-shirt with no shoes and his hair had the damp look of a man who'd just had a quick shower. He was dressed so casually and it didn't suit Fisher at all. It's hard to make a strong impression on someone when you're barefoot and your sagging arms are showing. He always needed to dress the part, too worn down to intimidate otherwise.

I looked at him for a few seconds, the two of us standing there silently. There was nothing we had to say to each other that was ever going to be said out on the doorstep. He nodded for me to come in, held the door open and let me pass. I could try and describe his house to you, but I can't honestly say that I remember much about it. It seemed plain and functional, nothing that even approached a personal touch to it. It was a house with a bed and a shower and a kitchen and maybe that was all he needed it to be. My house would have been the same if it wasn't for the effort I made to make it appealing to Becky. My abiding sense of Fisher's house was that it was a lonely place.

Once he was standing in the living room in front of me, I started to talk.

"I've come to deliver on our deal," I told him.

He raised his eyebrows, started to look like he was pleased with what he'd heard. Then the disgust ran right over the top of it. He was getting what he wanted but he was getting it from me. A deal with the devil, was how he saw it. His righteous horror was plastered across his face.

"Go on then," he said.

"I know where he's going to be. Tomorrow night."

The tomorrow night thing caught his ear right away. It was going to make him suspicious, of course. I had to tell him now because the following day was going to be very busy for me. I'd have the chance to phone him and tell him, but I didn't want my phone giving away my location. Not when I was planning to do things I didn't want the police tracking.

"Tell me then," he said.

I took a piece of paper from my pocket, passed it across to him. The address in Shettleston that Zara had written out for me. A man of Fisher's experience would know where it was. He could get a team of people, surround the place. Might have trouble getting round the back unseen, but that was his problem. If some of Barrett's people made a break and Fisher had to give chase then that was just something else to distract him from me.

"Not a great spot. From the front they can see along their own street and down an adjacent one, so it'll be tough to get close unseen."

"Tomorrow night, huh?"

"Tomorrow night," I said.

"So if I went round there now with a squad I wouldn't find Barrett and his people there?"

I gave him the look. The expression doesn't change, not in any way that I can sit here and describe to you, but there was something in the eyes that told him he was playing with fire. A man with stony face and stony fists, giving you a blank look that would scare the waves from the sea. That was the plan, anyway.

"We had a deal," I said. I was talking low, and my grumbly voice was turning into a growl.

"The deal was that you let me have Barrett and I let you have Cope. That deal stands. You have my word that if we sweep up Cope in these arrests I will make sure that she doesn't get time. I'll make sure she's out on the streets within hours, in fact. But the deal said nothing about timing."

He wasn't being smug, which was big of him. He was just saying that he needed to be able to carry out a big move like this on his time, not on mine. I took a deep breath before I spoke.

"I'm giving you the chance to stop a war here. You go and arrest Barrett and his men tomorrow night, sometime after nine o'clock, and you'll have that bastard off the streets. You'll also have helped avoid something much bigger, much worse. You go in early, and taking Barrett off the streets won't mean a damn thing. You have my word on that."

I didn't want him knowing that there was something much

bigger going on, but there wasn't an alternative. Now he knew that my priorities had shifted away from Adrian Barrett. Had to assume that he was smart enough not to ask, not to push me. Assume that he was smart enough to guess that whatever I was glaring at now was something he couldn't touch.

An intelligent man like Fisher would know that my demand for the timing meant the Barrett job was a distraction. The plod focus their attention on Barrett while big, awful Nate Colgan and his band of merry thugs do something unspeakable to someone else. He wouldn't guess who the real target was. Fisher would guess at Don Park, most probably. No doubt that sent his mighty little brain off wondering what an attack on Don Park might do for the city. Hurting Park would keep MacArthur in place; keep a lid on the tensions that were rising within that organization. And, let's face it, if Park took control the first thing he would have to do was establish himself as successful by picking a fight with someone he could beat. Me taking out Park might actually calm things down; bring a little peace to the world. What was Fisher doing if not trying to encourage people to calm the fuck down?

"I'll be all over this address at nine o'clock tomorrow night," he told me. "If anything happens in the meantime that makes me think I should go sooner then I will go sooner."

I nodded just a little, accepting and respecting that he had come to a difficult decision. "And Zara?"

"The deal stands," he said.

I had what I wanted, so I turned and walked out of his house. Breathed a sigh of relief when I got out of there, and I'll bet Fisher did too. Relieved that I was gone from his view. We were two men who could do each other a world of damage. Not just if we were caught fraternizing. It was a mental thing, after years of being on the opposite side of a bloody big fence. Years of conditioning. It damaged me in my own mind, associating myself with someone like Michael Fisher. God knows what it did to the mind of an honest cop like him to be working with me.

A hypocrite. That would be the right word for it. Each of us as bad as the other. You can't trust a hypocrite. If a man works his whole life to do one thing, then flips and stands against it in an instant, how do you trust him? Fisher shouldn't have been working with me. I shouldn't have been cutting deals with cops. And not just any fucking cop either. The one that put Jamieson where he was. It was rotten. It was also very late, so I drove back home. I would get in touch with everyone I needed to the following morning, early. One of the benefits of not sleeping at all. I would be up early, ready to organize a long day for everyone else.

29

It was Sunday afternoon and I should have been with Becky. The job was a means to support her, to provide me with a life where I could spend my weekends with her. That was what I told myself. Convinced myself. That was what good people did. They worked jobs they didn't like because it supported the people they loved. Here I was putting the job first. Fine, I could argue that it was an emergency, but there would always be an excuse if I allowed it. Maybe the job wasn't just a route to providing for her. Hadn't started out that way.

The day was going to come when I had to talk to her about what I did for a living. She was going to hear rumors, or I was going to get arrested or hurt, and I was going to have to try and explain some things to her. Scared the crap out of me, to be honest. The thought of her hating me for what I'd done. I didn't hate what I had done; I had always been able to justify and accept what I did and why I did it. What I hated, what I feared, were the things I knew I was still going to do. There were worse things out there than the things I'd done, and I knew it was a matter of time before I did them. The path I was on, with the Jamieson organization, made it unavoidable. That was why I didn't sleep well. Lying there, knowing that I was going to do terrible things. Knowing that the day would come when I had to explain those things to someone I actually cared about.

Now I was sitting with Ronnie and Russell Conrad in a car on the south side of the Clyde, watching a flat we thought Taylor

"Original" Carlisle might be in. It belonged to his girlfriend, and we knew he wasn't at his own place. It was a four-story old building on a short street that probably used to be industrial, back in the days of industry. Now the buildings were converted into other things, but those other things made the place seem lifeless compared to the old industrial work. Her building was on the corner, looking down on the once industrial site turned dumping ground badly hidden behind a thin mesh fence across the street.

"There," Conrad said quietly.

Original was running across the street, hands in his pockets, hair flapping behind him, looking cold and eager to get to his car. We were back along the road, watching the front door of the building that he hadn't come out of. If he hadn't parked his car across the street we wouldn't have seen him go. I nudged Ronnie and he started the car, moved down to the corner and pulled alongside Original.

The bastard could have run if he was marginally more stupid. He was a lot of things, but not dumb. He knew that running was the first step in getting chased, and getting chased was just a sweaty way of getting yourself caught and punished. He stopped on the pavement and looked down into the car; saw us looking back at him. Conrad opened the back door. None of us said anything. Original stood on the pavement and looked around, maybe hoping that someone was going to magically appear and rescue him. There were no white knights around. He dropped down into the back of the car; as soon as Ronnie heard the door close, he pulled away.

Nobody said anything for a while; we just drove through the city. I adjusted the rear-view mirror so that I could watch the floppy-haired fraud from the passenger seat, but there wasn't a lot to watch. He had his head turned sideways, looking out the window and trying to stay expressionless. I think there were nerves there, a little bit of fear, but not as much as there should have been. He was being taken to God knows where by a gunman and two dangerous muscle. That lack of fear told me that this was going to be easy; Original Carlisle had already decided to tell us whatever we wanted to know.

We went east, Ronnie picking a route that I wouldn't have used. He got away with it because his route wasn't terrible and it was Sunday so it was just a little less busy than it might have been. But the kid wasn't a driver; this wasn't what he was employed for. As far as I knew the organization still didn't have a full-time driver for jobs, not since Kenny McBride took a walk in the woods with Calum MacLean over a year ago. Something else that should have been arranged by now. The organization needed a driver that we knew we could safely use on jobs, instead of every senior man having his own chauffeur. So it took us a little longer than it should have, and we might have been seen by more people than I would like, but it was no big deal. Original wasn't leaning out of the window, screaming for help; he was just sitting there, accepting what was happening to him.

The up-and-over garage door was open when we turned onto the street. It was a wide street, built to be used by big vehicles and heavy industry. I don't know how long the intended use had lasted but I'm guessing not very. Some of the buildings were still used for storage, including the one we were pulling into, but the street was quiet and there was nobody to see us arrive.

Currie had told his man to have the door open for us but not to be there when we arrived. The place was empty and it needed to stay that way. We were going to get details from Original and there were ways of getting details that you don't want witnesses seeing. People think they're loyal to an organization, they think there's nothing that's going to turn them against you, and then they see the dirty side of the business. They see you do something that turns their stomach and suddenly they're desperate to get out, desperate to unburden themselves. It happens. It's not everyone that's blessed with an iron stomach and Teflon memory.

Ronnie got out and pulled the door down behind us, dipping the place into darkness. The three of us stayed in the car while Ronnie presumably fumbled around to find a light. If there was a window in the place then it was caked in a wall of muck sturdy enough to repel daylight. A strip light flickered above the car; I opened my door before the light had decided to settle on staying on. I went and opened Original's door, waited for him to get out. Ronnie was over beside me, Conrad getting out of the other side of the car. Original was sticking with his conspicuous effort to look nerveless.

"This way," I said to him, leading him up three short steps and through a door into a large open back room. Must have been a workshop at some time; when I switched on the lights you could still see the markings on the floor where machinery had been bolted. The place was gloomy, even with a row of small windows along the top of the walls. There was dust everywhere; the place hadn't been cleaned in years. I naturally assumed that this had been a pretty miserable place to work.

It was places like this that led me into the life. All the men in my family worked in places like this, bigger or smaller variations of it anyway. They were ground down by it, every single one of them. Welders, joiners and sparkies, all working long hours for little reward and suffering health issues because of it before they hit fifty. I watched those men and I knew I couldn't be like them. The pride they felt in the good, honest work they did just wasn't enough for me, never would be. Pride was no substitute for a life I could be comfortable with; that was why I took the shortcut the criminal industry gave me. I wanted better. I thought I could have better.

There I was, standing in that abandoned workshop with some kid I was willing to torture to help an employer. Not once did the thought run through my mind that it really wasn't any better than the life I'd turned my back on. Certainly didn't occur to me that it was far worse. The place was grotty but it was towards the back of the building; the walls were thick and the only windows were high and faced out back. There was a small chair with a plastic seat, metal legs and the back missing sitting in one corner, a row of cabinets and a sink along a side wall. It was a smaller, dirtier version of the place out by the airport that Marty owned, these kinds of places being very useful to men like us. At least some kind of industry was using them. The chair was all I needed. I grabbed it, skidded it along the floor into the middle of the room.

"Sit down," I said to Original in a low voice.

"You don't need to do this," he said to me with a hint of his usual cocky tone.

"Sit."

He did as he was told with the kind of smug look that told us all that he was going to do whatever we asked and we were wasting our time in being aggressive. Being superior because he thought we hadn't realized it yet. We had. He sat on the chair, arms folded, and looked at me. He made eye contact and held it. This guy in his late twenties, trying to look younger, thinking he knew just exactly what he was doing. Never been in a fight. Never done anything darker than rob some gullible halfwit of their cash over the phone. He thought he understood. When you're grassing your boss, giving away damning evidence against someone who gave you your living, you do not look smug about it. You make an effort to be sad, to be reluctant and you at least have the balls to show a little defiance. This little bastard thought he knew how this was going to play out, and the certainty of a victim is never a good thing. Certainty is a strength that you have to take away from them.

I walked over to him and punched him in the face. Little backswing, a rabbit punch in the mouth that tipped him backwards on a chair with no back. He tumbled onto the floor, rolled over and got quickly onto his knees. He was a little disorientated; falling over always makes a punch seem much worse than it really is. When the world does a somersault your mind tricks you into thinking it was the punch's fault, not the backless chair's. He was gasping for breath for no reason that I could guess at other than shock. I grabbed the collar of his presumably expensive thin jacket and lifted him up, dumped him back on the chair.

Ronnie was leaning back against the sink, watching and keeping any sign of emotion off his face. That was something I had tried to teach him. Don't let the victim think that you sympathize or that you're bored and want this to end as much as they do. Don't give them anything that they can cling to. Conrad was standing back towards the door we had come in through. There was an expression on his face that went somewhere near to disgust. He wasn't muscle; he wasn't a guy who knocked people around or liked to watch people get knocked around. No, he was just a guy who shot people in the back of the head. Everyone had their own little standards, I suppose.

"You're going to tell us everything we want to know," I told Original quietly.

"Yes," he said quickly, still gasping. "Yes."

30

Getting a man to talk is one thing. Getting him to tell the truth is another. Original was ready to blab because he was scared of another shot to the mouth. Scared of getting his expensive clothes any dirtier as he rolled across the floor of the workshop. He wasn't a fighter. What he was an expert at was talking. An expert at running off at the mouth, lie following lie until you were wrapped in so many of them you were forced to accept them as truth. That was his skill. It was why he was in the organization. It was why I still didn't trust him now.

"Tell me about the Christie killing," I said to him.

He took a few seconds. Showing some long-overdue reticence. Trying to think of how much he should say. This was him working out his own place in the story he was about to tell, making sure that he didn't say anything to incriminate himself. What he said next would certainly be lies whenever he talked about himself. He was going to gloss over his own role in all of this.

"I wasn't really involved then, you see. Right, your man Lafferty, he called me up when he was organizing the meeting. That's when I got pulled into all this."

"But you knew him before," I said. A test of honesty. He knew Lafferty before; there was no way Lafferty would have used him as a mouthpiece at the meeting if he didn't. No way he would be using Original as a senior man. There had to be history there, but it was a history Original thought he had kept hidden.

"Okay, yeah, I knew him a bit. I'd helped him out with some

stuff. I got connections. See, you guys, you think I'm just sitting there scamming old ladies, but I need to make a lot of connections to do what I do. I got skills. I mean, not your kind of skills. Tech skills. I had helped him out a bit. Helped him make a bit of money. But it was for the organization," he added quickly.

"Lee Christie."

"Like I says, I wasn't working close with Lafferty then. So, you know, this is just what I heard from others. The boy Jake, people who were around. He found out about Christie giving info to that two that work for Billy Patterson. Summers and the other one. Those two. Lafferty found out about all that and he was pissed off. Didn't like Christie grassing on him, didn't like anyone spying on him. It was trust, you know."

"But that wasn't it, was it?" I asked him. "He didn't just want to kill Christie?" The other two were silent, letting me get on with what had to be done. They didn't much want to get involved. Just me standing over Original in the middle of the floor, him sitting carefully on the backless chair.

"I don't know," he said, shaking his head. "I told you, I wasn't around. I don't know how it started, right. Really, okay. I don't. Maybe he already planned to make moves against people. Seems like, I don't know, he saw Currie and Marty getting all pally and thought he was being excluded, something like that. He thought other people were trying to push him out. He figured, I don't know, that the organization needed a strong hand, you know what I mean? A single person in charge. He thought it should have been him."

I knew how it had started. How it had to be. He had Barrett and his crew on hold, waiting for the chance to use them. Working in the city to make a name for themselves, but not pulling the trigger on a takeover until he had the excuse he needed. Waiting for something to come along that Jamieson would have no choice but to back. One of Lafferty's men killed so Lafferty gets to lead the investigation. Didn't matter that Lafferty was the one who had him killed.

"So Lafferty's using Barrett and his crew to try and take control." I said it as a statement, not a question.

"Yeah," Original said, nodding his head. "Got them in quick. Had them here already, I guess. I don't know. Like I says, I wasn't involved at that point. Had to use someone from outside. Someone from the city, that would have been too obvious; people would have known them. There would have been leaks. Had to use outsiders. They killed Christie and then he called the meeting so that he could start leaning on people, get them to back him. Force them to, I suppose. The meeting, that was all a set-up. Some of us had been told what to say beforehand."

Didn't bowl me over with shock. He was talking fast, spurting out the words as he tried to ingratiate, show what a good little helper he was being. He had stopped now, breathing heavily and looking up at me. Scared. He knew that one wrong word was going to cost him.

"Tell me about his crew."

"Lafferty's?"

"Yeah, Lafferty's."

Original snorted, and then almost choked on the blood that was in the back of his throat. He spat a blob of it out onto the floor.

"Lafferty doesn't have a crew," he said. The attempt at cool derision had been wiped out by the blob of thick blood and spit in front of his chair. "The guy doesn't have a clue. Okay, all right, that's not fair. He has a clue. He knows how other people run things, with people around them, but he thinks he can do it different. Like he can keep doing things the way he always has. He's got all these legit businesses and he plays at being this legit businessman and he thinks he can keep that up." His voice was getting more Glaswegian as he talked.

"So who's around him?"

"Like, permanently around him?" He exhaled loudly. "There's a bunch of people who're around him a bit, for business I mean. Around him all the time? Only the boy Jake, really. He's not there now; he's fucked off somewhere. Work, is what I heard, getting support for something. I don't know. Maybe he's pissed off back to Bratislava or whatever shithole his people came from. Lafferty doesn't trust most people, doesn't like having anyone near him."

"His family?" I asked.

"They're not there. I don't know where they are. He sent them away someplace, keeping them safe I suppose. I heard it was just a marriage of convenience these days anyway, but I don't know. He doesn't talk about them much. They ain't at the house though, I know that. I spent a bit of time at the place last week so I know all about it."

"You do, huh?"

"Yeah, I do."

Almost begging me to ask him about it. So proud of the fact that he had something useful to tell me and desperate for the chance to share it. Wanting to be the most helpful little bunny in the world.

"Go on then."

He paused, realizing from my tone that he'd exposed his gratuitous enthusiasm. Time to pull back a little.

"Go on then what?"

"Tell me about his house. Let's say I wanted to go there tonight and I wanted to get in without him knowing."

Original nodded. "Yeah, sure, yeah, you could do that. Lafferty, he doesn't have a great security system. Just the same sort of thing his neighbors have, so that it doesn't stand out, you know? He's got cameras, but you can get up to the house without being seen by them. And it ain't like he checks them much anyway, because he doesn't have staff, right? Doesn't have someone watching them for him. His driveway, right, has these trees and bushes up either side of it. Looks good, but the cameras don't pick up what's behind them because he doesn't have a camera on each side of the garden. His neighbors would see them. That gets you up to the house. Go round the right-hand side and you can get to the back door without being picked up."

I was frowning, shaking my head. This was contemptible. A man like Lafferty, making a play to take over the organization but keeping the same security he had before. That was unacceptable. Original must have thought I was shaking my head at him, rather than his words. He started babbling.

"It's true, Nate, it's true. I'm telling you, on my life it's true. I said it to him already. I said, Angus, man, you got to get some better security now. Fuck what the neighbors think. He said he would, but he still hasn't. All about appearances, you know? He got this new alarm put in, but he had Jake put in the password for it and I saw it. It's two three six five. That's it. And I got a key. Jesus, Nate, yeah, I got a key." There was relief in his voice, joy, like he'd just found the golden ticket. "In my wallet. There's a few keys in there. You take it out; I'll show you what key is the right key. His back door, Nate. His back fucking door."

Smiling with bloodied teeth. Leaning forwards for me to reach into his coat pocket and take out his wallet. There were four keys; he told me which got him into Lafferty's house.

"That gets you into the sun lounge at the back. There's another door with a lock into the dining room, but he never locks it. Or it's never been locked when I went there. Maybe late at night, but I don't know. The alarm box is just inside the dining room. Little white box on the wall beside the light switch. Just type in two three six five and *enter*. That's it."

Grinning now. Convinced that he must have done enough to win me over. I didn't like that, however true it might have been. A guy like Original, he just wanted to be on the winning team. There was no loyalty there. He was loyal to John Young and Jamieson when they were on the outside. Became loyal to Lafferty because it looked like Lafferty might take charge. As soon as power changed sides, so did Original.

"Tell me about his routine, late at night."

Original started shaking his head. "I don't know. I only been there a couple of times at night, bunch of times through the day. I don't figure he has much of a routine at a time like this. I know he's got a meeting with Stuart Crockley at six tonight. Stuart told me. Stuart's well on side with all this. His money-cleaning: man, Lafferty needs it and Stuart's well up for a change of leadership. Thinks he'll be sitting pretty. After that meeting, I ain't got a clue."

I nodded along. He was being honest about not knowing, and that was something to treat as a positive. Exaggerating what he knew could be as dangerous as lying to me.

"He expect to hear from you today?" I asked him.

"Yeah, sure," he said. "Works me like a dog. All of us. Always has things for us to do, always wants to know what's going on. He's properly serious, you know."

"So if you don't get in touch?"

"I don't know." He shrugged. "Maybe he wouldn't be too bothered; I'm not working on anything, like, urgent, right now. But, you know, he's a bit paranoid, so I think he'd be worried about it." Nodding his head and inflating his punctured ego with the thought that he was important to Lafferty. "I could, uh, call him up, spin him some yarn about an emergency coming up or something. Tell him I wouldn't be available for anything tonight."

At least he was trying. God bless him, he was giving it a shot. Trying to get a phone call so that he could drop some code word or something, help the boss out. I hated him a little less for confirming my assumption that he was a lying little shit.

"No," I said.

"But I could help you," he told me. "And I wouldn't say anything to him about you, Nate, I wouldn't. Come on, I just gave you the key to his fucking house. Once you give away the key to a man's house, you ain't getting back in that house. I'm dead to Lafferty. You got to trust that I wouldn't shaft you now."

"No," I said again. Same low tone, firm enough to make it clear that the talking stopped now.

I looked away from that dickhead and round at Ronnie, still leaning on the sink. He looked relieved that only one punch had been thrown. There was still a softness there, and I would have to work it out of him. Time would do that for me, I figured. He'd learn.

"Go call Conn. Tell them to come round here right away," I said.

Couldn't have Original out on the streets until we were done with Lafferty. That meant I needed good people to babysit him. Conn and Mikey were overqualified, and that was the sort of reassurance I wanted. There was nothing to gain from killing Original. Okay, it would make the world a slightly better place. Might even make me a little happier. But those weren't good enough reasons.

The kind of awkward silence you get when you're hanging around with people you hate fell in the room while we waited for them to come. We couldn't talk work in front of Original. Ronnie didn't have the confidence to say anything. Conrad seemed determined to hang around in the shadows like fucking Batman.

Conrad heard them first, opening the garage door and bringing their car in. Ronnie and Conrad stayed where they were; I went out to talk to them.

"What's the gig?" Conn asked.

"Staring at Original Carlisle for a few hours."

"Seriously?" Mikey asked.

"Seriously. Enjoy."

Original had been useful, but that usefulness had run out. We had one more visit to make before we went for Lafferty. Another useful but awful link to Lafferty.

31

He drove past the address a few times and didn't see any sign of life there. It bugged him, nagged at him, that maybe Nate Colgan was playing him for a fool. Giving Fisher a fake address while Colgan went to the right place. The detective could have a squad of men surround this house while Colgan and his fellow thugs were at the actual safe house, killing off Barrett and his crew. Fisher had to be sure before he committed himself to it, to this act of corruption and hypocrisy.

There had to be a way of identifying that this was the right place, but there was no outward sign. For hours he agonized about it, killed the morning that way. The address was, as Colgan had warned, in a spot where they could see along their own street and down an adjacent one. He parked at the top of the adjacent street for ten minutes. Just sat there and looked down at the front of the house, a white semidetached in the middle of a well-populated residential area. There were steps up to the front garden, raised up from the street. It wasn't the sort of place he had seen professionals use as a safe house. Not nearly safe enough, he would have said. Too many people to see them coming and going.

Unless the address was bullshit. Fisher was tearing himself apart thinking about it when the side door of the place opened and out walked a woman. He wasn't close enough to pick out exact features but he didn't need to be that close to know it was Zara Cope. She went out with a bag of rubbish and put it in the green bin that was pushed against the front of the house beside the path.

She turned and went back into the house, closed the door. Just that one glimpse, those few seconds, told him that Nate Colgan had given the right address.

"Right, I have a lead and I want a squad on top of it before it slips away," Fisher said loudly to anyone who was listening, when he got into the station.

It was only after he said it that he stopped and looked around to see who was there, see who might be part of the squad he was assembling. DS Louise Forbes wasn't there, which was a disappointment. She was the brightest of this bunch but she must not have been working. It was Sunday, well into late afternoon. It would be damn close to nine o'clock before they had everything set up and ready to go. That was enough to keep his promise to Colgan. A promise he didn't feel deserved a lot of effort on his part.

DC Davies was sitting at his desk, looking like the arse had just fallen out of his world. Fisher was enthusiastic and determined to drag people along on a big job and that scared Davies. Always did. The saddest part of his laziness and fear of the job was that he wasn't a terrible cop. Not great, sure, but not terrible either. DC McGowan there as well. Another one as soft as jelly, easily pushed around but not often pushed into doing something useful. Didn't matter—Fisher intended to provide the steel and leadership for this. What he needed more than anything was numbers, and he could get that with suspicion of Adrian Barrett's location.

The one question that was running rings around his mind was weapons. If people started to suspect that there might be guns there then they might suggest that there was a need for armed officers. Fisher didn't want that. Didn't think firearms officers would do anything other than escalate the situation with a man like Barrett, and didn't want them taking away control. This was a score that owed its existence to the work of Nate Colgan, and Fisher did not want to have to explain that to anyone. He needed complete control. Actually, he needed people like Davies and McGowan who wouldn't dare question him.

It took as long as he had assumed it would to get everything he needed to sweep the front and back of the house. It was such a bloody awkward location. Had to be an accident; no way they had picked it because of how tricky it was for the police to get to. Those bastards must have run there in a hurry after their gunman was taken down. Once he was gone they would have moved. Fisher still believed it was Barrett who had had the gunman, Nasif, killed. He didn't know why, but it was a fair guess that only his own side could set him up as cleanly as that. They killed him and then moved quickly before anyone could trace the killer back to them. It wasn't a nice thing to admit, but he was a little bit glad that they had gotten rid of their own gunman: it made Fisher and the rest of the team he had assembled much less nervous about what they were walking into.

He said nothing about guns to anyone and none of them had the guts to say it to him. But there was a chance Barrett and his crew were in there, armed to the teeth, ready to fire on any intruder. Fisher didn't think so. Not with Nasif dead. He convinced himself there wouldn't be a gun there. He had everyone lined up where he wanted them. One van at the bottom of the adjacent street, round the corner and just out of view. Another group were going to go in through the back of the house, but they had to get through the garden of the house that backed onto the safe house. Fortunately there were trees between the two gardens and they thought they could get close without being spotted. Fisher and his group were waiting until the ones going in the back were in position before they moved up to the front of the house.

He looked at his watch; it was just after half past eight. They would be in before nine, but that was just too fucking bad. He could have done this in the morning, when it might have been safer. He could have done this any time he liked, but he had left it until damn close to the time Colgan wanted. That thug didn't have the right to expect anything more than damn close.

"There are lights visible at the back of the house," someone said over the radio. "Downstairs and up." There were no lights visible at the front of the house; they'd sent someone round the corner to check.

"How close are you?" Fisher asked them.

"Nearly ready, sir."

It took another thirty seconds that felt like thirty minutes before they messaged through again to say that they were prepared to jump the fence and ready to go on his orders.

"All right, everyone move, now," Fisher said.

The van they were in screeched into life and round the corner, down the street to face the house. The doors slid open and the cops jumped out, running up the steps to the garden and up to the front door. They weren't going to waste time knocking; these people were too dangerous for that. They had their own little can opener: the battering ram that just about took the door clean off its hinges with one swing from a bulky PC. Another example of how this wasn't a good safe house. A good safe house has a sturdy door that takes a few bangs to knock down and buys you a few more seconds. Seconds can be a lifetime.

They went in through the front. As they moved along the corridor Fisher saw someone disappearing upstairs. A male, thirties, jumping two steps at a time. He disappeared round the corner at the top of the stairs while uniformed officers poured into the downstairs rooms. There was shouting and bawling, two men pinned down on the floor in the living room. Officers shouting that rooms were clear, the downstairs secured in a twenty-second flurry of confusing sound and movement. They got to the bottom of the stairs.

"There's at least one up there," Fisher said to the officers, who started to go up ahead of him. "Who have we got?" he shouted over his shoulder into the living room.

"Two male, neither Barrett."

Shite, he was the one Fisher wanted, the head of the snake. Get Barrett and they could talk the rest of them down out of their tree. As long as Barrett was ensconced upstairs, whoever was with him would follow his lead. Cope, she had to be up there. She was in the house, he knew that, and she wasn't one of the ones they'd secured downstairs.

The officers went up the stairs; Fisher pushed up behind them, wanting to take the lead. He wanted to be seen to take the lead — that was most important to him. If there was danger up there then he wanted to be the one who faced it. And, yes, if there was glory up there then he wanted to be the one enveloped by that too. For better or worse, this was his investigation, his score, and he wanted the consequences to belong entirely to him, either way. One of the officers had a door open, a light on, shouting clear. There was still noise downstairs, someone shouting abuse at whoever was bundling him out the door and down to the police van. There was movement upstairs, and it took just a second for Fisher to isolate the sound coming from the bedroom along the short corridor. He pointed at it, led the officers toward it.

A couple of steps and he could hear that they were moving furniture, loading it up against the door to stop the police getting in. A pathetic last-ditch attempt, he thought, but it was only penultimate ditch. They had the two downstairs, there had to be another four up here if his info was correct, and that meant anything they did now was temporary. Four people had no hope of getting out of there, but desperation could hide any inevitability when it was big enough.

"Open up," Fisher shouted, trying the handle. There was no lock on the door but it didn't budge even a fraction; they must have had someone with their boot against it.

"I'm armed," someone shouted. "I'm armed and I have a girl in here."

That was the moment Fisher's heart just dropped. He had rolled the dice and bounced them right off the fucking table. Maybe it was the high of the Jamieson score, the last wash of adrenaline that success had given him, that had persuaded him to take the risk. It was unforgivable, taking officers into that house with a man who could have been armed. "Could have" was enough to play cautious, but he hadn't. Michael Fisher had rushed in, and now he was going to pay the price. Whether the bastard in the room was serious about using the gun or not, Fisher knew his argument that there was little reason to believe he would be armed wouldn't wash. And if he shot Cope, what the hell would Colgan's reaction be?

He pointed the officers back down the corridor, told them to go. But Fisher stayed. He was already in the shit; there was no point trying to wipe it off now. He stood outside the door, leaning against the wall in the corridor, listening to them. The people in the room were trying to move something heavy across the floor to further block the door. He listened to urgent whispers, mostly male and occasionally female. He picked out a few words, just a few. The female whispers were the ones that mattered. They were reassuring, calm, smart and the ones in command.

32

It said a lot about Lafferty that he insisted on hiring complete wankers. You can judge a person by the people he employs. We were driving to Mark Garvey's house, a place I already knew too well.

"You want to take the lead on this, being the customer?" I asked Conrad. He was in the back seat, Ronnie in the passenger seat beside me.

"Uh, maybe you should. If things are fragmenting, we might need you to persuade him," Conrad said. Sounded like an excuse to me. Wanted to make sure that I took the lead in everything so that anything that went wrong was my fault. Fair enough.

We weren't looking for one gun. Not when we were walking into the unknown. The least we needed was one for our gunman, but I wanted a second. You walk into a house belonging to someone like Lafferty, with only the words of someone like Original to guide you, and you better bloody have cover. Conrad would take one gun, I would take the other. I wasn't going to put one in Ronnie's hand; he had too little experience to handle it. I hadn't shot a man either, but that's not the sort of experience I mean. The more pressure you've been under, the more you understand how to handle it. It's not the ability to shoot someone that you learn; it's the ability to stop yourself.

I led the way up to Garvey's front door. Three of us, standing out on this little suburban street where people cloaked themselves in respectability. Rang the doorbell and waited. Hoping that no neighbors would spot us. A man like Garvey would have all sorts of visitors. The kind of people that the rest of the street would notice. Seemed like common sense to me that he should be moving house more often than he did. Maybe the fact that he didn't was down to Mel and her ample charms. Wanting to keep her happy, give her stability. Or maybe not. Easy to blame the wife for your own mistakes, a luxury some of us didn't have.

It was taking too long. I rang the doorbell a second time. That hurried him up, Garvey pulling open the door and looking at the three of us. He recognized me all right; I could see the hint of disgust that ran across his face before the trademark smile found its home. He recognized Conrad as well. A client. Looked a little puzzled when he saw Ronnie, but didn't say anything about it.

"Come in, lads, come in," he said, holding the door open for us.

I led the way, Conrad and Ronnie dropping in behind me. My turn to take the lead, remember.

"Come through to the living room. No point in us all standing in the corridor." He dutifully led us into the living room, trying to keep it as casual as possible.

Mel was nowhere to be seen. Didn't take long to find out where Garvey's delightful wife had gone. Noise burst from upstairs, a TV with the volume a long way up. She wasn't hard of hearing, so that was just petulant. Part of an argument, I figured. Mel trying to make Mark Garvey feel a bit stupid in front of us. He glanced up towards the ceiling, the smile falling off his face for just a second before he looked back at the rest of us.

The noise was still booming away upstairs. The TV only needed to be that loud if she was trying to listen to it from somewhere down the other end of the street. Told me something about the state of their marriage. When it got to the point that she was trying to embarrass him in front of people like us then you knew it was perched on the cliff edge. They were standing on the brink of divorce, looking down into the darkness and screaming loud. Maybe she hadn't been playing games on his behalf the last time I was there. Maybe I was harsh. Still didn't want to have sex with the woman, but I could have been more polite about it.

"What can I do for you gentlemen?" Garvey asked. Speaking with a little more volume than he would normally have needed.

The question pulled our attention away from the noise upstairs. Conrad hadn't batted an eyelid, a man who had trained himself to ignore everything. Ronnie wasn't that subtle. He had spent a good ten seconds staring at the ceiling, his gaze only broken by Garvey's question.

"Handguns, two," I said.

I shouldn't have been the one who answered the question. This was Conrad's territory, and no matter who was in charge of the job overall, the gunman should have been handling this. Garvey knew it too. He gave me a little look. The mouth was still smiling, but the truth was in the eyes. This meeting was uncomfortable. Garvey didn't know that things were falling apart in the organization, and me taking the lead didn't reassure him at all.

"Two small pieces, of course. Anything else?" he asked, looking at Conrad to make it clear that he thought the gunman was the one that should be answering the questions.

"Nothing else, just the two," Conrad said quietly with a shrug.

Garvey nodded at that. The sort of jolly, smiling nod that was supposed to make everything seem just fine. But he'd asked Conrad because he didn't trust my word.

"Why don't you guys take a seat and I'll go have a look at what I've got for you. Can I get you anything?" he asked, meaning tea or coffee.

"Yeah," I said. "Two handguns, quickly."

He nodded, still smiling but managing to look miserable at the same time. He hated me. Whether it was because I was taking the lead on something I shouldn't have been or because of the thing with his wife, I don't know. But Mark Garvey hated me. He left the living room, went out into the corridor and upstairs to get us our guns.

Normally, the three of us would have been chatting to kill the time while we waited. This wasn't normal. If it had just been me and Ronnie alone, we would have talked. There was something about Conrad that just sucked the life out of us. You couldn't talk in front of him because it felt like he didn't want to be part of a conversation. If me and Ronnie talked around him then it would be insulting. You couldn't fucking win. But that wasn't just Conrad, that was a lot of gunmen. You meet a few, Frank MacLeod was one, who are easy to talk to. Comfortable in their own skin. But most of them are guys who don't like talking to you. Don't want to get anywhere near people like me because they think people like me will end up getting them arrested. I can understand that. They have more to be nervous of than most.

The noise from upstairs lowered, someone turning down the volume on the TV. Ronnie raised an eyebrow. Seemed like Garvey was taking his time because he was having a loving conversation with dear wife Mel first. Telling her to stop embarrassing him, probably. Making her turn down the volume. We all stood where we were and listened, trying to pick out their voices. Couldn't. Garvey was smart enough to keep his voice down, although I thought I heard Mel's at one point.

Another minute passed and the volume went back up on the TV, louder than it had been before. Ronnie scoffed. Conrad didn't react. That would have been her reaction to Garvey leaving the room. Getting us our guns, I hoped, because he was taking more time than necessary. It was another minute and a half before Garvey came bounding down the stairs and back into the living room, padded envelope in each hand.

"Right, lads, sorry about that. Had to make sure I picked out the best stuff for you," he said with his sad grin.

He passed one envelope to me and the other to Conrad. The

gunman didn't look in his, just held it at his side. I wasn't interested in sticking to protocol so I opened the flap and looked inside. A small handgun.

"Both loaded, full clip," Garvey said to us. "Both as clean as a whistle, never been used. You won't get better than that, lads. Not a chance."

I didn't like the man. Didn't like the fact that we were tying the organization to him either. But I would never sit here and pretend that he wasn't good at what he did. There were very few places better to source a piece than Mark Garvey.

"Right, let's go," I said. I didn't make any effort to thank him; didn't seem like he deserved or wanted it.

I stood back and let the other two go out first. Ronnie led the way. Conrad gave a little nod of thanks to Garvey. He was the gunman; he was going to have to deal with Garvey again. Maybe he had dealt with him before. That was a thought that hadn't occurred to me before that night. I had assumed Lafferty hiring Garvey was a way of placating Marty, bringing on board his mate. Perhaps he was Conrad's mate as well.

That was the second time in a week that I'd left that house with a sense of relief. There was something deeply unpleasant about standing in the wreckage of other people's lives. I was beginning to feel a little bit sorry for both of the Garveys and that was an ugly feeling too. We got down to the car and left.

I noticed Conrad checking his envelope now that we were out of Garvey's view. Apparently a gunman didn't check in front of his dealer. Might make the dealer think he wasn't trusted. I don't know, there are quirks to every part of the business. Always have been. If you don't live in it, you're not likely to understand them all.

Conrad, sitting in the back with the envelope in his lap, wasn't going to say anything. Nor was Ronnie. He was sitting in the passenger seat, looking out of the window. I glanced at him. Was he ready for this? He'd been involved in violence before, but this was something different. You never knew how a person would react to it. Never. My old mentor Gully Fitzgerald used to say that some of the toughest people in the city weren't tough enough for death. They could fight. They could put people in hospital. They couldn't cross the line into killing.

"You know Lafferty's house, Russell?" I asked over my shoulder.

"Yeah, I been there once," he said.

"We ready for this then?" I said, hoping for some reassuring answers.

I got two mumbles of agreement. It would have to do. It was time to go and kill Angus Lafferty.

33

We were so close to death, it was no wonder they were nervous. Conrad I couldn't tell you about with certainty; I didn't know him well enough to judge whether he was truly nervous or not. Actually, he'd seemed a little nervous since the moment he saw me in his house. A gunman in this situation had a lot to be nervous about. Pick the wrong side and you're dead. Pick the right side and screw up the job and you're dead. I can't claim I knew him well enough to judge him though. Outwardly he might have looked a little nervy; inside he was ready to do whatever it took to get the job done.

I'd met him before this but neither of us mentioned it. You don't. You kill and dispose of a man like Potty Cruickshank and you keep that information to yourself. Our meeting back then was brief. Spent a few minutes together beforehand, both working on Marty Jones's orders. We went into a derelict pub, Potty in there waiting for us. Pushed him through to a back room and Conrad shot him. Big fat fellow, was Potty, so removing him wasn't easy, but you could get a van to the back of the pub without anyone seeing what it was doing. Good location, easy job. I tried to remember if Conrad had seemed nervous back then. Not that I had noticed.

Ronnie was obviously nervous. Little jerky movements and darting looks. He was wandering into uncharted territory. He would either lose his nerve completely on the job or the pressure would settle him down. I was banking on the latter. He had been under pressure before and handled it well. On at least one occasion he had been too relaxed, went and put himself into a hell of a lot of danger because of it. People got jumpy before a job. That didn't mean they couldn't handle it. Pressure's a strange thing. Brings out the best in far more people than you might expect.

We had left Garvey's house and gone to pick up another car. A safe, clean car. The number plate didn't mean anything to the police. The car would be made safe after the job at a garage somewhere. We were going to switch drivers at my insistence. Give Ronnie something to do, something to focus all that energy on. One thing I learned early in my career was that there was nothing worse than being the third man in a two-man job. You're there for insurance, there to give the impression of strength of numbers. That's fine, but it's no fucking fun. There's nothing to do. You spend the whole time waiting for something to go wrong so that you'll have a part to play. Ronnie needed to be kept involved.

"The car we'll use is in here," I told them, pulling into the forecourt of a large garage.

The guy who ran the garage was an acquaintance. There are some people in the business that I know only through my reputation. They do favors for me because they're scared of what'll happen to them if they don't. Ross French was one of the few who didn't fall into that category. It was just money with Ross. You couldn't frighten him; he was one of those people stupid enough to think that not being a career criminal somehow protected him. But he always took the money, and he never asked questions. I wasn't the only one who used his services. He had a few cars that were passed around criminals, repeatedly resprayed and retagged and sent out to do more dirty work.

We parked the car we'd been using so far and got into the new one, a car we would use only for this job on Lafferty. French had, at my request over the phone that morning, left three sets of thin surgical gloves and three balaclavas in the glovebox. We were going to wear them, no matter how safe we felt, in the knowledge that Lafferty had security cameras in and around his house. If Original was lying about security, underplaying it, or if we took a wrong step, we would be caught on camera, and we couldn't guarantee that we would be able to wipe out all the footage afterwards. We thought we could, but thinking something and knowing it are two different things, and on a job like that we had to know.

It was silent in that car as Ronnie drove us up to Lafferty's house. He seemed focused on that. Grateful, I think, to have something in the present to think about. Took his mind off the near future. There was so much about that boy that reminded me of myself when I was starting out. He didn't have my instinctive toughness, sure, but he was a fast learner and a good judge.

Lafferty was a legit businessman, most of the time. He had a lot of businesses that did a damn good job of covering up his criminality. That meant that he didn't have to hide his money. Everything had a ready explanation, including the mansion. It was in Milngavie of course, on a street we knew wasn't going to be easy to get in and out of unseen. For a start there was nowhere nearby that we could park, because the road up to the house was single-track. All the houses on the street had their own driveways; there wasn't one car parked out on the street itself. These weren't people who usually needed to park on the street when they had double garages and wide driveways for their fleet.

"We can't risk bumming an empty driveway," I said. "If the owners come back with the car there they'll report it. Get round the corner; see what's there."

Nothing much better. Another street with money and more driveways. There were at least a couple of cars parked up at the side of this road, leaving just enough room to pass. Must have been grubby visitors. I was keeping my eyes open, looking for somewhere suitable. I wasn't complaining though because this wasn't a surprise to me, wouldn't have been to Conrad either if he'd been here before. I'd visited Lafferty's house once before and I knew what the approach was like. There was never a great chance that we'd get to park close.

"We're getting too far away," I said quietly. "Just park over there." There was a passing place we could risk stopping in. If we were quick, we would get away with it. "We'll have to risk walking back up."

"Better have our balaclavas on from the start," Conrad said from the back seat. "Good chance a lot of these houses have cameras pointing out to the street."

Ronnie parked the car carefully, making sure there was enough room for any car or van to pass us. Last thing we needed was someone getting our car towed while we were in there. Come out and find it gone. Everything had to be careful from this point on. Precise, that's a better word for it. Timing was vitally important, communication, all the little things that would add up to make a job well done. And it had to be well done. It wasn't enough to go in there and kill Lafferty. Anyone could do that. Killing a man is a challenge that any old halfwit could meet. Doing it well was the difficulty. Doing it well meant walking away without anyone ever knowing that we'd done it.

We pulled our balaclavas over our faces and stepped out of the car. Three men walking along a wealthy street looking like the guiltiest people you ever saw. We must have been quite a sight. You wouldn't have been able to identify us, but it was a better world for everyone if you didn't see us at all. There was urgency now. If anyone did see us they would report us and as soon as we were reported the police would be swarming the area. This now had to be a very quick job, and that wasn't really what I had in mind.

We could kill him quickly, but that, as I just mentioned, was not the same as killing him well. We needed him dead and then we needed to get the body out of the house and out of Glasgow. Bury, burn, sink, whatever: it needed to disappear. With enough time we could gather up everything Lafferty would take if he was doing a runner and destroy that with the body. Give every impression that leaving was his decision.

Round the corner and up the street, not passing anyone, no cars passing us. It was a quiet area; that was one of the reasons people paid good money to live here. That didn't mean we hadn't been spotted, didn't mean we weren't on the clock. We reached the approach to Lafferty's house, a big place with a manicured front garden and a brick driveway. There was a double garage attached to the house, which looked like a new build to me. Last ten years anyway—a splurge of new money.

Whoever had designed the garden was fond of trees and bushes; tall trees were all round the edge of the garden and up to the side of the house. Five-foot bushes ran up either side of the driveway. That was an easy route to get us close to the house, but the information Original had given us didn't look the same in person as it had in his speech. I'd been here, seen the place before, but didn't remember it well. The bushes ran up the sides of the driveway but they stopped before they reached the side of the house. There would be about eight or ten feet where we had nothing to hide behind. We moved in a shuffle, ducking and running up the edge of the driveway, tucked behind those bushes. We were on the grass, running down the side of the house, looking for lights. There had been none visible at the front. I was tired that night, mentally drained, but I was at least alert enough to spot that. We reached the corner and I ducked my head round.

The back garden was as dark as the front. No lights in the garden. The security was bad. Even for a man who thought he was safe and didn't want to alert his neighbors, this was pretty fucking dreadful. I didn't stop to think about it. Should have, but couldn't. We were in a hurry. I glanced up at the back of the building and then pulled my head back.

"Two lights on upstairs, none down," I whispered to the other two.

"His office is up there," Conrad whispered to me.

I was puffing a little, which Ronnie wasn't. We'd only run from the car. It was the sort of run the boy could make on his hands, but me and Conrad were panting after it, stopping at the corner to get our breath as much as to take stock. I had never thought of being older than him as a disadvantage until that moment. Experience comes with downsides.

"Right, we have the key and we have the code for the alarm. Let's get this done fast and get out," I said in a growling whisper.

Ronnie nodded, Conrad probably did too. I had said it for the boy's sake. Conrad, a gunman after all, didn't need to hear that sort of basic instruction. I would be lying to myself to pretend that there wasn't a thrill in what we were doing. Standing in a traitor's back garden with a balaclava on, ready to break into the mansion under cover of darkness. It was a thrill I knew I would hate afterwards, something else to add to the mountain of regret and recrimination, to rob me of my sleep. But for that moment the thrill was perfect. I led the way round the back, and the other two followed.

34

We were silent and slow. Rushing would make noise and we were still trying to be stealthy. The path round the back was narrow, up against the wall. I could see a path leading up to a raised patio, another leading down the side of the garden towards a shed. The whole place was pristine. However much Lafferty was paying his gardener, it wasn't enough.

I'll tell you just how tired I was at that point. As we crouched and waddled along the back wall of the house, I was thinking about how nice a garden like this would be for Becky. Somewhere she could play, have her friends over to play in. She was getting to the age where playing in the garden with her friends was baby-ish and uncool, but still, that's what I was thinking. I was jealous of Lafferty's kids, that they had something Becky lacked. It was un-professional.

The two behind were still letting me lead the way. Ronnie must have thought I had experience at this sort of thing, which I didn't. Sneaking around, setting up a hit. This was gunman's business. This was where Conrad should have been in charge. We were sec-onds away from me taking a backward step and pushing him into the lead. Out in the city, setting things up, organizing, intimidat-ing, I was the senior man. Conrad didn't question that. He let me get on with doing what he knew I was good at. But this was his ter-ritory; this was his life. I needed to step back and let him do it. All I could do was try to seem convincing, make sure I did nothing that drew a snort of derision from the gunman.

That's the thing about the job I do: it gives me no practice at stepping back. Same for all muscle with authority. Our job depends on the respect and fear we get from others. We're the sort of people who feel that taking a single step back is a sign of weakness that we must never show. That made working with a man like Conrad on a job like this more difficult, like it wasn't difficult enough already. It was that sense of needing to show control that had me up the front now, approaching the door of the sun lounge. Ronnie didn't know any better, but I should have handed over the reins to Conrad by now. The superiority was naturally his.

This wasn't how I usually went about my business, Conrad either I would guess. Sneaking around mansions in the suburbs is not how you kill a man in this business, not unless you're in a movie. This was, by every reasonable measurement, a one-man job, but obviously I had to be there. I was the security consultant; I was Currie's eyes on the job. Fine, a two-man job then, but there was no justification for a third wheel. Ronnie was there because I wanted him to learn, because I felt more comfortable having an ally in tow.

My gun, at this point, was tucked inside my coat. It felt heavy and uncomfortable. I had handled a gun before, but only a couple of times. Never fired one. Not once. Hoped I wouldn't have to that night either. A gun doesn't make you tough. There's a saying I heard a few old hands in the industry use: the man with the gun isn't scary, the gun is. Anyone can point a lump of metal at anyone else and pull a trigger. Child's play. I wanted no part of the bastard things, but this was different. We could be outnumbered; Conrad might need backup.

No lights came on as I stopped beside the door. They should have; an automatic light should have been shining on us all at that point. A basic security feature even his neighbors couldn't have objected to. I reached into my pocket and took the key out. Bloody gloves were too small for me; I could feel them tight on my hands.

They were always too small when someone else picked them for me. I have large hands, and people don't think of these things. I slipped the key silently into the lock.

Anything could have happened at that point — the key jamming because it didn't fit, the alarm going off instantly, someone opening fire on us. It was a good point for a set-up to bite us on the arse. But nothing happened. The key slid into the lock, I turned it and slowly pushed the door open, stepping inside. The sun lounge had a couple of unused couches and a door through to the house proper. If this was locked I was going to have to break it. Turned the handle and the door kindly opened for me. The alarm panel was on the left-hand side, just inside the door. *Two three six five.* I tapped the code and the *enter* button. A flashing red light turned to stable green before any noise started screeching round the house.

The three of us were inside. This was the worst part of any job to me, and that might sound like a stupid thing to say given that every part of the job was noxious. Creeping around in close proximity to a target is lousy. Stepping silently through a house to try and get the jump on someone, knowing that a single noise out of place could blow the whole job. I hated that. It was out of step for muscle, rare and awkward. As a big man I much preferred any job that let me walk right in, batter a man and walk back out again.

We went through a large utility room and into the kitchen, a long room with an island and large windows looking out into the garden. We were banking on Lafferty being alone in the house. If he was upstairs in his office alone then we were fine. He wouldn't hear us from up there; this house was full of large rooms and you probably had to shout to be heard from one end of them to the other. But that was dependent on there being no clever bastard skulking about in the darkness downstairs, waiting for us.

I led us out of the kitchen and into the hallway, a wide and long space with a staircase down near the front door. There were doors along the corridor, the sort of places just about anyone could have jumped out from and attacked us. We were all treading slowly on the polished wooden floors. A carpet that cushioned our footsteps would have helped. We moved silently to the bottom of the stairs. It was time to shuffle the order. I stopped, looked behind me for the other two. The plan was for Conrad to go first, but Ronnie didn't realize that. He moved in front of me and started to step carefully up the stairs. I waited and let Conrad get into the middle and I went last. I didn't think about it at the time; I just went up the stairs behind the other two, all of us as silent as the grave.

Ronnie was moving too slowly up the stairs, too worried about making a small noise as he went. Understandable and acceptable in a small house, but this was not a small enough house for a footstep on the stairs to reach Lafferty's office. But Conrad wasn't going to nudge him, push him along a little faster; it would only have scared the kid. The one thing you want the awkward third wheel to be is predictable. He reached the top of the stairs and we were in the upstairs corridor.

The light was on in the corridor, and the door to the large office was ajar. We were walking slowly on carpets thick enough to lose a cat in, approaching the door and hoping that he was going to be where we assumed he would be. It had been, basically, textbook so far. We had used the key and the alarm code; we had made it upstairs without any sign of anyone other than Lafferty being in the house. This was exactly what I wanted, exactly what any gunman would want on a job like this. This was reassuringly perfect.

I was thinking about Conrad at that point. Strange. Should have been thinking about Lafferty. We go in there and we kill him. Then we need to remove him. A lot of work to do to get that done properly. Go through the house and find his personal belongings. Find his security systems and switch everything off before we bring a car up to the house. It would need to be done inside thirty minutes. That's where my mind should have been. This one time, with the tiredness and the awkwardness of the job, it wasn't. I was thinking about Russell Conrad, and what a dangerous little man he was.

You can call me whatever you like. You can call me a bad person, a sociopath, a stain on society. Fine, I wouldn't bother my arse arguing with you on any of those points, because they might all be true. What I never was, not from day one in the business, was stupid. I knew that Conrad, the man with the gun in his hand, the man with all the experience of pulling triggers, was the most dangerous person in that house. I was not the man that anyone should fear most. Ignore my reputation. Ignore the fact that I was big, angry and had a gun of my own. The man who knew how to pull the trigger was the man to fear.

I'd slipped my gun out of my pocket at the top of the stairs, and I was assuming that Conrad had done the same thing with his. Russell Conrad with a gun in his hand, creeping through the shadows of another man's house. That was the stuff of many a person's nightmares. Ronnie had the sense to stop before he reached the door, glancing back. He paused, letting the gunman move in front of him. That was how it should have been from the start. You go to a shooting and you let the gunman go in first. Conrad stepped past him up to the door and paused for just a second, listening. Ronnie was right behind him; me another foot or so back, feeling the weight of the gun in my hand. There was movement in the room, sounded like someone shuffling something, pushing something across a desk maybe. Conrad turned back and nodded to me and Ronnie, the kid standing in between us. He blocked some of my view, but I looked down long enough to catch a glimpse of Conrad's gun held loose and confident in his right hand.

The gunman turned back to the door, still hearing someone moving conspicuously inside. Sounded to my ears like a man who wanted to be heard. That set off an alarm. Lafferty wasn't experienced at set-ups; he was trying too hard. I was too late to notice.

Conrad took a quick step and pushed open the door, entering the room with the gun half raised. Lafferty was opposite the door, on the far side of the long room, standing at the side of his large oak desk. He had a piece of paper in his hand and dropped it as he looked at the door. He and Conrad made eye contact just for a split second before Lafferty looked over the gunman's shoulder at the two figures behind him. Conrad spun round, faced Ronnie, raised the gun and shot him in the forehead.

35

Shouldn't have run upstairs. Should have put their hands up and let the coppers take them in. Didn't think Dyne would react the way he did. He should have seen what the best way out of this was, but he didn't. Now Elliott was stuck in the room with his best friend and his best friend's girl. The woman who had gotten them into this.

Barrett and Elliott were pushing the bed up against the door, trying to block themselves in. Zara was standing back by the window, looking nervous. Dyne looked like he was panicking as he pushed the bed, wide-eyed and sweating. This was the one thing he couldn't stand, the thought of a long stretch. Better to be killed than this. The gun was lying on the bed in front of them. The gun Henson had brought back from the house Nasty had died in. The gun Nasty had died for. Elliott did as he was told, blocking the door, doing a poor job of hiding his reluctance.

Barrett shouted out at the cops when they reached the door. "I'm armed; I have a girl in here." That, Zara and Elliott both knew, was a stupid thing to shout. He was making things worse when they needed to engage in some damage limitation.

They had the bed against the door but that didn't matter — that was only going to slow the police down if they chose to push their way in. The whole idea of resisting, of trying to get away, seemed stupid to Elliott. You don't fight your way out of a corner this tight; you try and talk your way out. He backed away towards the window, towards Cope.

Elliott Parker hated that girl. He had hated her from the first day because he knew Zara Cope was bad news, but now...Now he knew that she was the reason for all this. She had gotten the crew to come up here. She had told them there was a deal here where they could make good money and get out quick. Set up some third-rate loser, kill an easy target and then whatever thug the first guy's boss sends to chase them, and get out. She had been full of shit from the start.

Zara set up the deal and they had all gone along with it. His old mate Dyne had led them up there and Elliott had followed because their friendship ran far deeper than his hatred of Zara. Now Nasty was dead because of it. She wasn't mourning. Wouldn't get any tears out of her for the death of their friend. Nasty had been like a brother to Elliott and Barrett and he was dead because of Zara and her stupid fucking deal.

If only he had been able to make Barrett see how stupid this was. Going up to Glasgow like a bunch of mercenaries, doing a job in a city they didn't know for people they couldn't possibly trust. It was always going to be a disaster, always. Common sense was blinded by money. Blinded by her reassuring words.

Elliott was trying to piece things together. Trying to work out how much the police knew. Must have been when Jess got out that the cops found out about them. He had liked Jess. She looked about fourteen without her makeup. He could have kept her for ages, had a lot of fun with her. Would have been good for her too, he was convinced of that. She just didn't understand. She didn't know that Elliott was the one who stopped her from being killed by Nasty. She didn't understand, so she ran. Ungrateful and stupid. Didn't think she had it in her to go to the police. If she told them all she knew then the police knew a lot.

That idiot Henson shouldn't have let her get away. Neither should Cope. She was in the house with them when it happened; she should have been able to do something about it. Maybe she did do something about it. Maybe she was the one who let the girl out. That thought had been floating through Elliott's mind for a while now. Wouldn't have surprised him if he was correct. He was never surprised to be right.

Didn't matter a damn at that point. This was over. Elliott knew it as soon as the cops came crashing through the front door. Knew it before then. Knew it when Nasty got killed. They should have been out of there then, but she persuaded him to stay. Her, again. Little Zara Cope, whispering bad ideas that sounded oh-so-good.

"We need to hand ourselves over," Elliott whispered to Barrett. He figured the cops would still be outside the door in large numbers, trying to listen in.

"No, we can get out of this," Barrett said. He knew that wasn't true; you could see in his eyes that he knew. He just wanted to believe it so much.

He blamed himself, that was why. Himself was a good place to start, Elliott thought, but she was as much to blame as he was. And, fuck it, they all went along with it, didn't they? He didn't put a gun to their heads to make them go up there with him. Elliott and Nasty could have stayed in Birmingham if they'd really wanted to. The money lured them north. The need to be a part of the group. The need to protect each other.

"We can't get out of this," Elliott said to him. "They got us surrounded. They ain't going to let us out. Either they take us by force or we hand ourselves over. Looks worse if they have to use force. Come on, man, we have to give this up."

He hated saying it. Hated it. Couldn't believe that they'd reached the point where they were going to give themselves over to the cops. Since day one of their careers Elliott was the one who thought they would always get away with it. He thought they would have no problem staying one step ahead of every enemy in town. Their mix of skills, his strategic mind. It would always work for them. Now he had to admit that they were done.

"Don't…Just fucking don't," Barrett said to the room in general. He was whispering, trying to keep his voice down and failing.

Elliott didn't say anything for a few seconds, but that was as long as he could leave it. The longer this went on, the worse the consequences would be for them. They were getting damn close to the time when the police could start to dress this up as some kind of dramatic stand-off and use that against them in court. If they walked out quickly they could make it look like a misunderstanding. Make it seem like they were just scared by the cops crashing in, didn't realize who it was. Their mate had just been killed and they were scared witless, that sort of thing. Maybe not a great excuse, but better than the nothing Barrett was offering.

"Come on, man, you know this ain't happening. We're in the corner, right, and the only way out is with our hands up. Live to fight another day, that sort of thing."

"We'll get time, big time," Barrett said to him, the sort of whisper that made it clear he wanted to shout.

"What for? Nasty killed that Christie guy, that was it. We haven't done anything else, not really. We get done for possession of the gun, it's a few years, I don't know what they give you up here. Give it three years and we'll be back down home, chanting 'Shit on the Villa' and pretending Birmingham and Wolves aren't an embarrassment to us. There's nothing else they can do us for. The girl that ran, she could be a problem, but maybe our employer keeps her quiet to help us out. Keeps her away from court," he said, more in hope than expectation. "Least he could do."

"Exactly," Cope said, the first thing she'd said. "There's no way that girl is going to stand in a dock and point the finger at any of us; he won't let that happen. There's nothing major that they can pin on any of us. Maybe possession of a weapon, but they can't prove who it belongs to. It'll be a short term," she said.

Elliott wanted to say, yeah, it'll be a short term for you. They got nothing on you, sweetheart—you'll be walking free in months.

But he agreed with her, so he fought down the urge to provoke and kept his mouth shut.

"Give it a few months and we'll all be back down south," she said. It was hard to tell if Barrett believed her; maybe he was hyper enough to believe anything just then. He was walking in a small circle, blinking heavily. "We can be down south and forget about this," she went on in a calm voice. "We can start again. We still have half the money from this job. That's something. We can start again, Dyne."

She was persuasive. In that little room, with decor that had fallen out of an eighties catalogue, the bed pushed against the door, the cops surrounding the building, you would have believed that everything was hunky-dory. Zara Cope could persuade you of just about anything you wanted to believe. It was easy to see and hear why Barrett had fallen under her spell. If she had been speaking to him like this all along, Jesus, it was no wonder. She might even have gotten inside Elliott's head if she'd bothered to try.

"I don't want to have to start again. I don't want to be always starting again," he said to her. His tone wasn't rough though, not as rough as it had been with Elliott. He was relaxing. She was getting through to him.

"It wouldn't be starting again," she said to him, going across and intercepting him as he circled. She stopped him and put a hand on each arm, looked him in the eye. "It would be starting for the last time. This would be it. Get this out of the way, serve whatever time they give us, and when we get back together in Birmingham we have the chance to make proper plans. We'll have enough money to plan what we want to do, not what other people want us to do for them. We won't need other people's help, other people's jobs. This'll be it. We just have to pay this price first."

He was looking into her eyes as she was talking. It was impossible to tell if he believed her or not. Barrett was always too smart to really believe that sort of thing. If they went down, they would go down for different terms. Him and Elliott, maybe months if they were lucky, years more likely. If Zara was lucky, she wouldn't get anything at all. She could plead ignorance of everything and Barrett would back her up. She would be long gone before they got out. At least two of the people in the room knew that, maybe all three. But Barrett wanted to believe her. He wanted her to give him an excuse to end this thing because he was smart enough to know, once the panic and anger faded, that they were finished.

"Yeah," he said, "we can build something."

"We can build something amazing," she said to him.

Elliott stayed silent, watching the witch pouring a little more poison into his best friend's ear. He watched it and he didn't say anything, because it suited him to say nothing. He needed to get out of there in one piece as well and that meant winning Barrett round. Meant Zara winning him round, because she was so much better at it. Meant her getting even more power. When Barrett looked at Elliott, Elliott nodded. Barrett nodded back and they began pulling the bed away from the door, leaving the gun where it was.

"We're coming out," Elliott shouted into the corridor. "We're unarmed. We have our hands up." Everything he thought they wanted.

There was only one cop in the corridor, Fisher. He was doing his best to look tough, not much of an expression on his face. He looked at Zara longer than he looked at either of the other two. That rather gave away the fact that he knew her. The look he gave her wasn't friendly, and that was all the reassurance she needed. She was going to be fine. Nate was as good as his word. Fisher had her under arrest, and he was furious because he was going to let her go. Some uniformed cops came running up the stairs and cuffed the three prisoners. They swept into the bedroom to look for any more trouble.

The three of them were taken away in separate cars. Fisher went in the car with Barrett, presuming that he would be the one with the most interesting things to say. Elliott watched them putting Zara Cope into the back of a car. She looked so relaxed, like she already knew the ending. She owned this whole thing. That woman was the most dangerous person he'd ever worked with.

36

It didn't register. I knew what had happened, but I couldn't allow myself to think about it. I had less than a second to react, and if I lost my focus I would be the next man dead. Everything shut out. All I could think about was the threat to me and how I could protect myself. I couldn't think about Ronnie being killed. It makes me seem like a horrible person, I know that. The idea that I could ignore such a thing. But it was that or die. I didn't choose to ignore it.

Instinct. That's the thing that experience brings you, that exhaustion overwhelms. I should have known. I should have seen the signs. That survival instinct is different from normal instinct, different from anything else. Doesn't matter how tired you are, it can still kick you in the brain. It can wipe away every other thought, every other fear, and leave you with just one focus. Stay alive. Don't kid yourself into thinking that it takes a certain kind of person to think that way. Maybe some would freeze, or react too slow, but many would react instantly. You don't know.

Conrad turned and raised the gun. He shot Ronnie in the forehead, dead center. The shot so loud, so close. Ronnie was between me and Conrad, between the gunman and his next target. I was right behind Ronnie. His body fell backwards into my arms. I threw my left arm around the body. I'm calling it his body because it wasn't Ronnie anymore. He was dead and he was just a body to me now. I held the body in place with my left arm, using it as a shield, and raised my right hand round the side of it. Conrad still had his gun raised but he was trying to pick a shot, taking time to avoid hitting Ronnie again. I raised the gun and fired.

Nothing. Not a thing. The trigger moved under my finger, but there was no shot. Little resistance when I pulled it. Garvey had sold me a dud. Given me, I should say, not sold. Quite happily ran upstairs and picked two guns from his collection. One for Conrad, one for me. He picked them carefully. Made sure the gunman got a gun that worked. Made sure that what I got was as dangerous as a banana. Garvey and Conrad, both hired by Lafferty. I went to Conrad, and I thought that meant I could trust his conversion. Garvey was a gun dealer; he would sell to Conrad because I told him to. They were both playing me. Working with Lafferty all along. That was why the gun made no sound. It was designed to kill me from the start.

The gun was always unfamiliar to me. Instinct told me to use it because it was in my hand, because it was the fastest way to remove the threat. Now my instinct was telling me to fall back on the thing that had always served me so well in dangerous situations. My brutality. I had to act in a heartbeat, knowing Conrad was about to fire. I shoved Ronnie forwards. His body crashed into Conrad as Conrad fired his second shot. It was meant for me; it hit Ronnie instead. Shooting a dead man. Conrad stumbled when Ronnie hit him, a dead weight, but he wasn't going to stumble when I hit him. I lunged as soon as I pushed the body. Threw all my considerable bulk at Conrad and hit him hard as he took a backwards step and pushed Ronnie's body aside.

I caught him mostly with my shoulder in his chest, the top of my head striking the underside of his jaw as I stooped. He tumbled backwards. I don't think I stayed still in any part of this. As soon as he was falling I lunged forwards again, down on top of him. He landed hard and before he could react, I hit him. I still had the dud gun in my hand and it was time for it to earn its keep. My arm was out behind me as I went down, using my momentum and the power of the swing to hit the gunman with my gun. I hammered it into the top of Conrad's head. Once, twice, and hammered him again. I felt a crack, and then with another blow I felt his skull crumple. I kept hitting him. I don't know why.

I had never killed a man before that moment. For all my reputation, and as close as I'd come, I had never killed a man before I killed Russell Conrad. I'd beaten people. Beaten them hard. But killing a man, that's something different. I killed him; I didn't murder him. To my mind there's a distinction. I killed Conrad because he was going to kill me. I defended myself. It wasn't self-defense that had me hitting him with all of my force, though, mouth tight shut as the sweat broke out across me. I was expelling energy, telling myself that I was making sure, telling myself that he deserved this for what he had done to Ronnie, admitting to myself that my fury was selfish.

That was enough. The top of his skull was crushed in. One eye was wide open, the other forced shut by the collapsed skull. His mouth was open, his balaclava twisted up to show it, but he hadn't made a sound throughout. I leaned back, still on my knees, Conrad underneath me. This was my fault. I could have stopped this. I should have seen it. That's where the anger came from. Smashing the butt of the gun into the top of Conrad's skull was no kind of catharsis. I was just following my instinct. Violence was the only language in which I was ever truly fluent. I was a master of it, every syllable, every pronunciation. Every noun and verb was under my command, and I was singing it all in perfect clarity in Lafferty's office. It made no difference. Nothing would make me feel better. This was one of those failures that would settle down to become a lifetime regret.

Lafferty was still standing there. Standing still at the side of his desk, watching me kill his man. His eyes were a little wider, but that was his only reaction. His plan had failed. Get me there with Conrad, have Conrad kill me. It was a smart little plan. Having

Ronnie there was the only thing that saved me, the only thing that stopped Lafferty getting exactly what he wanted. Would have been a great plan. Big horrible Nate Colgan, working for Kevin Currie, tried to kill him, which proves that little Kevin Currie is a traitor.

He didn't try to run. Despite all that had happened, despite the time it had taken me to kill Conrad, Lafferty hadn't made any attempt to get out. I was blocking the only exit and Lafferty had no hope of fighting his way past me. He didn't have a gun of his own, probably didn't want one. He had a gunman, which he had thought was better. He knew what had to happen next, and somewhere in his conniving mind he had accepted it and didn't fear it anymore. The fear had been in the approach, not the destination. When he finally realized that the business he'd chosen was about to kill him, the fear walked away and left Lafferty to face the moment with a sliver of dignity.

The only sound in the room was my heavy breathing. Down on my knees, looking across at Lafferty. Watching him and thinking that he should have made a dive for Conrad's gun. That's what I would have done, because I might have had a chance of succeeding. Not Lafferty. Too old and podgy and used to sitting behind a desk. Diving for the working gun would just have been a quicker way to die, and he wasn't in any hurry. A dying man always wants to take a few more breaths. Lafferty wanted to look around his office at the pictures of his wife and children, to see that he had created something good among all the bad. Those last few seconds mattered to him and he wasn't going to throw them away in some pathetic attempt at proving his courage and manhood by challenging me.

Conrad's gun was out of his hand, lying on the floor beside the two of us. I could reach out and pick it up. And I was alert; you must understand that. I wasn't swinging my arm wildly throughout, wasn't screaming and shouting as I killed Conrad. I was hammering the gun into the top of Russell's head, killing him, giving his dead body more punishment than the body cared about, but I wasn't completely out of control. As I leaned back, blood dripping off the handle of the gun in my hand, I watched Lafferty through the eyeholes of my balaclava. Watched him watching me. Watched him wait for me to kill him.

There was eye contact. Just a split second where Lafferty met my steady gaze and we both knew where the next step took us. Lafferty would have known that I'd never killed before — everyone knew that. It was one part of my reputation I was happy for the world to know. But Lafferty wasn't daft and he'd have heard all the stories about the times I beat people bad enough to make them wish I'd just killed them instead. I was a man of violence. A man who not only practiced brutality, but controlled it and was in turn controlled by it. That was the reputation. Also, I had a gun and he didn't. Lafferty wasn't some fearless giant, some warrior who'd been through every terror the world had to offer and would stand up to a gun. He'd spent most of his adult life behind a desk, filling in paperwork and giving orders for dirty work to be done by others when dirty work was required. Put a gun in the hands of an already frightening man and he was paralyzed by it.

I was finished with Conrad. I dropped my gun, more useful than Garvey had ever intended, onto the floor, reached across to pick up Conrad's and got slowly to my feet. My legs were stiff, my back as well. I could feel a throb developing in my right shoulder. That wasn't age, that was the intensity of the event. Every muscle had tightened; my head was starting to throb. I stood up straight, maybe stretched a little. I wasn't going to rush. There was a chance that there were other people in the house, hiding somewhere, ready to run in at the sound of a gun. That's how I would have worked it. Have them waiting to remove the body as soon as the body hits the ground. That's how a pro does it. Not how Lafferty had plotted this out. I stood near the doorway of that silent room and I didn't hear anyone coming. Lafferty wasn't a pro, whatever he had told himself. He hadn't organized this properly. He was going to wait until I was dead and then call someone in. Or him and Conrad were going to do the removal themselves. Bad strategy.

So I had time. The only part of me that he could see would be my eyes and I wasn't letting him avoid them. I stared straight at him. There was hatred in my eyes, I'm sure. Angus Lafferty was stupidly rich. He had more money than he or his kids were ever likely to spend, a big house, a happy family. If he didn't like what the organization was doing then he could have found some path that would lead him away from us. You can always find a way out. Might have been complicated, he might have had to leave the city to feel safe, but he could have done it. Instead he went the other way. His greed and his stupidity led him to try and take the organization for himself. That made more sense to this rich man than walking away. That greed was why all this had happened.

I was breathing heavily, holding the gun down by my side as I walked across the room towards Lafferty. I wanted him right in front of me, to get a good clean shot. Lafferty didn't react. I wanted to look him in the eyes, wanted him to be afraid and to see that he understood this was his fault. I wanted to see some sort of guilt. Fear was easy. I didn't need to stare him down and wave a gun in his face to achieve that. I could coax fear to the surface of any man with very little effort. But that bastard wasn't going to give me any satisfaction; he could see the end coming and he was determined to be defiant. We both stood still and looked each other in the eye like we didn't know what to do next. He seemed to be looking for some sort of emotion in mine that he wasn't going to find. Professionalism, I've heard a lot of them call it, when you go into the emotional dead zone and care nothing for anyone else. That's not what I would call it; it's closer to some sort of psychological disorder if you ask me, but there were some who were capable of it. Gunmen, mostly, but not exclusively. I had found that place and I had put myself there.

Lafferty opened his mouth slightly, trying to come up with some last words. He wasn't trying to save himself, but everyone wants to have some smart last words. Nobody had said a word since we were outside the house. There had been a blast of noise from Conrad's gun and my reaction, and then silence for the last minute or two. The last words that come out of anyone's mouth should be taken with a massive pinch of salt; I had heard some ridiculous begging from people who thought they were going to die. People would say anything they thought would make you pause, any desperate lie that might buy them several more seconds or an end to their pain. I wouldn't listen to a word that came out of the mouth of a man looking down the barrel of a gun, but I was letting him live just long enough to say it.

"You don't understand what they've done to you," he said to me. Said it quietly, and I was surprised at how calm and steady his voice was.

I kept my dead face. No expression in my eyes that would give away what I was thinking. I raised the gun. His expression didn't change either; he seemed determined to take his exit with the same carefully constructed dignity with which he had lived his life. Always saw himself as a step above the rest of us. Always saw himself as legitimate. When he had tried to move away from that, this is where he ended up. Trying to conjure what little grace was left to a man on the wrong end of a gun. He was well dressed; in the mansion his efforts had bought him; his family were as safe as they could be and would inherit well from his legitimate businesses.

I shot him in the head. He fell back beside the desk. The first man I'd ever murdered. This one I couldn't explain away as self-defense; this one was murder. I had walked up to a man posing me no further threat, raised a gun and shot him in the head. I was a murderer. A cold-blooded killer. I had crossed the line. They say that once you cross it, you can never go back. Once you become a gunman, you stay a gunman. Not because you want to, but because your employers make you. A good gunman is hard to come by and they don't let people walk away. Wasn't going to work out that way for me; I had the power to make sure it didn't. I would find another gunman for the organization, and I would go back to hating myself for the one time I murdered a man.

There was a lot I would have to do. A clean-up that would be far bigger than expected. Should have been Conrad doing the killing and me and Ronnie doing the clean-up. Now I was alone in the house, looking at three bodies, thinking about getting Lafferty's belongings. We had considered a burial, but that would have to change now. Three bodies meant burning them: find a furnace somewhere, properly get rid. Couldn't do it alone. This was a four- or five-man job now.

I would have to use Lafferty's house phone to call Conn. Him and Mikey could come round, bring some help with them. It would take too long, there was a good chance of being spotted and the aftermath was going to be near impossible to explain. There would have to be repercussions for Mark Garvey and Original Carlisle. People who had backed Lafferty, like Stuart Crockley, would be out of the business. More changes coming and I would be at the center of it. I needed to move fast, but I didn't. I stood in that office and I breathed out slowly. I was Nate Colgan, murderer.

37

The clean-up, in the end, was easy. Conn and Mikey brought along a kid called BB and the four of us moved fast. Got the three bodies into a van they'd brought, got a good bundle of Lafferty's belongings to go with them. Two bags of clothes, financial documents, credit cards, driver's license, passport. We managed to find his security room, deleted footage going back a few days to try and make it seem as though the security had failed long before we got to it. It was by no means perfect, but it was a good start.

"What about Original?" I asked Conn as we locked up the house.

"Let him go. It's finished, isn't it? Figured it was fine to let him go."

The uncomfortable shrug he gave me said as much as the words. I sat in their van, went with them to the industrial park to get rid of everything. They dropped me a few streets from my house and continued on their way to clean out the van. I walked back to the house, went inside and took off every item of clothing I was wearing. Should have been incinerated, but nobody had brought spares for me. I would do it myself.

A change of clothes did nothing for my mood. There was so much wrong with it all. I could sense the errors as they floated around my mind, the little clues that told me I had been part of a very different act to the one advertised. People were performing parts, and I hadn't quite worked out who was playing who. Too tired.

Not too tired to think about Ronnie though. That likeable, harmless young man that I had seen at the hotel. Pushed him to come work for me, because I got it into my head that I needed someone to work with me. Convinced myself that I would be a mentor, he would be my little protégé and I would transform him into the person I wanted him to be. It was arrogant and childish. It got him killed.

Every time I thought of Ronnie, I thought of his girlfriend. Esther Mayberry, her name was. A young woman I had met only very briefly, but had heard an endless amount about. Ronnie had loved to talk about her. Loved to brag about her as subtly as he possibly could. How pretty she was, how smart she was, how funny she was. She would be sitting in their flat right now, waiting for him to come home. She wouldn't be nervous yet. He would have told her he was going to be late so she would still be confident that he'd come home. I couldn't get the picture of her out of my mind. I could hardly remember what she looked like, but in my mind there was a pretty young woman sitting in a flat, watching the clock tick and beginning to wonder.

She was innocent. One of the genuinely innocent people whose life had been scarred by me. There were plenty who called themselves innocent but weren't. Plenty who knew the risks they were taking. But this girl…she started dating Ronnie when they were practically kids, and they were going to spend their lives together. Now she was sitting in their flat, the fear starting to creep up on her.

I pulled on a coat and got into my car. Drove straight round to their flat and parked down the street. My professionalism was screaming at me, telling me to turn around and go home. Just because she deserved to know, didn't mean she needed to. She would find out eventually, or work it out. Someone could tell her, someone from the organization. Make sure she didn't make a noise going to the police about it. But it didn't need to be now and it didn't need to be me.

None of that mattered. I couldn't stop myself. I owed this much to Ronnie, if not to the girl. Esther I didn't know. I'd nodded to her once when I was round at their flat after Ronnie got beaten up on a job. Ronnie was my responsibility. I pulled him into the business; he was learning from me. Whatever decomposing shred of decency I had left told me that I had to go up to that flat and tell that girl that Ronnie wasn't coming home. It was one of those very rare occasions where that shred won.

Don't know how long I stood outside the front door of the flat. A few minutes, probably, long enough to look very suspicious if anyone saw me. A big guy, standing outside the door, arm resting on the wall while I tried to pluck up the courage to knock. Courage. That's a laugh. I never feared a job. Every scumbag I beat up, everyone I pushed toward destruction, not one of them scared me. That was work and work was what I did. This? I don't know what this was. Guilt, I suppose, and that scared me. Hadn't felt it before.

I knocked on the door and waited. It was dark out there, after eleven o'clock I think. Maybe she was getting ready for bed, just starting to worry about Ronnie. Took her a while to get to the door. When she did, she opened it an inch and peeked out at me. She gave me the look most people do when they see me on their doorstep. The look of a person intimidated by my size and my expression. She was smaller than I remembered, a short, thin little thing with dark eyes and dark hair tied back. She looked younger than Ronnie, and he was just a kid to me. She had a decent office job somewhere, according to Ronnie. A smart girl.

"Esther?"

"Yes."

"Can I come in? I have to talk to you about Ronnie."

Esther was already trying not to cry. I didn't need to talk to her about Ronnie; she had instantly guessed correctly about Ronnie. She opened the door wider and stepped back. I walked in and closed the door. We stood in the corridor. She hadn't moved an inch, standing there with her arms folded, looking up at me. She didn't want me any further inside the flat and I didn't much want to go any further. Didn't want to see the reminders of Ronnie's happy life before I got involved in it.

"I work with Ronnie. I don't know if you remember me, I was here before."

She nodded slightly. "I remember you." Said in the sort of tone that made it clear she'd like to forget.

I nodded to that, accepting that she had every right to speak that way. Ronnie was weak and I had pulled him into the industry. She hated me for it, for exploiting him. Something we could agree on. I tried to keep my expression as steady as possible, but I knew my guilt was horribly visible.

"Ronnie isn't coming home," I said to her. My tone was sad; there was no way she wouldn't know what I meant.

Esther started to shake, trying to wrap her arms more tightly around her to stop the shaking. When I spoke again I don't think she heard me, don't think she paid any attention to it. She was off in a world of her own in which there was only room for her and her grief.

"Obviously I'll do all that I can to help you at this time," I said, speaking low, my voice turning into a growl. "Ronnie was very important to us, and we'll do anything we can to help you." I was rambling. I didn't know what to say to her, and I don't think it mattered. She didn't hear any of what was said. She was just staring straight ahead.

"Please leave," she said. It was a whisper with a sob in the middle of it, but I understood her.

I turned and left the moment she told me to. I wasn't going to hang around, traumatizing her further. I made my way back downstairs and to the car. Drove home, feeling things I didn't often feel. I had lost people before. I had seen people that I could describe as friends being cut down by the industry. Sad as it was,

it left little mark on me. That might be callous, but the business re-
lies on men as grim and unpleasant as me. Ronnie was not a grim
or unpleasant man.

This wasn't over. God, that sounds clichéd. Sounds like I was
sitting there, hell-bent on getting revenge for my fallen friend.
I wasn't. Revenge isn't something you go after in this business.
You'd never get anything else done. Wouldn't live very long either.
But there were a few more things that needed to be sorted out be-
fore I could move along with my life.

There was something I could do for Ronnie. Or for Esther, which
amounted to the same thing now. He would want her to be safe
and financially secure; he would want his friends to be looked after at a time when they were under pressure. I would have one last
meeting with Zara. Make sure she was leaving for good; make sure
she understood not to come back.

When all of that was sorted in the back of my mind, I was able
to push forward my other doubts. Looking back at the whole situation, from my employment by Kevin Currie onwards, was like
looking at a picture slightly out of focus. I could see the people, I
could see the places, but the details were all smudged. It felt deliberate. It felt like the things that didn't make sense were supposed
to be confusing to me. It felt like I'd been lied to. Follow the money.
That's what they always say. You want to work out who's behind
something, you sit down at the end of it all and you follow the
money. Whoever's benefited most is the person you're looking for.

38

I slept that night. It was broken, sure, but it was more sleep than I'd gotten for days. Maybe I'd foolishly persuaded myself that I'd hit rock bottom, that I couldn't possibly do anything worse. Maybe I had just reached the point where I was so tired that sleep couldn't be avoided. Whatever the reason, I woke up the following morning feeling as refreshed as I had in days. It cleared my mind.

I got a phone call a little before eight o'clock. I had only just gotten out of the shower at that point, much later than usual.

"She'll be out at nine o'clock." That was all Fisher could bring himself to say before he hung up.

So Zara would be my start to the day. Better to get her out of the way early. Have whatever information she could give me before I confronted the bigger beast. Fisher would go easy on her. Whatever he was, he was trustworthy. About the only person in my life at that point that I could say that about. The poor bastard probably wouldn't even interview her, let someone softer do that. If he was following her around as she suspected then he had to hate her. Hate was about the only thing that would motivate a man like Fisher to traipse around the city after a girl like Zara. Now he had to let her walk away.

Because the call was so short, I had no idea who else he had arrested. Word hadn't reached me yet, but people in the business would know. If he got Zara then he must have gotten Barrett. That part of the plan had worked then. Barrett would be looking at years, the rest of his crew as well if Fisher had gotten them.

I managed to get parked just along the street from the sterile-looking police station, and waited. It was bang on nine o'clock when the front door opened and she emerged. She was a little disheveled after her night in the cells, but she always looked good disheveled. A man was holding the door open for her, talking to her. Fisher. Neither of them looked impressed with the conversation; neither of them saw me.

Zara moved away from Fisher onto the street and started walking. She had the look of a woman with somewhere to go. Looking for a taxi, eager to put some distance between her and the police station. Eager to get somewhere valuable, I figured. Even then I thought about leaving, letting her get on with whatever she was doing. But she was the one I had to confront, for the sake of my own peace of mind. Fuck's sake, even then I could hardly face her.

She walked past the sandwich shop on the corner and disappeared out of view. I started the car and drove after her. She was walking briskly along the street, scrolling through her phone. I pulled up on the road beside her, lowering the passenger-side window.

"Get in," I said, because I couldn't think of anything smarter or friendlier.

Zara stopped and looked at the car. Looked like she was thinking of refusing and then thought better of it. Refusal was an option, but it was a hell of a long way down the list. She opened the door and dropped in. I pulled away so that I wouldn't block the traffic, but I had no idea where I was going. I started with the chit-chat.

"Fisher play soft with you?"

She shrugged. "Fisher didn't play with me at all. He arrested me, but it was another cop that interviewed me. Got a night in the cells, then a gentle pawing from DC Davies. You heard of DC Davies? Chubby little guy."

I hadn't.

"Soft as a good pillow," she went on. "Asked me some questions I could have asked myself, they were that obvious. Asked me about Dyne, about his crew."

"Dyne?"

"Adrian's nickname. I told him I didn't know anything about why they were up here. Told him I was scared of what they were doing. He believed me. Sympathized with me by the time I was done with him." There was a smile in her voice by the end that I didn't like. Her plan had been a stupid one, and if it hadn't been for my deal with Fisher she would be looking at years inside.

"What did he ask you, exactly?"

"Nothing about your lot. Didn't mention them. Asked about Adrian's crew and I gave them names and basic information. Asked about what I knew, I told them nothing. Asked about the stand-off at the house."

"Stand-off?"

"Adrian, Elliott and me blocked ourselves in a room. Adrian's idea. We had to go along with it. He had a gun. I tried to play it down, make it seem like a misunderstanding. Police kicking in the front door and screaming at us, we didn't know who they were, Nasty had been murdered. Told him we panicked, that Adrian was trying to protect me, that sort of thing. Help Adrian out a little; least I can do."

"Uh-huh. Fisher was talking to you at the door."

"He was. Walked me out, gave me a little lecture about bad things happening to the men in my life. Do you think bad things happen to all the men in my life, Nate?"

She was getting playful. "What else did he say?"

"I had prepared myself for some tough questions, but nope, nothing. Told me that it would be in my best interests to leave the city," she said with a sigh. Didn't like that I wasn't playing along. "Made it clear that if I stuck around he'd be watching out for me, waiting for an excuse to arrest me."

That sounded about right. Also sounded like nothing she'd be concerned about. She had no intention of sticking around; even Fisher had to realize that. There were so many more dangerous people that he could have gone chasing after, people doing far more damage. What was his obsession with Zara? There was something about her that he couldn't get out of his head and I don't think it was the fact that she was a pretty, though deteriorating, young woman. Zara represented something that he couldn't stop hating, couldn't stop thinking about. She was the kind of person that turned others into the criminals he hated so much. He saw her as the creator of the kind of evil he spent his life chasing down. Which led me on to the next awkward moment of conversation.

"Where's the money?" I asked her.

She paused, trying to think of a clever answer. Maybe some reference to the money she'd taken out of the bank account I had created for her.

"What money?" was the best she could come up with after a six-second pause, which was disappointing. Expected better of Zara.

"That crew came up here working a job. They didn't do it on a promise. They were paid half up front, right? Half up, half after. I'll take a guess that they were offered a good amount as well to come all the way up here and provoke a war, start something that would bring down a whole organization. What was it, six figures?"

The glance she gave me said I was close enough to the truth for her to assume that I already knew everything. I was guessing, but we'll call it an educated guess because a man of my experience knows how these things work.

"So?" she asked. Going down the petulant route, another disappointment.

"So Barrett and his mates are looking at a long time inside. Double-digit years, I'd guess, depending how much of the Christie killing they can pin on them. They were paid half up front. That's where you're going right now, isn't it? Going to get the money so you can disappear out of the city."

I was driving, watching the road, so I didn't see the look she gave me. I doubt it was wreathed in smiles and intended to compliment my brilliant deduction.

"So?" was her answer to it.

"So I'll give you a lift to your money and we can chat on the way."

"No," she said quickly. "No offense, Nate, but I want to get out and I want to get out as clean as possible. Someone's holding the money for me. I don't want you to know who because I don't want you leaning on them. We can chat, fine, but I'm leaving here without dropping anyone else in the shit, right?"

So we drove aimlessly. Didn't make much difference to me — the conversation was all I was here for.

"So did you call him or did he call you?" I asked.

"Who?"

"Kevin Currie. At the start of this, I want to know who pitched the idea first."

I wasn't supposed to know. They would have been keeping this between as few people as possible, and they obviously preferred the idea of keeping me in the dark. Perhaps because I was so close to Zara, or because I wasn't a senior man in their eyes. Didn't matter. I knew enough, and I wanted to know more.

"Me, I suppose," she said with a shrug. "I called him first."

That's what I had figured. She pitches the idea of having her own crew, asks if there's any money drifting around they could work for. Kevin thinks about it, takes it to Jamieson, the boss decides to use them to get rid of Lafferty, a man he no longer trusts. Their mistake was using me to make it happen.

"Wasn't much of a plan," I told her. "Relying on luck to get you away from your man like that."

"I wasn't relying on luck," she said. "I had other ways of doing it; you just complicated matters. I dealt with it."

"Yeah." I nodded. "You did."

I looked at the clock in the car: nine fifteen. I blessed those few hours of sleep; without them I couldn't have handled Zara. Couldn't have handled any of the things that I still had to do that day.

I made the decision to stop turning to look at Zara, even when we were stopped in traffic. Every look was a reminder of other times, and every reminder was a lie. We had never been happy, not really, not in the way normal people were happy. We could never be together again. I had to stop looking at her before the lies caught me out.

We drove in silence for a few more minutes, before I got frustrated with how the non-conversation was going and pulled into the car park of a large DIY store. This wasn't some attempt to stop somewhere quiet and out of the way where I could say or do something terrible; even on a Monday morning the place was quite busy. I parked, switched the engine off, swallowed my emotions and talked.

"You need to leave the city," I said to her.

"Seem to be hearing that a lot today," she said with a smirk. The look I gave her in reply killed the smile and she got serious instead. "I know."

"The money you're getting, that'll start you off?"

"Should do, yeah."

"How much is it?"

She paused, didn't want to mention the price she had put on people she was supposed to care about.

"Well?" I asked.

"Fifty grand," she said, and I believed her.

It was a decent price, enough to persuade a person like Zara to betray anyone and everyone. She could start again with that money. Get out of Glasgow, out of Scotland. Find another city, another life. I knew her well enough to know that the next phase of her life wouldn't work out very differently from every other phase she'd gone through. She only knew one way to live.

Maybe she'd have done it for less. Wouldn't surprise me if Zara had been planning on throwing Barrett overboard from the very minute she met him. That was Zara's default setting, trying to exploit every person she knew. It told me that every instinct I'd had about her in the last few years was correct. I needed to keep her away from Becky.

"That was a nasty thing to do, Zara," I said quietly. Don't know why I said it. I was probably trying to set up the demand I was planning to make of her, trying to justify something I hadn't yet said.

Zara Cope was willing to take criticism on a lot of subjects and from a lot of people, but she wasn't willing to be dismissed as a nasty piece of work by the nastiest piece she'd met.

"You have a problem, Nate," she said to me, all the playfulness falling out of her while she gripped her courage and criticized me to my face. "You think you're the good guy. You think you're a good man doing bad things reluctantly. You think you're forced into these things by the actions of others, the reluctant anti-hero. You're not the good guy, Nate. Only you think you are. The rest of the world knows that you're the bad guy. You're the threat that richer people use, you're the creative punishment for the really unfortunate, the man that the beasts are scared of. You could walk away but you don't; you keep on doing the job. I know you want to protect Rebecca from me, but who protects her from you? You need to stop kidding yourself, Nate. You're the bad guy."

There was silence in the car for what felt like an age. It was awkwardly long, and any words that broke it would have to fight through that tension. She was right, obviously. I don't need to tell you that. She was articulating the very thoughts I'd had about myself for the best part of fifteen years. In those fifteen years I had never found a good answer to those criticisms, so I moved us on to my demand. Perhaps threat would be a better word.

"Listen Zara, you need to get out of the city and you need to stay out. Find somewhere else to live, somewhere else to run to, somewhere else to be you. This city isn't safe for you anymore."

I wasn't just referring to the police. They were in the mix, but there was a growling undertone that told her the greatest threat came from the man she was looking at. This was my way of telling her that I wouldn't let her back into my life. I wouldn't be the safety net she came falling towards if her next adventure failed. It wasn't the same macho nonsense as Fisher telling her to stay out of his city, like he was some Wild West sheriff and she was an admittedly adorable Clint Eastwood impersonator. This was me making it clear that my life was now officially off limits. She was out, and she had to stay out or I would push her out. When I push people, they fall far. There was a little threat in there, which from me was more frightening than any big threat from anyone else in her world.

"I know," she said to me. "Goodbye, Nate."

She looked me in the eyes and I could see that it hurt her, even if only a little. I didn't want to do this to Zara, throw her out of my life. We were silent for a few seconds, showing each other our regrets. Zara opened the car door and got out into the car park. I drove away, not daring to look in the mirror. She was out of my life.

39

You get used, in a very short space of time, to having people chattering in your ear. The boss wants something done, an inexperienced guy is asking your permission for something, a colleague wants a hand with something. Phone calls and knocks at the door. It had been frantic, the whole of the previous week. That day was nothing.

After I left Zara I went back home. It was Monday morning; there was nothing happening in the world. The place was groggy, back to work after a weekend off. Now was my time to rest. Back to the house and into the silence of a long day filled with nothing. No phone calls. No knocks on the door. That seemed wrong to me, the day after something so big. People should have been in touch. Kevin Currie should have been calling to talk about it before he got in touch with Peter Jamieson.

I knew why he wasn't. The kernel of it had formed when I called Conn and asked him and Mikey to come and help with the clean-up at Lafferty's. They had let Original go. That had surprised me, but it shouldn't have. Original was a plant. He was Currie's man, working for Lafferty. He went to Ronnie's friend's shop so that he would get quickly rumbled and questioned by me because that would speed things along nicely. They let him go because he'd played his part to perfection. That meant one or both of Conn and Mikey were in on it.

I would guess only Conn. You didn't need Mikey to be in on the secret; he would go along and do the work no matter what.

But Currie needed Conn to know so that there would be a man on the street who understood what was happening. Didn't want me to know. Maybe didn't trust me. I wasn't his choice; I was Jamieson's. That worked against me, kept me in the dark. So Conn knew. Which meant Billy Patterson, his boss, had to know. But Marty didn't. No way would he have let me batter his brother like that if he did. He thought Adam was working for the enemy. His brother thought he was working for the enemy. Only a chosen few knew.

Showed how little trust there was. Showed that Kevin wasn't fit to be the leader of this organization. He had gotten away with it, after a fashion, but it would have been a much smoother piece of work if Peter Jamieson had been on the outside to work it. There's a lot to be said for keeping as many people in the dark as possible, but you have to give a little light to the right people.

Could have been a good little job as well. Use Barrett and his crew to lure Lafferty into making a push for leadership. They knew how he'd react when Christie was killed. So they got him running around, trying to put himself in power, and then had Barrett and his people make it seem like Lafferty was behind the killing in the first place. Suddenly you have Lafferty painted as the guy who created all this in the first place. Killing him is the only thing you can do.

Fair play to Lafferty—he fought a good fight. Naive, but good. Got Conrad on board, which was, on reflection, a good move. Didn't seem like it at the time, but that's because I didn't know Lafferty was being set up at the time. Got Garvey on side and used him well. I would bet a reasonably useful body part that Garvey was the one who fingered Nasty. Nasty would have been looking for a gun after shedding the one he used on Christie. All along Lafferty suspects he's being set up here, so when I turn up on Conrad's doorstep they decide to use me. Nearly worked. Nearly's not enough.

I got a phone call, late afternoon.

"Nate, it's Kevin. How are you?" He had that sad and sympathetic tone in his voice. He didn't sound wary though, didn't sound like he'd been warned by Zara. She was cutting ties and getting out; she wouldn't have called to warn him.

"I'm fine," I said. My tone wasn't sad, wasn't friendly, wasn't anything.

"Good. Well, I wanted you to know that I'm sorry about what happened to the boy, Ronnie. He seemed a good lad, and it's a damn shame that we've lost him." He sounded uncomfortable now, but that was natural when men discussed death.

"It is," I said.

"Eh, the reason I called, Nate, is that we need to have a face to face. Need to find out all the details of what happened, you know. What do they call it, debrief."

I had a few hours to sit and work out what I was going to say. The meeting was that night, at Marty's office above a gadget shop. Didn't mean Marty would be there. I hoped not. I really hoped not. What I was going to say was confrontational, and I didn't want that to extend to Marty as well. He didn't need to know that he'd been kept out of the loop.

How scared would Currie be? He had to know that I would find out, and he had to be terrified of my reaction. That wasn't a good thing. A senior man who's scared of what you might do to him becomes dangerous. Tonight I would calm those fears, but only a little.

There was nobody to call, nobody to talk to. Couldn't call Ronnie and get him up to speed with events, tell him where the meeting was going to be. Couldn't call Conn or Mikey either; didn't trust them. Conn had been in on it, had to have been. Mikey went along with Conn, and that left me on the other side of the fence from them.

I kept going back and thinking about why they'd used me for

this. I kept coming back to Zara. They used me because she knew all about me. She could tell Barrett and his crew scare stories. They would pull stunts like the one at the hotel with Zara drugged up; try to scare me because they were afraid of me. A public way of presenting them as Lafferty's crew, and I fell for it. There was a problem with Currie's plan. Not Currie's, actually; Jamieson's. The problem with it was that they put me front and center as their man, and ditching me now would make them look unstable. So now they had to keep me around, after the performance had closed.

I killed the day in silent thought and then drove to the meeting. I didn't recognize the cars on the street. Rang the buzzer and was let into the building, made my way up the narrow stairs and into the office. It looked like I was the last man to arrive. Kevin was there, Ben Carmichael with him. Conn and Mikey were both there, both looking tired. Looked like men who had worked a long night and not gotten enough sleep off the back of it. Billy Patterson was there too. He was Conn and Mikey's boss, but he was supposed to answer to Marty. Marty wasn't around. Just the people in the know, and me.

"Nate, good to see you," Kevin said.

The five of them were congregated near a desk on the far side of the room. I made sure I stayed a little nearer the door. It was the only exit, and I wanted nothing between me and it. Violence wasn't likely, but you put me in a room with people who've lied to me and there's a chance.

"I know I've already said this," Kevin said, "but I really am sorry about Ronnie. I was shocked when I found out. That bastard Conrad."

The others nodded solemnly and watched me while I watched them back. There was a heavy silence in that room, a bunch of people trying to keep their nerves in a headlock while they waited for my reaction. There was a little bit of implied criticism in Kevin's words. Conrad had been my mistake. This was Kevin making it clear that Ronnie being killed was at least partly my fault. He was right, of course.

I nodded a little, and didn't say anything. Let them drown in the quicksand of their silence.

"I had a talk with Peter a couple of hours ago," Kevin went on, trying to take the lead. "He was very sorry about Ronnie as well, of course. He was also relieved and pleased that we managed to sort out Lafferty, get it done. So, uh, yeah, he was pleased. There's still some work to do," he said, looking across at me.

I stood in resolute silence and looked back at him. Left it long enough to make sure that whatever I said next didn't need to be a response to the bullshit he'd just spouted.

"I went to see Ronnie's girlfriend last night. Told her he wouldn't be coming home."

That added another layer of depth to the silence. All of them looked at me. Mikey and Carmichael were doing their best to show no expression, Kevin and Billy were shocked and Conn just looked sad. Looked like he sympathized with me for making such a mistake. Even the best of us occasionally lets humanity trip us up.

"I think the least we can do," I went on, "is see that she gets something from us. Something to keep her quiet, but also something to express our sorrow. Ronnie had a friend, Owen Turner. You own a slice of his business. I think it would be a worthwhile gesture to hand that slice over to Esther."

Kevin looked at me, nodding very slowly. I had spoken in a steady voice; there was nothing there to give away my rising anger. But I was still standing by the door, still facing the rest of them. It felt like me against them.

"Of course," Kevin said, "that's the least we can do. I'll make sure it happens as quickly as possible. Does he have anyone else, family?"

"No, none that he mentioned."

"Okay." Kevin nodded, probably relieved that he only had to compensate the girl. It was a twenty-grand compensation, generosity not usually forthcoming in this business.

Silence made its way back into the room and filled the place. Kevin was watching me, waiting for me to say something else. I was watching him, letting his discomfort grow. He must have known by that point that something was wrong. They all did.

"Everything's clean then?" Billy asked, directing the question at Conn.

This was an attempt to move away from bad news. I think Kevin would have hugged him for changing the subject if he could. Get them off Ronnie and Conrad and onto the things that went well. The clean-up, for one.

"Yes," Conn said quickly. He was smart enough to grab hold of the opportunity to change the mood. "Couldn't have gone better. Bodies are gone, a lot of Lafferty's key items as well so it looks like he ran. Maybe they'll believe it, maybe they won't, but it was well done. We think we've cleaned away all the security footage as well."

"We haven't had any word from our police contacts yet either," Carmichael said, Kevin's right-hand man trying to move the tone towards something conversational. "They haven't been tipped off about any of the three being missing yet. Shouldn't be long before someone starts asking questions."

A few more nods of the head, a few more glances towards the doorway where I was standing.

"Barrett and his crew have been charged," Kevin said. "Bunch of stuff, but the murder of Lee Christie is in there. That might not stick, because it was Nasty that did the deed and he's not around to be charged with anything, but they're still looking at good time. Been charged with possession of the gun, charged with resisting arrest."

"We might need to lean on anyone that was supporting

Lafferty," Conn said. They were so determined to carry this conversation to a non-explosive conclusion.

"Don't think we'll have much trouble with them," Kevin said with a shrug. "I'll have a word with one or two, the more senior guys who backed the wrong horse. Doubt there'll be any trouble though. Once they know Lafferty's gone and he's not coming back, they'll be queuing up to lick Peter's boots again. Should make them more loyal, in the long run. They'll be desperate to prove their loyalty as well, so we can use that. Might have to push one or two out, I suppose; we'll see."

They were moving towards the end, and they wanted to draw me into the conversation before it finished to make sure that my grim mood wasn't directed at them. Billy looked at me before he started to talk.

"Garvey's done a runner," he said. "Myself and BB went round to his house and the place had been hastily cleaned out. Nobody there. We'll keep looking though." Said with a smile and a shrug, designed to let the room know that that was the last point of business.

They had dealt with the treacherous Lafferty and the English thugs he'd hired to attack us; we had lost one of our own but otherwise could all move cheerfully on. Everyone else in the room seemed to accept that, but their opinions didn't matter. I wasn't finished.

"You make sure the girlfriend and his friends are looked after and I won't make trouble," I said. "I'll keep working for you, because employers will always lie to people like me. But you made a mistake in not telling me. A dangerous mistake. I don't like being kept in the dark. Maybe it wouldn't have changed anything, but you played me like a sucker and I don't like that." My tone wasn't good, not as calm as I wanted it to be. My mouth felt tight.

The rest of them looked at me, but only Kevin had the seniority to say something. He could have tried to deny it, but he was smart enough to see the ugly cul-de-sac that lie led him into. Instead he went for conciliatory.

"You're right," he said, looking down at the floor like a guilty schoolboy. "You're right and I apologize. There's no excuse for it, only an explanation. Zara suggested using you, said your…history together would make the whole thing more convincing. It was her opinion that you would work the job aggressively because she was involved, and that the rest of the industry would be convinced by it. We wanted to hire you anyway, so…She asked that you be kept in the dark. She said if you knew, you would walk away and leave her stranded. I don't know, I didn't want to argue with her, not when she was taking the risk she was. We went along with it for her sake and that was a mistake. It's just…I don't think it changed anything, Nate. Not really."

That was it. That was his justification for stringing me along: the fact that, in his mind, it didn't change anything. Well, it changed things in mine. Changed the way I looked at Kevin and Jamieson and the rest of the organization. But I couldn't stand there and say that to them, because I still worked for them. I would keep working for them. But things had changed.

"Fine," I said. "Just so we're clear, you don't have to tiptoe around me, or hide Original from me. I know what happened, all of it. You should have told me. You want me to be security consultant or some other bullshit name for having me run round the city being your clenched fist. Fine, I'll do that, but from now on I'm an insider."

Kevin nodded faster than he should have. The others were silent. I gave them all a look. The sort of look that told them they'd made a mistake with me that could still prove very dangerous. Then, because I'd had quite enough of them, me and the rest of the world, I left the office and went home.

In the past, as if the past meant anything, I had been able to put people, events, anything I wanted, behind me and just move on. Not this time, and it took me a long time to understand why. It had all been my fault, that was the main reason. I had employed Ronnie, forced him to come and work with me when I knew he didn't want to. I wanted someone beside me. Shit, maybe I wanted someone in front of me. I spent hours that night trying to work out if I had hired him for the role he died playing, acting as my shield. I let him go in ahead of me; I allowed him to stand between me and Conrad when I should have known that Conrad could still pose a threat. I still don't know the answer. Maybe I did hire him just to have him stand between me and a bullet. Maybe, subconsciously, I was just that cynical.

Zara was on my mind as well. She was another example of my weakness and stupidity. If she had said to me that she wanted to stay, if she had made a play for me, I might just have given in. I told myself all the time that I was strong enough to say no to the things I wanted but should avoid, but that day I could have been won round by her. She was still beautiful and dangerous and capable of damaging both me and Becky, but I would have found a way of ignoring that. I wanted her, but she didn't need me. I was glad about that. Maybe I would give Kelly a call. Maybe a fragile relationship was better than none at all.

But my mind kept coming back to Ronnie, lying dead on the floor of Lafferty's office, just inside the door. I shouldn't have gone to his girlfriend, shouldn't have told her. That was unprofessional and I surprised myself with my behavior. But some good came of it, because it forced them to do something for the girl, something that Ronnie would have liked. Handing over Kevin's share in Turner's shop to her would put money in her pocket, buy some silence perhaps, but also help Turner. Ronnie was worried about his friend, worried that he'd made a mistake by introducing the boy to Currie. This was a chance for Currie to make sure it was a mistake that didn't come with regrets.

They would give her the share in the business, as well. I would make sure of it. They understood, I could see it in them. Kevin understood that when I told him he had to hand over the share of the business I would be checking; I would make sure that it happened. If they didn't hand that share over, I was going to take a short cut through every single one of them. Currie, Billy Patterson, Conn Griffiths, even Peter Jamieson himself. There isn't one of them I wouldn't have taken down if they had held out on paying Ronnie's girl.

I didn't bother going to bed. No point, not with everything that was running through my head. People and their faces, the things I had done and things I knew I was still to do. I thought about Ronnie, obviously, but I thought about Rebecca a lot. Thought about her father being a killer, a man she needed to be protected from. That's what Zara had said, and she was right. I protected Becky from Zara, but maybe I needed to protect her from me as well. I wouldn't though, because I was both protector and danger in her life, the person most likely to ruin her and the person I was least capable of scaring away.

I thought about myself, thought about the life I needed to build for myself. I thought about Kelly, and maybe building a life with her. But it would have been a life with her in it, not a life built around her. I wasn't capable of committing to anyone other than myself, not really. Maybe Becky, but I was at least smart enough to know that she had to be kept with her grandparents to lessen the damage I could do.

The night turned into morning and some light crept into the living room as I sat in my chair and let my misery and doubt consume me. This was what I deserved, this sense of failure and uncertainty. This was what I'd earned with my life. Remembering Lafferty as I shot him, remembering his choice of last words. *You don't understand what they've done to you*, that's what he said. He died being right, as little as that means to him now.

Hours passed, I suppose, with me just sitting there letting them go. I had nothing to add to them, nothing to spend them on. Time was better without me at that moment; the world was. Anything I did in that exhausted, depressed mood would have been hateful and violent because that was all that was in my mind. I had been played like a puppet by men who now feared me. It's a very dangerous thing, to have powerful people terrified of you.

ABOUT THE AUTHOR

Malcolm Mackay was born and grew up in Stornoway, where he still lives. His much-lauded Glasgow-set novels have won the Crime Thriller Book Club Best Read Award and the Deanston Scottish Crime Book of the Year Award, and been shortlisted for the CWA John Creasey New Blood Dagger, the CWA Ian Fleming Steel Dagger and the Scottish First Book of the Year Award. *Every Night I Dream of Hell* is his fifth novel.

Follow Malcolm on Twitter @malcolm_mackay.

MULHOLLAND BOOKS

You won't be able to put down these Mulholland books.

Visit mulhollandbooks.com for
your daily suspense fix.